Granddaughter of

Marchlands

A NOVEL

Karla Kuban

Karla Kuban (signature)

SCRIBNER

SCRIBNER
1230 Avenue of the Americas
New York, NY 10020

SCRIBNER and design are registered trademarks of
Simon & Schuster Inc.

Designed by Brooke Zimmer
Text set in Granjon
Manufactured in the United States of America

1 3 5 7 9 10 8 6 4 2

Library of Congress Cataloging-in-Publication Data
Kuban, Karla.
Marchlands: a novel/Karla Kuban.
p.   cm.
I. Title.
PS3561.U183M37   1998
813'.54—dc21   97–37254
CIP

ISBN 0-684-83165-1

For my mother and Barney Karpfinger

Acknowledgments

Madison Smartt Bell, Gillian Blake, Liv Blumer, J. M. Coetzee, Andrew Cohen, Stephen Dixon, Moira Egan, Ken Foster, Lawrence Frank, Nan Graham, Joe Gramm, Richard Hartfiel, Mikhail Iossel, Nancy Jean, Thomas King, Joyce Lamb, Paul Lavoie, the MacDowell Foundation, Alison McGhee, John Nagel, Ben Neihart, David Nichols, John Nichols, Mark Poirier, the Ragdale Foundation, Louise Redd, Brant Rumble, Barbara Stooksbury, Janet Thomas, William Trowbridge, Jennifer Unter, and William U'ren.

Marchlands

part One

L ET ME TELL YOU about our ranch. Sheep roam the high beautiful plain, and not too far away is the silver camper. In spring rain comes, and when the sun shines the red dirt on the road hardens and cracks. On top of the high flat land there are antelope and cows. There is nowhere to hide. The sheep move across the plain, and Demetrio on his horse watches from a distance. Sheep heads are bowed, thin legs moving them through sage. The dogs run at the edge of the flock, cutting back and forth, and at night when Demetrio sleeps, his horse is tied to the back of the silver camper. His dogs lie underneath. Demetrio dreams of his flock.

What do you dream? I ask.

Wolves come, he says.

There are no wolves around here.

I dream there are.

There are coyotes.

I dream that too, he says. But the wolves. The eyes are yellow.

In his silver camper I warm my hands on the flame over the stove and spread jam across bread. The coffee is black and thick, and I drink three cups. When I ride home I'm restless. I'm not fond of going home.

At home my mother and Aunt Alice drink wine and smoke cigarettes. They watch television and wait for the news. They switch from channel to channel, looking for my brother and my cousin Billy, who signed up to go to Vietnam when they were eighteen. The boys have been there a month now, since the end of March. Boot camp was eight weeks at Fort Leonard Wood outside of Waynesville, Missouri. The first American fighting troops went last year. Those boys couldn't know what to expect.

Aunt Alice comes over two or three nights a week. She and my mother watch war footage, hoping to see their boys. A crazy thing. When the news is over, they sit in the dark for some time on the couch, not talking, facing each other, watching the orange of each other's cigarettes. My mother keeps Winston cartons in the refrigerator or over the fireplace mantel. There is a gray cast to her face. The television has thrown gray on her and it has stuck.

The sun hangs overhead, half hidden away in the clouds that move like flocks of sheep. On our ranch you can walk or ride or drive for long distances and never see another person. My white horse is Pablo. He has dappled flanks and is big-boned and seventeen hands high. I whistle, saddle him, and make him run. Sometimes I give him apples after our times together. The road angles steeply and veers off to the north toward Tin's ranch. We cut to the left off the road and go north into the sage. We go across the red dirt, move down along a stream, up and over the ridge, up another hill. We stand on a high flat land and see the camp a distance away. Demetrio's horse is tied to the back of the silver camper, where the sun hits against silver. Six white heart antelope stand along the flat. Pablo trots on. As the antelope run, their white heart antelope buttocks pulse. The antelopes' slender legs lope ahead, and they grow small, then vanish down the gully. It doesn't have to rain for you to smell the sage. Sometimes it smells like bleach.

When I get to the sheep camp, I slide off Pablo and come around to the front to tie him up. His nostrils flare red inside. The camper door is always open. Demetrio runs his tongue along my fingertips.

Pelo negro.

Your hair is black too.

You are the laziest girl I have ever known.

No.

Say the word. *Pestaña.*

Pestaña.

He lifts my finger to his eye and blinks. Eyelash, he says. I wonder if he loves me. His eyelash is soft. He puts my hand between his legs where it's very warm. I close my eyes.

Going home, the air is cloudy with dust and I feel grit between my teeth. Pablo is sweating under my thighs. I let him out to pasture. He canters to the patch of dirt, sinks to his knees, and rolls. The other horses watch, then shift.

Mother comes from the house carrying a thermos of iced tea for the men. She wears a red mini dress with fringe balls at the hem. She sewed them on herself. Her shoes are red ballet slippers. Sheep shit has ruined many pairs of her ballet slippers. She steps around carefully.

Don't forget to water the tomatoes, she says.

I began the hotbeds last week, and they'll produce seedlings that I'll set in the garden in June. I'll set them four feet apart, and we'll have pounds of red tomatoes in September.

I can see that my mother tries to look elegant in her red mini dress. She tries to walk lightly on her ballet slippers. She's as tall as Julian and I'll bet the money in my envelope she weighs the same. She's not fat, but big and strong. She's much bigger than Aunt Alice. Julian and Piraté respond gratefully when my mother brings them iced tea. They take down their silver cups hanging by nails on the pen walls and drink. Willy. *Muchas gracias. Muchas gracias.* Mother's name is Wilhelmina, but she goes by Willy.

Inside the corral, the ewes run about on skinny legs and bleat. They're afraid. Near the gate a ewe lies on her side in the dirt. She groans and pants. Piraté stands over her and lifts his bode bag to his mouth. He drinks an arc of red wine. Julian comes from the tool shed with a hammer. His arms are bowed. He walks to the pens and pounds nails. Piraté pins the ewe with his knee and slits her throat and slices her belly. From the belly of water he pulls one lamb by a leg and another by the neck. The lambs wobble and look for a teat. Piraté picks up the lambs, one under each arm. He drags them into a pen, then calls for Julian to bring the bottles.

An ewe stands bleating at the pen. Her rear bones are sunken and she paws the ground. Her white bag tells the men she's about ready to have her baby. It hangs from her back end. Piraté touches her under there and laughs, his teeth brown and gapped. She runs off and he follows her. He turns around once to look at me. His eyebrows rise and fall and he blinks as if dirt has gone into his eye.

There are fifty-one days left until my tenth-grade year in school is finished. Going home, my bus stops at the railroad crossing. I wish you could see what I see: a man walking down the tracks, passing my school bus without looking our way. Straight yellow hair uneven at the ends, swinging down his back to his buttocks. Beige pants hanging belted and loose around narrow hips, and feet striding along in brown lace-up shoes. His chest bare. Brown as a berry and broad enough that I would like to sit on his shoulders, my legs dangling over his dark chest, and go awhile where he's going. In the eleven years I've ridden the bus, we've only had to wait six or eight times for a train to pass, but we always have to stop anyway. It's the law.

This time of year, April, the air is fresh and clear. Sunlight shimmers on a dozen or so white rocks that cluster together this side of the tracks. The day is unusually warm. The tracks head east and west. The bus lurches forward over the tracks and bears south.

Guy Larksman's alfalfa field is in bloom with purple-blue flowers. Kidney-shaped seeds sleep inside curled pods. Last summer my mother stopped her truck on the shoulder to speak with Larksman who was checking some fence on the edge of his property. I walked to the edge of his field and tried to pull an alfalfa plant up by the root. It was impossible. When my mother was ready to leave, she called for me to get back in the truck. I was still pulling. I wonder how far the roots stretch into the soil.

There are plenty of kids to drop off on the way to my place. Mine is the second to the last stop. The bus driver's name is Jack. He's my mother's age and bald as a bulb with a red beard and skinny body like our standing brass lamp in the living room. He was in prison once. He was the getaway guy for some other guys who robbed a bank. Those criminals must have thought he was quite a safe driver, and I feel safe with him behind the wheel of our bus. He and I can talk about anything on the last leg of the ride if nobody else is in the bus. There's one stretch of ranch that runs six miles, owned by Duncan and Gracie Barber's mom and dad. They're cattle people. The Glensmiths own seven miles both sides of the road. They run cattle, too. Their land abuts against the Picardys'. There have been some bad exchanges of words between the Picardys, who run sheep, and the Glensmiths. Tin Picardy says that cattle people are purely jealous of sheep people. Sheep have six grinding teeth at the back side of each jaw. They can cut short grass off at the roots. They can crop a measly field where cattle would starve, and mow through good pasture and leave a desert behind.

There's a nice breeze blowing through the bus window. The cottonwoods bend at their necks and limbs. The inside of the bus stinks like bubble gum and Jack's smelly underarms. I open the window a little more. A cool wind hits my face and brings tears to my eyes. It must be very beautiful to walk down a track for miles and miles and to rest when you like against a cottonwood tree. He might have been walking along until a train came by. Burlington Northern passes through, and the Chicago and Northwestern. Freight and cargo cars. He carried no rucksack or duffel bag. Just maybe his people live in Thayer or Rock Springs. His waist was lean and narrow and his shoulders and chest straight and fatless. The muscles of his chest are beautiful. His brown nipples.

I've never been awfully in love with my teats but since I've known a baby's growing inside me I notice them. I view my teats not as objects of beauty, but as bull's-eyes of food for the baby. The teats won't produce milk for seven and a half months, but the nipples have tingled since the first week, or it could even have been the first day, after Demetrio and I made the baby. The growing began when my right nipple puckered with three small goosebumps like seeds. I hadn't thought about this too much before the bare-chested man walked down the railroad tracks in front of the bus. I would have enjoyed the sun on my nipples and the air on my back, and my hair touching the skin on my shoulders. There must be other women who feel this way. There must be women who want to wander freely, wearing loosely belted pants and nothing on top so their chests and backs soak in the spring and summer sun.

I'm free to run away any time I please, as anyone in the world is. The truth is that I'm too lazy. I eat my mother's food and live under her roof. I have my horse and I sleep well in my bed on cotton sheets. I don't pay the electricity and land taxes, nor the hired hands. I have the sheep, the *ovejas,* to thank for their bounty, and my mother too, who directs a sharp eye on the gross and net. She figures the books, and every three months she figures the taxes. Her devotion to TV war footage could be dangerous. She fears the worst, and this kind of fear pulls like a magnet. She'd better watch out, for what you fear is bound to occur. My brother always thought he was tough. It would serve him right to catch a bullet in his leg, but when it comes down to it I'd hate to see him die.

We pull up to the junction of Pilot and County Road D, nine miles from my house. We have to stop at the four-way. A bitter smell of hogs. Bedeker's.

Once he drops off the Staples boys, Jack and I are by ourselves. I ask him to tell me about prison life. He always has a lot of stories about that.

First of all, he says, prison is wicked because you can't get no womanly love. Womanly love for a man is a very important thing unless you don't like women in the loving way. I love my wife, he says, but she says I don't tell her stuff from my heart. I can't do it every minute. You and me, Sophie, we don't need no one to tell us every minute, stuff from the heart.

Is that okay?

The door swings open.

Do your thing, Sophie.

Okay, Jack. See you.

See you.

Their jobs are to go out into the jungle and scout around. Every now and then they go back to base camp and eat and get rowdy. Ten days in and ten days out. It was Clements' idea when he and Billy graduated from high school that they sign up. The buddy system. Clements was never satisfied spending time alone, so he talked Billy into it. Even if Billy were right there with Clements near his foxhole every minute of the day or night, you wonder what good the buddy system does. Billy's written me two letters. Was I seeing anyone and was I still a virgin and where did my father go, he wants to know.

Clements sends Mother letters and sometimes they're addressed to both of us. Since he's been there, he's sent two letters addressed only to me. Clements and I have never been too close, but maybe letter writing will make us closer. His letter of March 29 was addressed to my mother and me.

He wrote Dear Mom and Sophie Loaf. He wrote about the trip over and the food. He wrote about his weapons and supplies. He asked if I'd seen Lillian. She was a girl he'd dated a few times. He wrote that his first lieutenant's name was Chris Skinner and that he carried a .45-caliber pistol with him and slept with it too.

I got a letter from my cousin Billy the first week he was in Vietnam. He saw a dead girl in a ditch. He cut a bracelet off her wrist. She'd been dead for some time because the flies were laced up over her face. She was a teenage girl wearing black pants cut to her shin and nothing on top. Billy keeps the bracelet in his back pocket.

We had to go to a funeral. This dead fellow was not wholly evil, but he did things to the ewes I don't agree with. Things that don't seem right for the purpose of pleasure. I'm not stupid. I know such things occur from time to time on ranches.

This dead man's name was Nicklow and he worked on Guy Larksman's ranch. Two nights ago, Nicklow penned a ewe and tied a rope around her neck. To do this right, he tied the other end to the water trough so there was a three-inch slack. When she was pushed forward, her head was level with the water. If a ewe doesn't want to drink, she doesn't want her head in water, and if forced into it she'll step back.

The two wetbacks at our door are good-looking men about Demetrio's age. They work for Ken Duggan, one of our neighbors. Julian takes them out to the corrals where the ewes are lambing. They know what to do. They work the lambing season at their place. We'll be back in three or four hours, Mother says. One of the sheepers wears chaps. I don't know why. Birthing lambs isn't riding the plain and busting horses. The pale brown leather is stained and cut, and he looks good in them. I have to say that.

My mother, Piraté, and I drive to the funeral in one truck. I sit between Mother and Piraté. Julian, Demetrio, and Antonio follow us in the other truck. Piraté has *borrega* shit all over his boots, and it makes a bad smell in the car.

Lo bueno es que Nicklow nunca supo lo que pasó, Piraté says. *Cuando* Larksman . . .

He says the good thing is that Nicklow never knew what happened. Larksman finding him that way.

My mother knows a good deal of Spanish. Her father taught her. He made her speak Spanish to the sheepers.

Lo malo es que el nunca comprendió lo que hizo.

She says the bad thing is that he never understood what he did. She means that he never understood the consequences in terms of heaven and hell because he was dead before he expected it and had no time to ask the Lord's forgiveness.

El pobre Nicklow, Piraté says.

My mother drives too fast. One night a deer will jump into her headlights, she'll have no time to swerve away, and the deer will crash through her windshield.

My mother looks to the left and lifts her hand against the window to one of Bedeker's hired hands walking toward the fence. The man doesn't lift his hand to wave back. I've seen him before in town. His face is so sad, as if everyone close to him has died and he's alone. We're about half a mile past him when I have a strange feeling of sadness and turn around quickly to see him, a small figure blending into the fence by the edge of the road.

When I look ahead again I see Piraté's hand in his crotch. He's looking at me from the corner of his eye and his mouth is open a little. He's an ugly man of about fifty. I turn away.

This dead man, Nicklow, before he died, put the ewe's hind legs into the fronts of his boots. His hands sank into the wool of her rump, he situated himself, then pushed the ewe forward to the water. The ewe backed up. Forward and back, forward and back. Demetrio is the one who told me how this works. When he told me, he spoke in half Spanish and half English. I'd know more of the fine points, but I don't understand Spanish too well. He wasn't there with Nicklow but he's seen this before. In my heart of hearts I don't think Demetrio has ever done it.

Sophie, light me a smoke, will you? my mother says.

If you wouldn't drive so fast you could light your own, I say. What's the rush?

Piraté, *dame* a cigarette, will you?

Piraté's hand comes up from his crotch and he takes a pack of Winstons from his pocket. He hangs a cigarette from the center of his mouth and lights it with his silver lighter, passes it to my mother. My nostrils catch airy scraps of lighter fluid. She cracks the window, and her lips push a line of smoke into the air outside.

¿Quieres? he says, pulling another out of the pack and holding it up for me. His thumbtack eyes squint in the patch of sun that's come over his face. His forehead is gathered with wrinkles.

¡Creo qué no! Don't corrupt her yet!

I can smoke if I want.

You'd better not.

I wouldn't want to. I'll bet your lungs are black. Like his teeth.

Honey, his teeth'd be black without the smoke.

He parts his mouth and laughs as if he's choking. He makes fun of his own black teeth.

Piraté acts as if he knows no English, but he knows plenty. He turns away and pretends to look with interest out the window. My mother's lips are pursed. She taps the steering wheel with a finger.

In a moment we pass the cemetery and we're only a few miles from town. My mother's mouth softens. *Quería acampar en las montañas este verano. Con Sophie.*

Bueno, Piraté says.

She wants to go camping. We went three years ago to the great park with its waterfalls and lakes and white peaks, and the longer we climbed the harder it was to breathe. Our second night at twilight just before nightfall, this occurred: I relieved myself in the woods, and walking back to the tent I saw Mother. Kneeling under the spruce, her head tipped back. She spoke in a whisper, Forgive me for I have sinned. These words repeated. On and on. The woods were still and quiet, save for her words. I pushed her over to knock her from her spell. She fell onto her side, still frozen in the kneeling position, arms crossed over chest, hands on shoulders, weeping: Virgin Mary. Virgin Mary.

I don't know whether the Virgin Mary appears only to Catholics. Mother's Lutheran but it seemed the Virgin appeared as real as anything in her mind. Her hands were delicate and pink, Sophie. On each wrist a corsage of pink dahlias. I shouted, Be quiet! My hands over my ears. Her mouth still moved and when at last the lips were spent I took my hands from my ears. A white moth on each toe, their wings open like Jesus' hands, not closed as resting butterflies whose wings come together like praying hands. I ran into the woods. Crazy. Crazy. My mother needed the Virgin's forgiveness and she made her appear in her mind and her eyes saw it all through the made-up. Forgiveness for what sins?

The mountains. Change of scenery's good, Mother says.

I'd like to go to the ocean, I tell her.

That's not a bad idea. We've never been to the ocean. Poor Clements had to see the ocean. Think how many hours he was on that boat on the ocean. I'll bet it's a drab old ocean. Gray and ugly and full of sharks. I don't want to go to the ocean.

I guess we won't be going, then. I've read about it in school. I've seen it on television. When you visit the ocean you aren't in the middle of the country any longer. You're a long way from Wyoming on a coast: east, west, or south.

At any rate, we'll go somewhere this summer, she says.

Maybe to Chicago, I say.

For God's sake! Don't try me, Sophie.

I'm going to call her.

You do and I'll.

What she doesn't know is that I already call my grandmother.

I'm going to, I say.

Her lips curl under. She slams on the brakes and pulls over to the side of the road and brakes harder. The gravel from the shoulder of the road is loose and it's hard to stop. The men pull in behind us. She roughly grasps my shoulders. Her eye whites are red-lined targets circled with black eyeliner. I'd like to poke both of them and make her shut up. Julian comes to my mother's window. She waves him off. He shrugs and walks away. I pick my mother's fingers off my shoulders. She sinks her fingers into my shoulders again. Talon fingers.

It'd be nice to know where my father is. He's my father. I've got a right. I'll bet you know where he is.

I know, too, about where he is, from my grandmother. But I don't tell her this.

Mother takes her talons off my shoulders. She pulls out onto the blacktop. She asks Piraté, *¿Donde está la ceremonia?* Neeling's funeral home or Bresloff's?

Sí, Bresloff's.

Bueno. And don't bring up your father again. God damn it to hell.

This dead man Nicklow had a heart attack while he was in the ewe. Guy Larksman found the two of them by the water trough the next morning. Nicklow was stone cold dead, the ewe bleating. Larksman told Julian. Julian told Demetrio.

We pull up to Bresloff's funeral home. We're the first to get there. Julian pulls in behind us. We walk into the brick building together. The men are dressed in clean shirts and jeans. Demetrio's jeans are stiff with newness. I tell him on the way in that I'll have to wash them with a little bleach. He smiles and I can see the silver tooth near the back of his mouth. The men wear dress hats. Two are made of straw and two are made of beaver felt. Antonio and Julian wear belts with their names etched in the back. Antonio grunts when we step inside. The air smells of mold and mint. I wonder if that combination comes from the chemicals they use to make the body ready. This is only my second funeral.

Nicklow's laid out in a casket in the front parlor, dressed in Levi's and a blue western shirt. Con Bresloff, the undertaker, a small old man, greets us with clasped hands and says we're early. The funeral doesn't start for two hours. My mother blames Julian. Earlier he called Guy Larksman for the service time and somehow misunderstood. Julian just shrugs.

I have a closer look at Nicklow while I'm there, and wonder what Bresloff must have thought getting him ready for the casket. This blue-eyed Greek has the biggest feet I've ever seen. His boots are polished shiny black. I have to admit that I'm curious about whether or not his nozzle shrunk up after he passed on.

We walk over to Calley's Doughnuts and the men take off their hats. We order two doughnuts each, and coffee, and sit down at the round table by the jukebox. Calley's about my mother's age, forty-three, and her husband's in Vietnam. Her face is pale and drawn as if she's been working all night and day, and worrying. Piraté puts some change into the jukebox slot and a man's voice sings oh, lone-some me. As he's walking back he shimmies his shoulders. Does he know I've been lying down with Demetrio? Does he know about my baby?

Julian takes a bite of his doughnut and my mother flashes him a look. He sets the doughnut back down on the paper plate and chews slowly as if this is penance. Mother bows her head and folds her hands. The men bow their heads. Her eyelashes flutter twice and she closes her eyes tightly.

Come Lord Jesus be our guest, and let these gifts to us be blessed.

The men say amen and cross themselves. They're Catholic and we're Lutheran.

Two eighteen-wheel semi-trucks pull into the parking lot. A man steps out of each one, and they walk in and sit down at the counter. One is wearing a cowboy hat like a mushroom and he doesn't remove it as he steps inside. His face looks as if it's been dragged through gravel. Acne scars. At school they tease you if you have acne and call you what they think are clever names. Clements didn't have acne. I don't. I think acne's determined by your genes. I'd like to see some pictures of my father when he was my age.

Now and then the mustached one turns around and looks at us. Calley refills our cups.

Julian gives tribute to Nicklow. He says, Nicklow sheared the lamb in one minute, no less.

In the Bible, Mother says, such heinous acts occurred with goats.

Caballos también, Antonio says.

Okay, well, I'm sorry I brought it up. I don't want to hear about it, Mother says, fanning her tongue.

I guess the coffee was too hot.

She goes on: Brothers, watch yourselves, or you also may be tempted. Galatians six one.

Julian creases and recreases the corner of his napkin. I think her religion makes him uncomfortable. But he's the worker. She's the boss. She can say and do what she likes.

With the riches of God's grace we will be lavished with all wisdom and understanding. We must forgive.

Demetrio's boot, under the table, touches my shin. I look into his eyes. I don't think anyone here other than Mother has thought about the need to forgive Nicklow. He deserved something, but he didn't deserve to die. Now his soul's gone and his big body lies stretched out in a chestnut casket. I hope for his sake it was worth it.

I wonder if my mother has read the one about judging others, for in the same way you judge others you will be judged yourself.

What does she know? Everyone sins from time to time or we wouldn't have a Bible and church and Pastor Fabila to tell us how not to sin.

Adios Nicklow, Julian says sadly. He made us a good spanako-pitta last Easter.

After a while, crocodile. Piraté raises his Styrofoam cup and the others raise theirs. But Mother won't toast Nicklow. I do, and she lets out a lungful of air through her nose. I think the subject of Nicklow is closed now.

The little mustached truck driver who's been turning around and looking at our table says something to his friend who's drumming the counter with his spoon to the song on the jukebox.

Hey, what's a man with lots of stupid lovers called? the mustached one loudly asks.

I don't know, the gravel-faced one says. What's a man with lots of stupid lovers called?

Sheepherder, the mustached one says, and the two of them laugh.

Julian looks down at his napkin, and Demetrio's nostrils flare.

Ignore the ignorant, whispers Mother.

But Demetrio stands and walks over to them.

¿Qué dice? he says to the mustached one, who doesn't answer but lifts his cup toward Calley. For a moment no one moves. No one speaks. Now the mustached one lifts his cup to his lips and drinks. Refill, please, he then says, but Calley doesn't move toward him with her coffeepot. He doesn't face Demetrio but says, his back to him, You can't speak English, man? Then to his friend: They come to our country and expect us to learn their language.

Hold your tongue, mister, Demetrio says.

Demmy, I call out, your coffee's getting cold.

Oh, for Pete's sake, Mother says, elbow on the table, hand on her forehead. Demetrio pulls his buck knife out of the leather case on his belt. Mother whispers goddammit. In one swift movement he takes the mustached one's head back at the forehead and holds the knife at his throat. The other one runs to the door. Calley's frozen.

My mother's face wears a look asking the men to step in, but the men don't even look Demetrio's way.

He fights his own war, Julian says.

Antonio shakes his head and blows air from his mouth.

I can't see the look on the mustached one's face. He must be afraid. I would be. Each day Demetrio sharpens the blade on the whetstone. The knife is six inches long with a hooked nose.

Demmy, I say. This honor thing. It's one thing that bothers me about Demetrio. All the ranchers and sheepers around our parts, it seems, save for old DeWolf who they say is senile. They have an honor bone to pick.

Demetrio is close to the man's ear, whispering words to him, and the man sits perfectly still so that I think he must've stopped breathing.

Demetrio turns halfway to me. It's the same knife we use to spread jam across the bread. It's the same knife he uses to scrape calluses on his palms, then spread petroleum jelly across them to keep them from drying and cracking. It's the same knife Demetrio uses to cut a length of rope and tie a ewe's leg to sagebrush so she'll stay put on the plain and the lamb will suckle from her. Those ewes who try to run away are called, by the sheepers, bad mothers. They abandon their lambs.

Chrissake, you're cutting me! the man cries.

I don't know if the gravel-faced man has gone to get a rifle from his truck, or to get our sheriff, or maybe he's already driven off and left his friend behind. They both seem like cowards. Demetrio lets go of his head and says, You want English? Fuck off, mister. Go fuck yourself and your mother, too.

The men at my table say words in Spanish and stand. Mother says we can wait at Bresloff's for the funeral to begin, that it will be good to take refuge in a Christian place. Who is she trying to fool? You can pull your knife out anywhere any time if you have to, and anyone can run in and fire a gun. The mustached man flies out of Calley's and gets into his semi. I want to walk with Demetrio, my arm through his, but then she'll know that he and I are more than friends. She'll Lord this and the devil that. I can be friends with the sheepers, but I can't have sex with them. Sex before marriage is sinful and rebellious. I have secrets from her. Most of the time I try not to make her angry.

On our way out, Demetrio sneaks a walnut shell from his hand to mine behind my back. While the others walk ahead, I untie the string around the shell. I lift the top half and take out a small piece of paper folded four times. *Te quiero,* it says. I smile. Then I stop smiling and think: I don't know if I love him. The list of people who love me isn't too long. When someone loves you it's a gift.

My mother's stocking has a run in it. A Christian like her could not hate a blameless baby, could she? My baby and I will stay on the ranch and escape from time to time to take walks down the railroad tracks. I'll teach my baby, when my baby is old enough, to ride a horse.

Piraté catches up with Demetrio, who leads the way to the trucks. Piraté's arm is raised in the air. He shakes his fist and speaks in Spanish. He says, You should have made him bleed. Next time you will make him bleed.

I won't meet him again, Demetrio says, spitting on the ground. He's not worth the blade of my knife.

I know this much Spanish.

The school bus is covered with bird droppings. I've never seen it so painted like this. We cross the tracks and I look both ways. Not a soul is walking the tracks today.

The two Masterson sisters have ganged up on Ivy McCullers. They are sitting up near the front, and Ivy McCullers made the mistake of sitting across from them. I'm sitting in front of the Mastersons, catty-corner from Jack, so I can look out the big front window at the scenery. The Mastersons' weapons are evil narrow-eyed glances and whispers behind cupped hands. I turn around and look at Ivy. She stares straight on as if she's paying no attention. Her face is very stoic and dimpled in the chin from biting her lower lip. Ivy's a beautiful brown-eyed girl with short curly black hair. She sits hunch-shouldered and walks pigeon-toed and never speaks unless spoken to.

Rudy Picardy is coming the other way in his orange truck. He lifts his hand from the steering wheel, and Jack lifts the palm of his hand.

The Masterson sisters have done the same thing to me. It was easy enough to pretend to ignore them in the bus, but hard to keep from crying when I got off. They take your worst physical trait and make it into the world's greatest sideshow. They laughed about my teeth. My teeth had never seen braces because I refused them. I bit the orthodontist's thumb when he tried. My teeth grew in crossed over on top, and pushed back. When the girls teased me, I took it, and decided I couldn't fix such stupid people. The world is full of them. Wasting my energy on girls like the Mastersons would be stupid. They try to make you into a circus show. I'm not too popular. So what.

I was born with deformities. These girls don't know this. When I was born my tear ducts didn't work, and when I was four months old I had to have an operation to open the ducts so that when I cried the tears would flow. Three toes on my left foot were webbed. I wouldn't have minded if Mother kept them that way. I would have been a faster swimmer in the river. I had an operation on my toes when I was nine months old, and they're no longer webbed. My mother isn't too fond of ugly people. She nearly sent Antonio the One-Armed away when he came to our house for a job. But she kept him because he can cook, oil guns, and fix fence, even with that one arm.

The Masterson girls talked almost every kid at school into making fun of my father leaving us. I wasn't an orphan or a bastard or a child of divorced parents. Just an abandoned. In Bluerock High, I guess no one's father ever parked his pickup by the train tracks and vanished into the sky. This happened when I was four, almost four. The kids at school feed on anyone's bad luck. They stick together. It makes them feel important.

The man I saw a few days ago on the railroad tracks didn't look to be going fishing unless his fishing pole and bait or flies were already at the lake or stream. He didn't look drunk and stumbling. He didn't look to be a madman. His arms hung easily at his sides and moved forward and back with his legs. His mouth wasn't rimmed with froth. He didn't look to be walking to a picnic unless he planned to meet his friends who'd already spread a blanket under the cottonwood. Imagine walking down railroad ties for an entire length of track. The idea of such expanse is almost too much to bear.

The wind on my face is fine, and I draw myself up in the baby growing inside. One hour and five minutes after the train tracks, there is the shrill song of brakes, and the door swings open. Jack says, See you, doll. Have a good one.

Here's how lazy I am. In the morning I drive one of the pickups a half mile to the edge of our property by the blacktop where the bus picks me up. The sign hanging off our barbwire fence reads MEAD- OWLARK CREEK RANCH. There's such a creek on the northeastern side of our property, but I call it a stream. We own a thousand acres, more or less, which were first owned by my great-grandfather on my mother's side. Before that a half Arapaho Indian owned the land.

The afternoon air has turned sharply cold and the wind has picked up, carrying the scent of sheep and hay to my face. Next to the truck's front tire I see a greasewood shrub. It's eight or nine inches tall with erect many-branched stems, and its leaves are stalkless and fleshy at the tips. Its fruit is reddish and nutlike. In big amounts it'll kill sheep. I pull it up by its root. I'll have one of the men spray around here tomorrow. I throw the bags in the back and climb in. I toss the root on the floor and sneeze from the dust on the dash. I think about Billy. In his second letter to me he wrote that he was dehy- drated all the time and it wasn't a good idea to try to collect the rain and drink it. They drink Kool-Aid made with sugar and water and purifying tablets. The truck smells harshly of garlic and onions from the men picking up the groceries Saturday. I collect rainwater in bottles and drink it. I think it will make me live forever.

Three times a week I go to Bilky's and get all their old produce for our sheep that are sick or weak and have to stay in the corrals. Brown lettuce, old apples, even eggplant.

The three dogs bark as I come in. They're Sharpa, Piraté's dog,

Pokey-Joe, and Rebby. The groceries are very ripe and maybe only hours from turning bad. I bring them right away to the pens. Mother's there, bottle-feeding two pure-white lambs. Their curlicue tails twitch and spin.

Hello, baby. How was your day?

I got a B on my social studies test.

Say. She smiles. All that studying paid off.

What she doesn't know is that I didn't study for the test. I'm not a genius, but if I pay attention and write notes during the lectures, I can usually get a B.

Soph, she says, looking up. The lambs are pulling on the nipples, pulling from their rear legs on top of the straw. You do a really good job with this produce. Thank you for taking that chore over after Clem left. Sometimes he'd remember to swing by Bilky's and pick it up, and sometimes he didn't. I appreciate the help, especially when we're busy like this.

You're welcome. Do you want something from inside? Something to drink?

I've got to come in in a minute anyway, and refill these bottles for the other two.

Do you want me to feed them?

If you'd like.

When I walk in the door, there's a new letter from Clements on the coffee table, and it's addressed to Mother and me, not just me. I think Clements and Billy, the warboys, write letters because it helps their hearts to get letters back. Maybe Clements has learned that if he wants people to write close things to him, he has to write close things to people. Ranch life is plain and safe compared with Vietnam. Before they left, Clements and I weren't close and Billy didn't want to be close to me and divide himself from Clements. Billy's second letter asked, Aren't you curious about where your father is?

I know he's somewhere in the mountains of Colorado. My grandmother told me. He moves around, my father, a leaver. Also, Billy's letter asks, do I have a boyfriend and have I slept with anyone. He's my cousin and I shouldn't get romantic with him when he comes home. If we had a baby it could have crossed eyes. Billy's a big handsome boy with a nose like a shark's fin.

I can tell you that Clem doesn't answer questions I ask in my letters. But I'm glad he writes at all. It's a start of friendship for us. His first letter to me:

Dear Sophie Loaf,
Week one in this hellhole. Sarge Fire and Ice calls it the war of
fuckers and fuckees. His real name is O'Connor but his girl
sent him a tube of her lipstick called Fire and Ice. He paints his
face before we make recons and it scares the shit out of the
villagers. Like to scare the shit out of me Fire and Ice.
Remember how I use to bitch when Antonio cooked cabbage?
It made the house stink like farts remember? But the goddam
jungle smells worse so I ain't complaining about Antonios
cabbage no more. Anyway I could use some of his cabbage
about now. You know what I found in the jungle yesterday?
Somebody's teeth. Not all together. But damn near a mouth
full, I bet you. Mom always made such a big load about
straight teeth. How is Mom? Sometimes I worry about her.
Billy said he wrote you a letter. Did you get it? Take it easy
and don't do nothing I wouldn't do.

                                                                        Clements

The black sky pours cold rain. I think of Demetrio walking his sheep in this rain. He'll know the rear of the flock is an important place, because straggling sheep or those who wander away searching for good grass, not sage, need to be brought back into the flock. Demetrio will call to his dogs and coo to the sheep. Maybe he'll have a thermos of coffee tucked under his arm. The rain will fall in rivers off his slicker. He came to our ranch because he knows sheep. He worked with them in Mexico where he slept and ate outside at all times with no shelter, not even a tin camper. He's proud of knowing the signs of bloating and colic in the sheep, that potato sprouts cause birth defects, that muscle tremors could mean milk fever. He's an expert shearer. He has a firm but gentle way of holding the sheep with his left hand under the animal's chin and around its neck, then shearing the right shoulder. Demetrio will stand on a hill in this rain, his arms outstretched to the east and west, and he'll look like a cross. He thinks he knows sheep better than anyone in the world. He can think that if he likes. I don't mind.

Television is an ugly thing. It brings no good news at all. It makes a lot of noise, and my mother's face adjusts in shades of gray when the footage is on. After the news, my mother reads to me from the front page of the paper where it gives the numbers of men killed that day.

Did you look for Daddy on television when he was in the war?

It's hot in here. Heat on or something? Hey, grab me a pack of smokes from the freezer while you're out there, will you?

I wrote to Billy that I cried when I read about the dead Vietnamese girl with the bracelet on her wrist, that the buds are coming out on the trees, that the sheep are going to Climax, Colorado, for the summer. I wrote that he should take care and stay alert. I love Billy, but I have to watch what information I give him. I don't know what will get back to his mother, and I don't know how much he tells Clements. Anything he tells Clements could get back to my mother.

I hand my mother a pack of Winstons. Then I step outside for some fresh air. The ewes bleat all night. In four days lambing will be over and it will be calm out here.

Do you know how long it's been since I've seen my grandmother? Almost eleven years. If it weren't for my grandmother, I wouldn't know anything of my father.

Town is where we pick up our grain and salt licks and grocery shop at Bilky's. Bluerock grows a little each year and shrinks a little each year. Buildings go up, and others sit boarded and vacant, or are torn down and replaced with new ones, or with gas stations. The main street has diagonal parking with meters where you have to pay a nickel for an hour. The street is very wide and in the middle is a strip of sidewalk. In summer it's lined with rows of flowers. The flowers are arranged according to color. A row of red and a row of purple and a row of yellow. There's a new owner of the barbershop. The old one finally died of Parkinson's disease. Before he got too bad with the disease, he liked to sit on the bench in front of his store, read the paper, and drink from his coffee mug, which he set down between sips on the sidewalk. When a customer walked up he would stand and set his paper facedown on the bench at the page he was reading, and when he was finished with the haircut or shave he'd step outside again to the bench and the newspaper and his coffee. I don't know the new owner's habits yet.

My mother forbade me to contact Grandma Irene. Three years ago I did anyway.

At the end of town facing Main is the limestone courthouse. Next to that is the post office. The American flag flies there on top of a silver post. Three years ago my mother went to the dentist to have a filling put in, and I had a Coke at the drugstore and leafed through the women's fashion magazines. I often stop at the drugstore and look at those magazines. I feel jealous of those beautiful girls. I suppose if you're a girl like that, you have many strange and wonderful things to talk about. Your adventures build and build. Maybe secretly I want to wear false eyelashes, but I don't think so. Maybe one day I'll have hand-beaded silk organza, as the caption says, flowing around my ankles. But my work boots would be full of horseshit.

Then I went to the post office.

There were no other customers. I stepped up to the front and said hello to the clerk, an old man with a gray mustache down over his lip. What can I do for you, young lady, he wanted to know.

You might have a record of a forwarding address for Joseph Behr, I said.

He twisted his mustache.

Who're you? Say, you're the Behr girl.

Sophie. I thought you might have a record.

He's been gone an awful long time, ain't he?

Eleven years.

Nosir, we don't keep records that long. Year, maybe year and a half. I don't remember a forwarding address. I think your mama's already been here to ask that, a long time ago.

I didn't explain to him that I was forbidden to ask about my father, that doing so would bring something bad, that my mother said there would be dire consequences if I ever mentioned his name. She didn't go into the post office too often. She burned the pictures of my father.

Do you remember if he got any mail here under general delivery? I asked.

Nosir.

You don't remember or he didn't?

None of the above, as far as I can see. Been eleven years.

I thanked him and went outdoors. I went into Bilky's. It smelled like ripe watermelon. I bought some food for Antonio to cook. Mother had given me money for this, and the change was a couple of dollars. I would give Mother some of the money, but I'd put a little of it in my envelope. She'd never know.

Then I called my grandmother.

Demetrio's camper is shining silver. It draws in the sun and is very warm inside. You take small steps and there's an oven small as a bread box. Two burners for making coffee and beans. A sink. The water comes from the barrel beneath the camper where the dogs lie. A single bed is covered with a red wool blanket. One pillow. The sheets are holey from too much bleach.

Bleach is very good when you want to get the sheepers' underwear white. They wear sleeveless ribbed undershirts below their work shirts, and they wear Jockey briefs. Their underwear is stained with various things. The aftershave bottle is greasy from their hands with what they put on their hair. The razor is rusty. Around the sink stands an aspirin bottle, salt for gargling, a bottle of pink stuff. They use toilet paper to blow their noses. The bathroom in their trailer next to the house has no running water and that's why they use ours. On Saturdays I scrub the sink, tub, and toilet with their dried drops on the rim. If you think my character is built with tasks like these, you're wrong. These tasks get me nothing. The men are paid well to run the sheep. One of these days I'm going to stop cleaning their bathroom. One of these days.

For three years I've been calling my grandmother collect once a month. Sometimes she knows where my father is, and sometimes she doesn't. I've sent letters to wherever it is that he supposedly lives, but I get no response. He never has a telephone. Maybe he's tried to contact us and my mother hung up on him. Maybe there were letters and she threw them away.

My grandmother had always sent presents for my birthday and Christmas. She stopped sending them when I was eight. I thought I'd done something bad, but I couldn't think what. But I sent you presents, she said. Were they lost? Why did they not come back to me through the mail? Has your mother taken them? In my first phone call to her I asked if it was true that she tried to take our ranch away when my mother divorced my father. She said no. I was at the phone booth. My mother was getting her tooth filled at Dr. Mercury's. My mother says you say terrible things about us. No, she said. If you say terrible things, then say them to my face. I don't, she said.

In the first phone call, my grandmother told me that my father, for a time, lived near Salmon, Idaho, in a shed. Uncle John went to see him there. He tried to get my father to go back to Chicago with him. My grandmother is Polish. She came to America when she was sixteen.

Saturday, midmorning, Piraté and Julian come in for coffee and shortbread. They listen to the radio, the Spanish station. The music has accordions and trumpets. Mother's out at the blacktop, at the mailbox. She likes to get the mail. Sometimes there's a letter from Clements and sometimes there are only bills. Twice I have seen letters from Grandma Irene. I don't know what my mother does with those letters but I've never read them and she's never talked about them. She said those letters were none of my business. I looked through the trash. They weren't there.

Antonio the One-Armed swings his arm as if conducting, and Piraté taps his fingers on the table. Piraté has a beautiful low voice. *¿Son azules los ojos de la novia? ¿Son azules los ojos de la novia?* The bode bag is full of wine, full like an udder across his chest. Spanish radio is so nice. I understand when the man on the radio says the names of some Vietnamese cities, but I don't understand the other words. Piraté jumps up from his chair and pinches his shirt at the breasts, then pulls the material and does a little jig, laughing with a snarl and singing his own words to the song in half Spanish, half English, "Titties, titties, titties," his eyebrows rising and falling. His eyes are on me, then on the others, his feet jigging, and with a quick swipe he pulls his filthy beret down over one eye. Antonio chuckles but Julian looks down. Then Piraté sits back on the cracked plastic chair cushion and pushes shortbread into his half-toothless mouth. Has he noticed that my teats have grown? I don't know if he understands why they're bigger. His shirt hangs on him like a scarecrow's. He belongs snorting in a pig trough.

Pablo, my white horse, is on the other side of the pasture. He canters to me because I have carrots. Then I tie him up by the sheep corral and make him wait because he thinks he shouldn't have to wait. I think I'm a decent master but now and then I need to remind my horse who's boss.

Julian turns on the spigot and watches the water come into the troughs. He looks like he's smiling but he's only squinting in the sun. There's sweat on his bald head. The ewes run to the water. They're thirstier during lambing.

I could saddle Pablo in the barn, but I enjoy the outdoors. Carrying the saddle the short way from the barn isn't so bad. I get my pick from the barn and go back to him and scrape out the shit from his hooves. I set the bit in his mouth, the reins over his mane, the blanket and the saddle on his back. We ride past the corral of rams.

Julian waves me over and I get off Pablo. He shows me the horn he's cut off a dead ram, and the worms curled inside. He pushes back the dead ram's lips. The teeth there are narrow.

Old ram, he says.

Maybe he ate too much dirt and his teeth got narrow. Maybe he's not that old. They eat too close to the ground.

Too many rams, he says.

How much you figure you could sell one for?

Two, three hundred maybe.

One of the old rams is hobbled with a broad leather strap on the fore- and hind leg. He's a fighter. Now when he gets close to the other rams, he pushes them, but he can't charge, he doesn't lower his head and butt so much. He used to jump the fence to get at the ewes. I named him Cosmo, but it's not good to name the sheep. By naming them you get close to them, and it's a sad thing when they die on you.

I get back on Pablo. The creaking of the leather saddle is so nice. Coming up on the ridge, the horse spooks and lopes sideways. It's only a rabbit who jumps and finds its hole. We dodge prickly pear cactus as if it marks a competition course. I asked my grandmother if she said bad things about us. No. Did you try to take our ranch and make us leave? No. How's my father? He's not the same man as when you were a little girl. He's not the man I raised. His own brother barely recognized him. I never knew him too well to begin with, I told her. She said, You were about four when he left. Yes. There was some kind of trouble but we don't know. Trouble. I suppose that's water over the dam.

The flock is in the valley eating sage and weeds. The sun shines on their backs and pushes them along. Grandmother has a trace of Polish in her voice. It was hard for me to hear her say my name— Sophie? Sophie? She spoke with such excitement and disbelief. I was undeserving of her emotion. I should have called long before I did. I think she was weeping. It was hard to bear. Sophie, darling, I wish you had called sooner.

Sheep have a deep gland between the two toes of their feet,

with a small opening at the front of the hoof on top. Goats don't have these. The gland drips waxy stuff with a faint odor of cabbage and salt. It scents the plain and keeps the flock together.

We had wolves last night, Demetrio says.

No wolves here. Not a one.

I heard them.

You were dreaming.

Sweatshirt, he says.

My sweatshirt comes off.

Pantalones, I say.

He unbuckles his belt and I drop to my knees.

This will stay on, he says bending to my ear and pulling the strap of my bra. His hand on my breast and his tongue circling my ear.

Huevos are fragile and you must take care when handling. You must cup them and speak nicely to them. Hello, beauties.

There are holes in the white sheets from the bleach.

The sun is angry and the plains are quiet. The sage is purple, not green. My horse's head comes up and he sniggers. Something in the air: Antonio's paella cooking or a pack of coyotes far off, or stiff lambs and old rotting sheep piled on top of each other waiting to be burned.

I ride over the ridge and drop into the yard. Piraté's kneeling in a pen with a ewe, cursing in Spanish. His knee is on her belly, and she moans. Her one eye bulges and the other is in the dirt. He rams his fist up her and pulls out the lamb's leg. He puts the other hand in partway and pulls out another leg. Then he braces his feet on her hollow back and leans back pulling on the leg and pushing against her creaking bones. The ewe groans and pants, her tongue half in the dirt. In his soft low voice he calls her *puta*. The lamb comes out. Piraté opens the pink mouth and runs a finger inside, then puts his mouth over the lamb's face and blows into it. He takes the lamb by the back ankles and holds it upside down. Its head is loose and waving, and liquid drips off its nose. He shakes it and says *hijo de puta,* and drops the lamb into the red dirt. He turns the lamb on its back and straightens it, slicing the skin at the belly. He wipes the blade first one side, then the other, on his pants, and slices some more. Then he peels back the skin and takes it dangling to another pen. Fits the ears and all over another lamb whose mother has died, and brings the bleating covered lamb with terrified eyes back to the pen, then guides the orphan's head to its new mother's teat. He doesn't guide the lamb's head gently.

The next night when the moon is past the first quarter, the men make a fire. They pour gasoline on the dead lambs and ewes and rams, and Antonio strikes a match on the bottom of his boot. The sound of burning sheep is bad. Piraté isn't a big man. He comes from the barn carrying, with some burden, a broken feather-filled smelly red chair, throws it on top of the heap, then frowns and lifts his palms to be warmed by the fire. We used to have a red couch that matched the chair. It was down-filled. I was sleepy-eyed when I found my father on the couch some mornings. How old was I? Three, going on four.

The pens are filled with floodlight. The light and fire seem to scare the night away. You shouldn't look at the moon two nights in a row. It will be the same size as the night before, and you'll only be disappointed. If you want to see change, you wait a few days or even a week, and then you're surprised when you look at it.

After my ride I go inside and take off my boots. They're muddy, but the mud will dry and I can brush it off tomorrow.

My mother and Aunt Alice are on the couch waiting for the news to come on. The room is dark except for the light from the television. Aunt Alice is very small and thin-boned and flat-chested. Her feet are narrow and my mother's are wide.

It's raining? says my mother.

Yep, I say.

A ball of thunder rolls across the plain. She looks up at the ceiling and shouts, The heavens declare the glory of God! Alice rolls her eyes but says nothing. She never says anything bad about my mother.

My mother is three years younger than Aunt Alice. Alice married Edward Sanderman who owns a beef cattle ranch. She wears her husband's shirts sometimes, as she does tonight with the tails out and the cuffs over her knuckles. She looks half swallowed up in the shirt. The air in the house smells of cigarette smoke and butter. It sends a wave of nausea through me. The nausea makes me want to lie down and sleep.

Where have you been, sweetheart? Mother asks.

Hello, Aunt Alice.

Hey, Sophie. Your mother says you got a letter from Billy. Has that fungus on his feet healed? I didn't get a letter from him this week. Do you know if he got his two days off?

My mother interrupts. Where've you been?

Thinking. He didn't mention the fungus in his letter this time.

Thinking. My girl thinks. She thinks and thinks. Where were you thinking?

By the catfish pond.

How many letters have you had? Aunt Alice says, wringing her hands.

That smelly pond. Come sit down with us and watch the news.

What? Oh. Three now. It's not so smelly.

Are you thinking up stories when you're thinking? Aunt Alice asks.

Nothing. A big fat nothing.

That's impossible, Aunt Alice says. You must be thinking about something. You're a smart girl. Popcorn?

She holds up the silver bowl. I shake my head.

Sshh. Mother hushes us.

The news has arrived. The rain has flown away and there's no more thunder. My mother turns up the volume.

He didn't say anything about that fungus? Alice whispers.

I shake my head.

A foreign-news correspondent in fatigues is speaking into a

handheld microphone. Behind him soldiers walk across the screen. A group of three is gathered behind and to the left of him, smoking and talking, their shoulders round. I sit down on the floor in front of the popcorn. Television-babble makes me crazy.

I don't know if my mother ever wore my father's shirts. I think she might have been bigger than my father. I imagine when she nursed me her teats must have been full and sore. She wears a size forty D bra. Her bras hang on the clothesline all summer, and they hang there during some of spring and fall, flapping in the wind like dead gulls. There's something I've always wanted to know. Why is the California gull not the state bird of California? It's the state bird of Utah. I learned this in geography class. I'd like to watch gulls dipping above the sea.

The bowl of buttered popcorn sits between them and they eat fistfuls of it. It's what I call nervous eating. It makes me nauseated to think of the butter. I should eat to make my baby grow, but I'm not hungry. The nausea says don't eat. I need to do what my body says not to do.

In the kitchen, the pans they used, one to make popcorn and one to melt butter, have been washed and dried and set on the counter to be put away by Antonio in the morning. The pans' copper bottoms are polished to a bright golden-orange. Antonio doesn't polish them. They're so shiny they stun our eyes and the eyes of the company that we have. You can't call the sheepers real company because they're here constantly. My mother polishes the copper bottoms. She calls it therapy. She likes the utensils in her kitchen just so. She likes her small electricals covered against dust when not in use. I pull the cover off the toaster and put a piece of bread into it.

There's some commotion in the living room. I slice my toast in half, and put it on a plate, and wipe up the crumbs before I go to the living room and settle into the news with them.

Whoa. This is up by that same ridge, Mother says excitedly. She's waving her hands in front of her face as if she might be trying to cool herself. Billy and Clements were there last week!

That's where Billy picked up that fungus, my aunt says. It rained for twenty-eight days straight. Even before they got there. Rain, rain.

I sit down again on the floor between them. Their legs are stretched out straight on the coffee table close to my ears. Mother's calves are round and meaty and Aunt Alice's legs are like sticks. I think the boys are probably somewhere miles away from this place. Almost every night that Aunt Alice is here, there's a cosmic catastrophe with the news.

Look at the two over there, Alice cries. The one with his shirt off. Doesn't that look like Billy's back?

I wonder if Mother's seen Billy's bare back. Probably not.

Does it look like Clements there with him? His nose, I'd say. I'd say! Oh my goodness.

They leap to the television. Mother comes in first place and nestles her face into the glow of the bright day in Vietnam. David Brinkley says something about the men in the clearing. My mother wants to go through the television set and travel on electricity to this clearing.

Oh, turn around. Turn around, young men, she groans.

David Brinkley talks about the villagers being so cooperative, and the villagers in the neighboring village being so cooperative. Suddenly we're back with the other reporter.

No. No, my mother says.

Back at camp the other reporter gives the news. He says the weather's fine and the men's spirits are up. He interviews one of the soldiers, a colored man from Oxford, Mississippi.

Oh, Lord, Aunt Alice says.

We were so close! We were so close!

It might not have been them, I say.

It might not have been them, Aunt Alice says sadly. She looks defeated. There's a chance it wasn't them, you know, Will?

My mother's eyes are sullen in the gray light. Bastards! she shouts.

They listen to the interview. There's no sense in changing the channels. They've found one that is so close to their boys, and they have to stick with it now. There's a hope of glimpsing them. They have not glimpsed them before, and they have never been so close as now. My mother has pulled off one of her socks. She twists it in her hands as if she can wring water from it. She has very large feet. Sometimes she buys men's shoes. Her saddle shoes are men's. After the interview with the colored man, my mother stops twisting the sock and waits. It looks as if her breath has stopped.

Back to David Brinkley, my aunt says hopefully.

Alice knows most of the reporters by name, and when there's a new one it upsets her. She wants to know how she's supposed to keep all their names straight. Some of the reporters are boys themselves, brave boys, and she admires them for being there.

Lady Bird Johnson fills the screen. She's scattered bluebonnet seeds in Texas. The camera cuts to a faraway shot of a highway median of bluebonnets.

My mother changes the station. A commercial for toothpaste. She changes the station. A commercial for baby powder.

They could come back to it at the end, Aunt Alice says. Sometimes they do. Some of the boys say hello home. Should we turn it back?

Mother can't take her eyes off the crying baby, and when powder is sprinkled on it, the crying baby becomes a cooing baby. A happy face as its mother changes its diapers. The mother's happy face. The mother's mouth making cooing noises back to the baby, then lifting the baby into her arms and kissing its nose. The mother and baby looking into my mother's, Willy Behr's, face.

My mother is up off her knees and in four steps she reaches the fireplace that we almost never use because that kind of smoke makes her cough. She picks up the poker and strides to the television and draws her big arm back and smashes the green screen. Pop! The glass doesn't spray, but falls in front of the TV, and there are a few sparks. One smash does it. The picture's gone. There's nothing left. Nothing at all.

I step back when she raises the poker again, and lift my arms over my face. I hear the poker hit the rug with a dull thud. Aunt

Alice has gone behind the brass lamp by the couch, but the lamp won't hide her. Mother would not hit her, but Aunt Alice seems not to know what to expect.

Dear, Willy. Jesus. Alice walks over to my mother who has dropped the poker and who stands slump-shouldered with a hand over her eyes. Her shoulders heave as she weeps. She falls to her knees and bends over as if she's going to kiss the rug. They're only boys. I want to march in a war protest. Where's a protest? I'll go there tomorrow. It's such a mess.

Sometimes, Willy, you scare me, Aunt Alice says.

He's so brave, Mother cries. He's so brave and ambitious.

Mom, I say. I put one arm around her shoulder and use my other hand to gently push the hair back from her face.

He's so brave.

Jesus.

Until she sits up, her hair will only fall back into her face.

Stop that, she says. Please.

I stop pushing the hair from her face.

Try not to take the Lord's name in vain, Mother says to Aunt Alice, her words muffled in the rug.

It's just a word, Will. Alice's voice is soft. It's just a word like any other word, but it carries more weight. Now what will we do about watching the news?

Mother sits up on her haunches. I run to the bathroom and bring her the box of Kleenex and she blows her nose.

Thank you, she says. She makes a clucking sound with her tongue. I'm sorry.

I get the broom and the dustpan from the pantry. I sweep up the glass while they talk about Aunt Alice's husband, Edward. How he doesn't want them at their house switching channels. It drives him nuts when they switch channels.

I'm sorry, Mother says again. Honestly.

I wonder if she's sorry that she brought up Clements' brave ambition. She often says how ambitious he is and how lazy I am. Her definition of laziness is different from mine.

Uncle Edward said you don't watch the news for soldier footage in hopes of catching sight of your sons. That's ludicrous, he said. My mother and Aunt Alice think badly of him for this. He isn't on their side. He's insensitive. He thinks only of himself. Alice sleeps on the couch some nights. She has a bad back because the couch is so soft.

My mother pours a glass of wine for herself and one for Alice.

I'll have to buy another set, Mother says. Let's call Donny Triet and tell him to hold one of his color TVs for us.

A Magnavox, my aunt says.

Let's phone him right now, my mother says.

He might be in bed, Aunt Alice says.

Mother checks her watch. She says, He's not going to sell all his color TVs first thing in the morning.

Still, her eyes look desperate.

Of course not, Alice says. Of course not.

Alice lights two cigarettes and hands one to my mother.

Thank you for cleaning up, she says to me.

Okay, Mom. I'm tired. I'm going to bed.

My mother comes toward me and I take half a step back. She embraces me around my neck and then my back. Her body's warm. I can't remember the last time she held me like this.

Good night then, sweetheart. It's nice that you're able to go off on your own and think, she says. At the catfish pond.

Yes, it's nice, Alice says. You're a very independent girl. I wish my girls were so independent.

Aunt Alice's two girls, Glenna and Sabrina, twenty and twenty-two, are housewives in Casper. Their husbands are certified public accountants. They make their mother miserable by not calling on Sundays. They could at least call on Sundays, Alice says. Glenna has a child with cystic fibrosis. Jeffy. He calls his disease sixty-five roses. He's a beautiful little boy with a splash of freckles across his cheeks and nose. I've never seen him cry. Only last Christmas I saw him fall down the stairs at Aunt Alice's, and he didn't cry. My mother can't look at him. Sickness is weakness.

I was up at five this morning, Aunt Alice says, yawning and making her way to the door. Call me in the morning. I'll pick you up and we can get that TV at Donny's. You've got to get a grip, Willy, she says leaning her head to the side. Really.

My mother begins to cry again. By now I'm getting impatient. I'm tired. Aunt Alice comes back from the screen door and sits next to my mother on the couch. She has a half-smoked cigarette in the ashtray, and she lights another with unsteady hands. Alice coos to her: Everything's going to be all right. Our boys are all right, Willy. Come now. Everything's going to be all right.

Everything, everything, everything, I think. Everything forever in the universe? I'm not such an innocent to think that's true, but it's nice to hear. I say good night and start down the hall for my bedroom.

Sophie, my mother calls. I know the voice. Her prayer voice.

I turn around.

Can we say a prayer?

I bite the inside of my mouth and fold my hands.

My mother stands straight and tall. Her legs together, hands folded, and eyes closed tightly: Who may ascend the hill of the Lord? Who may stand in His holy place? He who has clean hands and a pure heart. Lay you down to sleep, and pray the Lord your soul to keep. Good night, Sophie.

Amen, I say quietly. This is the way my mother copes. It's defective, but it's her way. In my bedroom I close the door, open the window, and breathe the night air. My eyes burn from cigarette smoke. I hear something in the trash by the barn. A raccoon? Maybe a cat. Get out of there! Go on! Shoo! There is one last clank and all is quiet, save for the bleating lambs. My mother is in her God world. Somehow she takes away the humanness of the world. I wonder if ewes are sick to their stomachs when they're pregnant.

In Billy's third letter to me he wrote that he's too tall to fit into the narrow tunnels of the Viet Cong where they hide like prairie dogs. Billy wrote me about coming back to his father's ranch after the war and looking after the cattle and irrigating a piece of land for barley. Barley can grow anywhere, even in the Himalayas or in Lapland. It's used in malt for brewing beer. What Billy would not have given for an ice cold beer that minute. Once a week helicopters brought cold beer in burlap bags.

I keep his letters in their envelopes between the pages of books in my bedroom. I check them. They're still there. The envelopes seem to smell like blood and mud, and I imagine they wear a hue of the same powdery orange-red dust that covers Billy's boots and fatigues and face. He's written me about all these things. When he was on the ranch he had a purpose in his work. He put his back into the cattle, the fences, and the land. Now he marches from village to village without purpose. He plods along in the heat and rain, up and down hills, into paddies and across rivers. He searches villages without knowing what to look for.

Pretty soon I hear Aunt Alice drive off in her station wagon. She has a bad muffler and it drowns out the bleating lambs, but I can hear them again, the lambs bleating for their mothers. I hear the ewes bleating for their lambs.

On the bus I talk to almost no one but Jack, and in the minutes of silence I wish and dream. I wish my brother would not come back for a long time. But boys change when they come back from war. Maybe it will be all right.

I can tell you a few things about my brother. He's not really ugly and he's not really handsome. He has red-brown hair unlike anyone in our family, and he has wide-spaced green eyes like my mother's that flicker like leaves.

Jack is sometimes in a terrible mood. He spits his tobacco juice on the bus floor and all the kids walk around it like it's poison. Today José Vargas, a boy who calls me bastard chick, goes down on his tail end on that juice, and Jack laughs, calling him a spastic little shit. Then he winks at me.

When I was six and Clements was ten, we were in the barn. A litter of five kittens had been born not a month before, and in the first month the tom came back to kill the kittens. The mother tried to save them and almost died. I put ointment on the wounds along her back. They were healing well. Clements knew I loved the cat. She was a small calico girl. All calicos are girls. Pudding was her name. She took opportunities in a beautiful way. When I lifted her, she put her front legs on my shoulder and looked up to see where she could climb from my shoulders. One day Clements took her from the barn and tied her back leg with fishing line to the backyard clothesline. From fifty feet he took shots at her with the rifle. First he shot her in the front leg. Then he shot her in the back.

I stood screaming, my hands over my ears, trying to shut out the noise of the gun. Clements wasn't such a good shot. He had to reload. The sheepers were out with the sheep, except for Piraté who stood near the barn, laughing. His dog Sharpa was a puppy and he had to hold him with both hands around his middle. The puppy yipped on and on. Clements stood with the rifle at his hip, and when I tried to get to the calico, he raised it. Pudding didn't die of one wound to the leg or back. She bled to death.

The tom came back and killed four of the kittens. I don't know if Clements had the kittens in mind when he killed the mother. He must have known the kittens might be killed if the mother couldn't defend them. The fifth kitten lived. On the school bus I hid the kitten beneath my sweater and gave it to the old woman who lived next to the school. She was pleased to have it, and promised to keep it indoors so it wouldn't get hit by a car.

For many nights I didn't come to supper. I couldn't stand the sight of Clements. Mother told me I couldn't ride Pablo as long as I didn't join them. She said Clements was going through a stage.

Not all mothers protect their young, but our calico girl would have. In Vietnam, maybe Clem is so intent on sighting human prey that animals no longer interest him. Human prey is his job there.

In the corral nearest our house stands a table with boxes and needles and medicine, and a bucket. Antonio's shirt arm flaps in the breeze. The pens are filled with bleating boy lambs. Julian comes to

Antonio, cradling a bleating lamb. Antonio pokes the lamb, and the medicine is pushed in. Piraté comes from the barn and pulls out his pocketknife. Julian holds the lamb's forelegs and hind legs, and the plump pink belly faces Piraté. He slices the ends of the *huevos* and throws the tips on the ground. With his teeth he bites the edges and pulls them out of the sac. The small balls are put in the bucket. Antonio will fry them with eggs and garlic and olive oil.

Aunt Alice and my mother eat TV dinners in front of the new Magnavox color television, and watch the late night news.

Aunt Alice wears Mother's slippers and Mother is barefoot. I'm a terrible person. I wish my brother wouldn't come back, although I wish my cousin would. Maybe I'll be happy if my brother comes back. Boys change.

The moon is in the last quarter. The light on the plain isn't very good. In a week I'll see the sliver of moon like the tip of my fingernail.

part Two

THERE ARE THREE weeks left of school and I'm driving the truck from the bus stop, going home. The horses aren't in the pasture and that's because they're in the shed out of the hot sun. I've been thinking about my father.

There are many possibilities as to where he is. He could have hopped a train, slept in the freight car, gotten off in Montana. Clements said my father used to talk about the perfect weather in Santa Fe, and the town square where the Indians sold their turquoise and silver.

I'm not too far from the house now. Mother looks spread out and stuck to the window. As I drive into the yard I see that she's washing up high against the picture window.

My horse separates himself from the rest and trots over to the place where he usually gets his bucket of grain. Patience is a virtue. He'll have to wait.

Let me tell you about Pablo. He's tall and dirty white with a little dapple on his rump. You wouldn't think a big boy like Pablo is too graceful, but I'm here to tell you he's about as swift and light on his hooves as a sweet breeze across water. Sometimes I get up early before school and ride him bareback across the plain. I'm too tired and lazy in the morning to go to the trouble of strapping a saddle across his back. If I ride him after school, I put a saddle on him. There he is in the pasture with the others, lifting his head and watching as the truck comes around the circle, and prancing in place as I drive in and park.

Not all boy horses are potential sires. Pablo isn't. He's a third Clydesdale with no pedigree. He stands on quite a few good qualities, though. He has flat bones and smooth muscles, and his legs square well under deep high withers. There's a fist's width between his jaws, and his eyes are low-set and wide, his forehead broad. His ribs run deeply in his chest and give him a lot of room for his heart and lungs to function. His hind feet are more oval than his front, as they should be. His imperfect qualities are a parrot mouth and fetlocks that are a tiny bit meaty. No one is flawless. When he runs, his carriage is elegant, and when he runs full steam he's straight and balanced. He's coordinated and sure on steep rocky hills, and his stride on the dirt road or the open plain through sage is long and true. He's a bold boy. He has, most importantly, a strong back. Pablo and I are the same age.

According to my mother, when he was a year old he was castrated, but one of his *huevos* was tucked up inside. In order to get the other *huevo,* they would have had to open him up, and Father decided not to. My horse is called a ridgeling because of that. Ridgelings vary in personality. They can be mean like stallions and they can be proud-cut with a rank disposition and unpredictable. They can also grow up gentle and well mannered, save for occasional bouts of impatience. That is Pablo.

Before I saddle Pablo up, I brush him down. After that, I start at his long nose with a flat hand and smooth it and between his ears. I smooth straight back over his big muscled body to the point where his tail begins. I smooth my hand over his whole body, including the legs, down to the hooves. I check for tumors. Two years before, he had a tumor in his back leg, and we had to have it removed. Uncastrated ridgelings get tumors more than stallions with normal *huevos.* Of course I can't feel what's deep inside Pablo's body, and maybe he has a tumor growing there right now. It might look stupid, my spending so much time at this, but nobody really sees. Mother, Julian, Antonio, and Piraté, anyway, do plenty of stupid things. We all do.

I dig the shit out of Pablo's hooves with a pick.

In bad weather or when the sun is too hot, the horses stand around inside the loafing shed on the near side of the pasture. The pasture is fenced with split cedar rails. My grandfather built that fence and it has lasted a long time. There are six horses. I feed them twice a day. I muck out the manure every other day. Parasites and insects love manure. In summer I fill the wagon with it, and in winter I fill the plastic sled. The manure is dumped in a pile on the other side of the pasture, and we use it for fertilizer on the garden, or I lime it down if I've built up a mountain of it. We mainly use sheep manure in the garden. In the spring and summer months, I sometimes spread the manure around in the pasture and turn it over every few days with a pitchfork. The birds eat the eggs and insects out of it. I like to see a flock of black crows bobbing over the manure. They look like chickens pecking at feed.

At the start of the summer Piraté hooks the camper to the back of his truck, and Demetrio follows on his horse. Then once a week Piraté drives to Demetrio's sheep camp and delivers coffee, flour, apples, canned goods, and such. From time to time Demetrio orders Aqua Velva. When he and his camper are on the high flat land Piraté unhooks the camper and says good-bye. The sheep are in the valley with their heads bowed.

Piraté parks his truck about fifty feet from us. He pulls down his fly and makes a wide arcing stream of urine into the sage. He could make the urine standing next to me, and it wouldn't be ruder than dropping his zipper fifty feet away. If he weren't rude he would have done his business on the other side of the truck.

The men go to sleep early now. During lambing they take turns staying up all night. They've gone back to their early-to-bed hours, rise at six, and get plenty of sleep. They're all worn out from slitting throats and yanking lambs and peeling skin and setting them on fire, and it takes many weeks to catch up on their rest. Piraté and Julian and Antonio's trailer is right next to our house. Its windows have no curtains and there are no lights on.

The old ram stands alone at one end in the shadow of the corral. The moon comes up yellow and hangs low, and something is strange about me. It's only my baby growing. The ram would like to jump the fence. It's wise to first tie the ram up to the corral so that when the hobble comes off, he'll stay put and you can then lead him from under the chin to the other rams, and he won't lower his head to butt. A ram butts from the top of his head, not his forehead. It's all my fault that the ram butts. When I was a little girl I petted him every day on the head. My brother warned me, if I petted the ram he'd butt. Now I untie him and walk away easily, my back to him. I have never been his target.

Every morning Piraté comes first into the bathroom. He sings in his rich low voice and gargles, and the toilet seat goes down. I'm in bed rubbing my stomach and I feel bloated down there.

The front door opens and closes. I eat a piece of bread and go outside. The sky is blue. The ram stands on the far side of the corral but he's out of the corral. Piraté is next to the barn, sawing wood and making pens. He goes into the barn and comes out lugging a salt block. His thighs half hold it up. He puts it in the center of the ewes' corral. The ram jumps lightly over the corral. Piraté's back is facing him. The ram lowers his head and charges. Piraté lands with his head against the water trough. He cries out, and the ram hits him again from behind. Piraté's face hits the outside corner of the trough, and he lands against the salt block. The ram comes for him again.

Piraté doesn't deserve to die.

I run to the trailer and knock on the door. I say, Piraté's hurt. Julian shades his eyes with a hand. Antonio steps out and runs to the corral. He wears no shirt and his stump is pointy. Julian goes back inside and comes out with a rifle. He shoots the ram, who falls hard, and dust rises. Julian carries Piraté in his arms. Antonio opens the truck door and Julian put Piraté inside. Mother comes outside, and her eyes are crinkled in the sun. She's wearing her blue nightgown. Julian says they must go to town *por que* the *cabeza* is caved in on one side and blood is coming from the ear. It was stupid of me. He doesn't deserve to die. My mother looks down at Antonio's one arm. Her mouth wrinkles up as if she's eating a piece of lemon. Go put your shirt on, she says.

When it rains, purple flowers come out on the sage. The sheep are white after the rain. They're full of burrs and ticks, but the dust on their wool is washed into the red ground. The water trickles down the dirt road and makes tiny rivers, and the stream fills. The stream washes to a river, then a bigger river, and a bigger river, and finally into the ocean.

The ram was such a jumper. He jumped so lightly over the corral. Now he's dead.

Pastor Fabila stands in front of the pew, his hands resting lightly on the oak ledge. Red-bound hymnals are lodged there facing me, and pencils and tithing envelopes. No one else is in the church.

Tell the pastor what you've done, Mother says, green eyes flashing.

My forearm is pinched in her white-knuckled grip. The church is cool and moist and dark. Jesus on the cross stands with his arms spread. His feet are joined by a nail, and he looks very sad peering down on us. She's tricked me into coming here. Lied. But lying for the sake of saving her daughter from sin isn't wrongdoing.

Pastor Fabila gives me a sorrowful look, as if things occur, and there are consequences. It's a kind of bored sadness. Piraté had a consequence and now I'm having one. Pastor Fabila's face is bunched up and pained-looking as if he has gas. His face is in a grimace. Grim-ass. It's the second time my mother has brought me to Pastor Fabila for a kind of Catholic confession, although he's the pastor of our Lutheran church. If I will do my part and admit my wrongdoing, and the pastor will do his part and say a prayer asking that God forgive our transgressions, then Mother will talk all the way home about my wickedness and how fortunate we are that we can take solace in the church. If I don't do my part and admit my sin and ask for forgiveness, we'll drive thirty-two miles in silence.

We're waiting, says Mother.

I throw off her hand with a flip of my arm.

The ram didn't just wriggle out of his hobble, Mother says. We know better than that, don't we?

Pastor Fabila says, gazing compassionately upon me, Our Lord is benevolent and forgiving.

Pastor Fabila doesn't look to be a man who can change the world. He's thin and frail and white in the face. While I imagine some pastors feel they can change the world, I think he is without that belief. I think it would be good for him to take some sun on his face.

He came this close to dying, says Mother. Permanently scarred.

I shrug.

If he'd died, you could've gotten murder in the first degree. He's too decent to make a stink. You could get attempted murder. Do you understand the seriousness of this, little girl?

Piraté's a pig, I say.

Mother and Pastor Fabila glance at one another.

Sophie. Look at me, please. We have only to genuinely ask God's forgiveness, and God forgives.

I don't have anything to ask from God.

All right, from the very beginning she was goat-headed. Sat in Dr. Mercury's chair, for crying out loud, refusing to open her mouth so he could examine her for braces. Tried to kill her brother with a scissors when she was only six.

That's an exaggeration, my trying to kill my brother. I was trying to keep him from hurting Walter Wiggy Walk. Clements made Walter cry. He stepped on Walter's tiny wiener dog feet.

We haven't seen you in church for quite some time. We miss you here, Sophie. Mrs. Welmar misses you. Do you remember her, our secretary? She asked about you only last month.

Wicked girl. The devil incarnate. Piraté's served our family nearly twenty-six years. Did Clements give me trouble like this?

Sophie. Sophie.

Oh, he drank a little too much beer in high school with his friends. That's normal.

Sophie.

I didn't do anything.

Very well, little miss. Very well.

What about it, Sophie?

No offense, Pastor Fabila, but eat shit.

You've got a filthy mouth, he says, and Mother shakes her head. Ticktock.

They quietly say the Lord's Prayer. After we walk out, Mother two stepping ahead of me and mumbling, it's the start of the silent truck ride for thirty-two miles.

Last February when he was in boot camp Clements wrote us a letter. He wrote that his army blanket looked like the blanket he and I used to make tents over the clothesline. With clothespins at the top and rocks to pull the blanket into a V and hold it to the ground.

In a letter from Vietnam Clements tells me that the only good thing about the night over there is that sometimes he settles into a hole in the jungle and watches the changeover from dusk to dark. He watches the stars come into the sky like pinheads and it's a very cool sight. How's Mom, he wants to know. I worry about her. She never used to be so religious. Religion don't solve everything but sometimes I pray. Tell Mom thanks for the care package, I'll write her next week, and tell that bastard Julian I'm gonna whip him at checkers when I get home. Also, forget about Dad. He's long gone and it's better that way. Clements. P.S. Have you seen Lillian around?

I saw Lillian in town during her break from Bilky's. She was walking arm in arm with Micky Shaeffer. Son of Bilky Shaeffer. They walked down to Calley's Doughnuts. I saw them all right. Necking. It wasn't my job to watch over Lillian in Bluerock and I didn't want to put this on Clements while he was over there. He was tough here, but I don't think he's so tough there. Maybe he is.

It's easy to pick on someone smaller, and not too hard to shoot animals who don't have much of a brain and who trust. Maybe he'll win a badge of bravery over there. I don't care.

The first of June, half our sheep were shipped by semi-truck to Climax, Colorado. The government sets a limit to the number of sheep we can graze there, but they'll be on Bureau of Land Management land until the end of August. They sweep across mountain pastures which have grown in from fires and avalanches. Demetrio lives in our silver camper there in the wooded mountains, and keeps two horses and two dogs. Piraté used to go there, but this is Demetrio's job now. He's been with us two years. He's eighteen. Mother pays a rancher from Loveland to bring him groceries once a week. If you think Demetrio came to me for love, you're wrong. I went to him.

Piraté has a long clean pink scab that runs across his forehead, over the top of his scalp, and down the back to the bottom of his ear. Most of the time he wears his filthy red beret over it. Otherwise he walks and talks the same as before the ram got him. He doesn't look my way if I pass him in the yard, and at supper he glares at me. When I ask if I might please have the meat or green beans, Julian or Antonio passes them to me. I don't blame him for not looking at me. He knows I set the ram free, but I'll never admit it. From time to time, I eat my supper outdoors on the front steps and watch the sky. The sky is sometimes every color at dusk.

I miss Demetrio already.

Julian, Antonio, and Piraté stay on our ranch building pens or mending fence. Sometimes they tune trucks and putter with the tractor. They watch over the other half of our sheep, who move along the sage and back through the yellow and gray-green fields and are, from time to time, herded into pens for graining and worming. We keep our acreage sectioned in parts and fenced off. We keep some land ungrazed for a time so it can grow in again.

While Antonio cooks, Julian and Piraté keep watch for coyotes and prairie dogs. The prairie dogs live on the plain in small underground burrowed towns. A male and his females live together in tunnels, making babies and competing with our sheep for food. The prairie dogs are sheltered in large parks, but not on our ranch. Julian and Piraté keep the guns oiled and clean.

I have not told Demetrio about the baby. I have not told my mother either. It's something I will keep to myself for another month, and when the pregnancy shows I'll tell her. I have an idea that Mother will Jesus this and Satan that. She'll take me to see the pastor again, although that isn't the worst thing. It's easy to sit and let them talk while I think of other things. After school I'm tired because of the pregnancy, and most of the time I go into my bedroom to lie down until supper.

Sometimes I'm sick in the morning, and sometimes I'm even sick before I go to bed when I push my toothbrush too far back on my tongue. I brush my tongue to get the bacteria off. If I put my hands on my stomach, I become queasy. There's a type of tea in the pantry, and I drink it when I feel sick. It's made of peppermint, raspberry, rose hips, and fennel seed. Also, I eat crackers. Mother might take the baby from me as it slides out, and send it away. I have to be careful.

Demetrio has no telephone in the mountains of Climax, Colorado. I thought of phoning the rancher in Loveland and leaving a message with him, have Demetrio call me. But if he calls me and Mother answers the phone, she'll wonder what's going on. I don't believe she didn't have sex before marriage. What does it matter? There are sins and there are sins. I steal money for my emergency envelope, but I don't steal aside from that. I don't honor my mother so much, but I might honor my father if I knew him. I want to honor my mother. I wish she'd honor me. Some days when I really miss Demetrio, I think I'll call the rancher in Loveland and get a message to him. I want to understand why I can't feel too bad that he loves me, and I don't love his soul. My missing him comes and goes. I can be sitting on the bus and looking out at the galloping antelope and miss him. I might brush Pablo's flanks and wish I could lie down with Demetrio. He's a good man who sends part of his paycheck to his mother and seven brothers and sisters in Guadalajara. He's the oldest child and feels a responsibility.

Demetrio treats his flocks with care, and scolds men like Piraté who are cruel to the sheep, although Piraté only laughs at him. He keeps his horses grained and in sure-fitting shoes. He changes his dog's water bowl daily, and each night checks the dog's fur for fleas. He touches me with tenderness and kisses me roughly and smooths my hair. He can tell me a story on a minute's notice, and I laugh until my side hurts. I'm not a religious person, but if I were, God might punish me for my selfishness. I don't think, though, that every bad thing that happens is a punishment from God. Things both good and bad happen.

One letter I got from Clements had been water-soaked. Rain? It dried stiff and wrinkled. It's a good thing Clements writes his letters in pencil. He was going to Saigon to have a woman. He wanted love. He couldn't go on leave for some time, but he wanted love, and he was ready to hightail it to Saigon. I was not to tell Mother about that. He says his lungs feel burned. Burned to shit, he wrote. He coughs all the time. Clements asked how Pablo was. He said, I think Billy has a crush on you. He's just lonely. I mean, he's never had a girl-friend. And are you less lonely, Clements? Clements wrote that he told Billy to knock off the questions about me. I'm his cousin.

I wrote back to Clements: Coughing isn't productive when you're hiding in the jungle.

The day is bright and warm and the bleating of distant sheep is always present. Next to the fence, north of us, there's a small grove of aspen trees. The budding flowers pop out each spring, and they're conelike with beautiful greenish-yellow two-winged nut-lets. Now in summer the leaves are dark green. The bark is smooth. Demetrio once told me my legs were smooth like aspen bark. Sometimes when fresh-baked bread comes out of Mother's oven, I think of Demetrio and the way he used to run his hand up my leg. We ate a lot of bread and jam in his camper.

Mother and I meet Julian and Antonio out by the pasture. Split cedar rail fences are strong for the most part, but one old section of the pasture fence is rotting away. When my mother was a girl, she and her father fenced this pasture. My grandfather was a big man with arthritis. He had tick fever when he was young, and I'm not sure he really recovered. He went to his grave from heart failure. I never knew him.

Julian points out the bad section, and Antonio grunts. Mother wants to know if we could use a cheaper wood to replace the bad part, and Julian says it would then not be a handsome fence.

I don't give a goddamn how it looks, Mother says.

All right then, Willy, Julian says.

She takes the Lord's name in vain all the time. She prays for forgiveness every night, though.

Antonio hangs a blade of grass in the corner of his mouth. Mother walks the length of the bad part of the fence, stops, stares at it, squats down, and touches it at the base. She walks with her hands crossed over her chest, back to us, frowning deeply.

You're right, she says. We'll have cedar.

In the late afternoon Julian goes to town and comes back with a truckful of cedar. Antonio and I help him unload it. We dig holes and pour old engine oil in them to keep the posts from rotting. The next morning a cement truck drives in and leaves a batch of cement to pour into the old holes. The poles are four inches around and eight feet long, and we set them three feet into the ground. Julian pounds long thin planks of cedar with ring-shank nails. If he used regular nails, the horses might push on the fence and loosen it.

Since school is out I sleep late in the mornings. I go to bed a few hours after dinner and try to fall asleep before the late news. From time to time I lie awake in my bed and wonder about the trouble I'm in. Songs murmur and come into my head. I can't push them away. The familiar songs sometimes play over and over in my mind, and I invent songs too that seem to come from waste, from my worry.

• • •

Hello, Aunt Alice.

Why, you're limping, Sophie.

I twisted my ankle. It's not serious.

She sets her eyes in the distance, my mother says, when she needs to pay mind to the foot in front of her. Is it still swollen, baby?

Not so much.

What happened? Aunt Alice asks.

I landed wrong when I got off Pablo. That's all.

Mother says, Come sit down.

The rug is thick and soft compared with my saddle. I slide my back up to the couch. My mother runs her hand through my hair, her fingers like five cigarettes sharp with old smoke. I don't dislike the smell so much, but I relate this old smoke sharpness to her.

The reporter on television is a familiar wavy-haired and squinty-eyed face. The concern is about the college campus. War protesters lift painted signs into the street-lamped night. They walk together ten, twelve, or fifty across, their faces stiff and angry. Baby killers. Baby killers. My mother's fingers have stopped moving on my head. Her hands close around my hair and pull tightly, lifting so my neck is straight. Water comes to my eyes and I say, Mom, that hurts. Sorry, babe. What a rotten to-do over there.

Is Clem a baby killer?

I sit on the front steps and read my assignment for chemistry. I played hooky on the day of the final experiment. Now I have to make up for it. I'm not smart at understanding how chemical reactions take place. There's an equation and there's a result. I have no interest in knowing how these equations come about. I understand I'll never be a wizard in that field.

I look up from my chemistry book. Julian is walking casually, a gun cocked at his elbow, out to the pasture. Slung over his shoulder is a burlap bag. The horses huddle together at the east end of the fence. I know what he's about to do. He walks to within ten yards of the manure pile. Some of it I've spread out and will turn tomorrow so the sun can dry it out and the birds can pick out the bugs. There are a dozen crows there, all black and stout-bodied with heavy bills. They're intelligent and wary birds. My mother told me stories of my grandfather trapping one and training it to talk. Julian has hunted the crows before. I have no sentimental ties to crows. I refuse to eat them. There's something about watching them pick at the manure, swallowing up eggs and insects. He sets his shotgun, pulls it up to his shoulder, and takes a five-second aim. When the gun fires, the horses jump a little and dance around and whinny. One of the crows is in the air when it slumps and drops heavily to the ground. He picks up the four dead ones and puts them in his burlap bag. He walks toward the house and stops when he comes to me.

You want to clean the dinner? he asks.

No thanks.

Antonio will make a lard crust with potatoes and the meat, he says.

No thanks.

¿No te gusta?

It seems unappetizing to me.

You don't eat much. Too skinny.

He shrugs and goes inside, closing the screen door easily. He doesn't let it slam as I've asked him politely, Please don't, and for this time that he does not, I'm more thankful than usual.

Antonio, in the kitchen, has begun to cook onions in olive oil, and the afternoon bread is baking. They speak in Spanish and I hear something about paella. I suppose they're going to waste fresh mushrooms and rice and tender canned shrimp by adding crow to it. I'll have to eat my supper outdoors or in my bedroom so I don't have to see them eating the crow. I'll have to pick the crow out of my supper. I might not eat supper at all.

I take Pablo for a ride to the catfish pond. It's as round as a water tower. A few years before Grandfather died, he built a dock ten feet into the water. Clements used to stock the pond every season, but in the last five years it has become overrun with minnows and fat-whiskered catfish. The water is dark brown and cloudy. Anyone can dip a hook in the bait can, drop a line in the pond, and come up with a giant catfish. They'll feed on anything. I wasn't sick to my stomach before I came here, but I see the barrel at the foot of the dock. I know without lifting the lid that there's half a can of bait in there. I almost get sick looking at the barrel. I can nearly smell the bait without pulling off the barrel top. The bait is a cheese mixture with something else added to make it rotten. It's one of those chemical reactions, and I don't know the ingredients, much less the exact equation, although chemistry has done its job well here.

Instead of making the final experiment in chemistry, I hitched to Wamsutter, a small town at the Continental Divide. It's only about fifty miles away. I went to the coffee shop, read the paper, walked around town. It was something different, to sit in the coffee shop for a few hours. A trucker took me there, and on the way back a roofing salesman picked me up. He was all right. He dropped me off a block from school.

The odor of catfish bait is sharp and bitter. I'm tired. I have gone without a nap and I shouldn't do that. When I'm tired I should sleep.

Pablo and I canter back home. The sage is more gray than green. To the east, the land falls and rises. Hills wrinkle into one another.

So that I'm polite, I sit down at the table with my mother and Julian and Piraté. The newscaster on television says: Leftist college students and members of traditional pacifist religious groups and longtime peace activists and citizens of all ages are opposed to the conflict.

Come, Lord Jesus, be our guest, and let these gifts to us be blessed.

Antonio, in the crook of his arm, brings the stainless steel bowl full of crow paella to the table.

There's an insect called the blister beetle, and crows eat them with intensity. Horses, too, can eat blister beetles off hay. The beetles have a powerful poison and there's no antidote. Their bites can kill within six hours. The poison causes blisters to form in the horse's mouth and on the lining of the stomach. Then the intestines rupture. Sores come out and cause pain and the horse becomes colicky. The colic is the only warning before the horse dies. I've seen many blister beetles on a single bale of hay. For some reason blister beetles don't affect crows. They feed on them, grow fat for the bullet, and end up on our table.

No, I'm not going to eat paella with crow. I think I'd better change a few things. I should eat vegetables, fruits, and eggs. Not catfish. I shouldn't eat fish that suck on stinking cheese. I hadn't thought about food within food before I got pregnant. I should eat tomatoes and cucumbers. I wouldn't mind a slice of ripe watermelon. I think cottage cheese would be good. If Demetrio were here, I would still be eating bread and jam, and that would be fine.

I excuse myself from the table and don't look back as I walk.

I open my window and the breeze waves in. I smell rain and electricity. My underarms are damp and my face is cold with sweat.

The breeze is cool, but it dries the sweat. I pull the wool cover off my bed and wrap it around my shoulders. I sit otherwise naked at the window facing west. There is the pasture, and the loafing shed, and to the right the outline of horses clumped together. Barely the spine of the first hill. A blanket of clouds. There is no moon. No pulsing stars.

I write Clements so he does not get his hopes up for Lillian's love. If he has to get love from Saigon girls, then he has to get love from Saigon girls. Try to think of any good things, I write. Try to think of the time we slept in the backyard under the blanket of stars. It was too hot for you under the wool blanket, and you moved your sleeping bag out and slept under the stars. I don't care who wins or loses the war. I know I should care because you and Billy are there. Don't take it wrong. But I think the war in itself is defeat. Mother still watches the news footage to try and see you and Billy. A crazy thing. Pablo is fine.

·   ·   ·

A meandering shimmering stream washes through the valley. The sun glints off wet rocks in the stream and the rocks nearly out of the water halfway up on the bank. The grasses around the stream grow tall.

Where there's a fork just past Demetrio's old camp, my horse and I turn north. The road makes a wide cut and winds through hills for a little more than two miles. The Picardys' and the Glensmiths' and our land used to be one ranch until it was divided and sold by the half Arapaho Indian who made a killing and moved to Cheyenne. On summer afternoons the heat slows everything down. I have to put the garden in tomorrow or the day after. I can't complain, except for the heat and how my back might ache afterward. My horse cuts wide tracks over the dusty road. His rump swings easily from side to side, and his tail strikes back and forth at flies. The line in the near hill just over that ridge is the start of the Picardys' ranch.

The antelope move along with the sun. When I get down into the valley, they have moved around a bend and vanished into the hillside. It's good to sit for a minute on Pablo's back and think about nothing, but let the things on the plain pull any sadness away.

The road to the Picardys' from our ranch is made of the same red-packed dirt about as hard as stone, cracked from the sun. I look west at the edge of our property to the place where Demetrio's camper was. I think of him and wish I could stop in at his place and eat with him and love him.

Tin Picardy asked me to come over and meet her niece. The afternoon light spreads yellow all about Pablo and me.

I lead my horse down the fence line, open the Picardys' gate, and bring Pablo through. A light breeze comes upon our back and pushes us along.

Their *borregas* are near the property line, cloudlike in the west. The sheeper sits rounded in his saddle at the back of the flock. His horse is red-brown. Three Border collies run jagged lines and sew up the sheep.

The road is steep. It levels off after a while, and the Picardys' yard meets it. It's not a yard with green grass. It's a yard of dirt and weeds and a cement driveway. Their house is two-story and the roof is bad on one end, caved in a little. The garden to the west of the house has been planted already, and a high fence has been built up around it to keep the deer and antelope out. Still, some get in from time to time. They always do. I slide the saddle off Pablo, pull off the blanket and bridle, and put him out in their pasture. He drinks water from the trough, then rolls in a patch of dirt. I can't see Tin's horses.

Tin comes out to the front porch. So does the girl who is Tin and Rudolph's niece. I walk up to the porch and greet them. The girl shakes my hand. Her name is Edwina. She has long stringy blond hair parted down the middle. It's the color of saltine crackers and hangs partway in her face. Tin goes inside to get me a glass of water. The girl crosses the porch, her body rigid, and sits down on the pine porch swing. Her short short skirt is made of white patent leather, and her nylon stockings have diamond patterns. Her boots are white. She might care or she might not that they'll attract some dirt here. Her shirttails are lifted and tied and I can see some of the skin of her stomach. It's a strange way to dress, but I've seen similar clothes in magazines at the drugstore. I thought it would take courage to wear clothes like that. If you wear clothes like that in town, people will say things like, Halloween's long gone. She might think I dress in a strange way, like a boy. I do. From her profile I can see she has a bump at the bridge of her nose. Her posture is stiff and she's rubbing, with one thumb, the inside of her other thumb. She sits unmoving, as if she's gone inside her body and willed away the outside. She's shut out the noise of the popping chain saw in the distance, the droning bees in the begonias, and the clip of the dog's nails across the porch floor. Her pale eyes carry a germ of anger, or else she's bashful. The big orange dog comes to rest its muzzle on Edwina's lap. Her name is pronounced Edwin like the man's name with an *a* on the end.

How long did it take for you to ride over? she asks.

Not too long, I say.

Maybe she doesn't want to be here. At any rate, that's the end of our conversation for now.

I borrowed my jeans from Clements' closet. They're big enough around the waist to take care of my stomach, and cinched with a black belt borrowed from his drawer. My stomach is the size of a girl who has eaten a big meal and who now has a bellyful of air.

Tin comes back and hands me a glass of ice water, then sits on the swing next to Edwina. We make small talk about the weather, the war, Clements. Edwina has come to live with Tin and Rudolph for the summer because she doesn't get along with her parents in Detroit, Michigan. She can't ride a horse, and she knows nothing about sheep. She can tend to the garden and cook a little. Tin's husband is our sheriff in town. Their two sons are grown and married, living in Fort Collins and Greeley, Colorado. Edwina is staying in the younger son's bedroom. She sleeps in the upper part of the bunk bed, and says she's never slept in a bunk bed before. Neither have I, but I don't care if I do or don't.

After another hour I tell them, It's time I get going.

The land rises and meets the sky gray with night, as I ride up onto the edge of the stream. Pablo grazes first, then dips his head and drinks.

At night there is a kind of alertness in the crickets' song. Lightning bugs twinkle, and if you look out along the flat, the stars come down to meet them. Pablo canters across the last hill and over the plain, then slows into a trot. Aunt Alice's station wagon is in the drive. I think it's too late for the six o'clock news, and too early for the ten o'clock news.

Pablo walks into the loafing shed where the other horses stand and shift. One lies on the straw bed. I go into the barn, scoop some grain into my pants pockets, and take it back to Pablo. I hold the grain out for him flat on the palm of my hand. His lips meet my palm and take up the grain.

I have a few friends from school, but I don't feel so close to them. Edwina is different from the other girls, but I don't know exactly how. The way she talks for one thing, and the way she dresses, for another.

The lights are on in the trailer. The windows are open and I can hear Spanish radio. The music is low. I'm tired of *música de acordeón* and trumpet. The men's voices rise over the music and laughter, and I know what they're doing. Playing cards, the three of them.

There's a moth the color of my fingernail on the screen door. Mother and Aunt Alice are sitting on the couch sipping wine, and Mother's cigarette burns in the ashtray. Alice's cigarette dances in her mouth, the tip glowing, dancing as if she's flicking the end with her tongue. She pulls it away and blows smoke that forms a curtain in front of the light of the brass lamp. My aunt is wearing white crew socks stained brown at the heels and toes, and her feet are crossed on the coffee table. The hall light is on. Then I see them. Billy's three letters spread out over the coffee table. Out of the envelopes.

He wants to know if you're a virgin, Sophie. Why does he want to know a thing like that? Mother rubs her hands, crossed, over her elbows. Do you have such a depraved reputation?

Has my son touched you, Sophie? Speak frankly with me. Has he? Oh, I'm sure not, Willy. This is all very innocent

My face goes hot with shame. I roughly gather the letters and their envelopes.

Do you know what it means to get letters like this from a cousin? Incest, Sophie. You are an incestor.

Don't, please, tell him you've read these.

Jesus, restoreth my faith. Oh, Jesus Lord.

It's so bad over there. Don't tell him.

You see what happens when you lose your faith.

Did my son make an advance on you?

The letters are private, goddamn you.

Mother stands, her chin quivering, and she raises her hand over me, the flat palm trembling close to my face. She calls me the devil's companion and a fool, and says that God gave me no brains. Then she lowers her hand to her side. The elbow is stiff into her ribs.

Go to your room and I'll pray for you. Where God gave no

brains, the Lord will be merciful and have pity if it's asked for, and restoreth. Forgive you, for you have sinned.

A terrible feeling of shame has come over me. I feel out of sorts. Have I been present under Billy's sex and have forgotten? This much is true: I must have done something very wrong. But then I reconsider. This is the way it is in my mother's house. Many situations turn out like this with my mother begging the Lord to have mercy upon me. I'm not bad for this. I never had sex with my cousin Billy. He kissed me once when I was seven and he was eleven. He kissed me on my nose. Then he bit it.

Billy and I weren't close before he left. He writes letters asking certain questions so I can give answers. Letter writing and letter receiving take his mind off the war.

In my room I pull back the bedspread and strip off my clothes, stand in front of the mirror viewing myself first right and left, then full on. I turn around and look at my backside. Everything is fine, in order, coming along. My hair could be trimmed up from the shoulders. It is black and glossy like wet ink. My shoulders are strong, and at my breastbone the ribs show as though they're pulled tightly across. The nipples have turned chestnut. My teats are gorged, but not with milk. They feel bruised. My stomach is a half moon above the black pubic hair, and my legs are lean and muscled in the thighs and calves. The expanse of my back is without fat. My buttocks are plump, but rounded and tucked and firm. It would be fine if my muscles and skin and face would always look this way. But my mother, who was once young and fresh and beautiful, takes on certain characteristics as she ages. Facial lines and the shape of the eyes in their sockets and posture and voice. When I was about four and my father had been gone less than a week, she was rocking herself in the chair and weeping, her face turned to the window, arms crossed, rubbing her elbows. It's one of my first memories of her.

Aunt Alice leaves after the news. The muffler on her car needs to be replaced. No I'm not a virgin, no I'm not seeing anyone, no I couldn't care less where my father is. To hell with them and to hell with my father.

The fan on my dresser moves right and left. It blows warm air around. Outside, the stars. When a star begins to die, its fate depends on how much mass it has. The outer layers are pushed out and the stars become red giants. If the star is twice as big as the sun, it's called a supergiant. It can explode. When a star becomes a black hole I wonder if any light can escape. If any object can escape. Astronaut Edward Higgins White II did space walk gymnastics for twenty minutes on *Gemini 4*. He wanted to stay out there. When he said he'd go back inside, he told Command Pilot James Alton McDivitt, It's the saddest day of my life. White spent twice as much time outside in space as Soviet Cosmonaut Aleksei Leonov did last March. All Leonov did was somersault around at the end of a rope getting dizzy while White moved around without getting dizzy. I'm at the open window in my bedroom and I hear the whinny of one of the horses, then, Holy holy holy, Lord God Almighty who made heaven—

I don't hear it from the yard, but from the hallway. She's in her bedroom, and I know that she's on her knees in front of her bed with her hands folded and her head bowed. She has eyes like agates in her strong face. She is rigid. Her pink thin mouth is the only thing moving. There are lines next to her mouth, and the start of two slugs of fat. That summer she said, Forgive me, for I have sinned. The woods were quiet save for her gurgling. I pushed her over and she stayed frozen in the kneeling position: arms crossed over. My mother crying: Virgin Mary. Virgin Mary. She's in her bedroom kneeling in front of her bed, I can tell you that. The first time I called my grandmother she said, Your mother—I don't like to say—but she hangs up on me. I wrote letters, Sophie, but they came back unopened.

My father moved to Salmon, Idaho. He drank too much. He put a man's eye out and went to jail. When he got out he lived in the hills. Uncle John went to find him. My father wouldn't go home with Uncle John.

My first collect call to her: But, dear heart, for your tenth birthday this year I sent you kidskin gloves. No, Grandma, I didn't get them. I didn't think so. There was some kind of trouble between your mama and papa. Did you try to take our ranch and make us leave? No. Did you say bad things about us? No.

The moon is up like the tip of my fingernail. The moon this week is not good for anything regarding light. My mother's in her bedroom. She can certainly quote quite a few long passages from the Scriptures. I can see mushrooms in the dirt near the grass. They glow white.

Edwina calls and asks if I want to come over and teach her to ride a horse. That's something better done by trial and error, I tell her. I can show her some things about the bridle, and she can ride bareback for a while. It's good to start bareback and learn about the body's balance. But I can't help her today because I have to put the garden in.

I won't go bareback, she says. I have to have something to hang on to. If I could ride a horse, I'd come over and help.

Can you drive? You've got a driver's license, don't you? How old are you anyway?

Sixteen. Rudy took the truck to work and Tin drove in to the doctor's an hour ago. Ingrown toenail. Bad pain.

Do you want to come over and help with the garden?

Would if I could.

I could use the help.

If I could get there, I would.

My whistle is shrill and long, and Pablo comes from the far side of the pasture. I lead him back to the barn, brush him down, and smooth my hand over him. I check his hooves because his feet are larger in the damp spring and summer, and smaller in the dry fall. I need to see if his shoes fit properly and that his hooves aren't cracked or full of fungus. In summer the weather is both dry and damp, so you have to check. His feet seem right. I put the bit in his mouth and the crown piece over the ears. I lead him out to the fence, line him up against it, then step onto the first fence rail and swing my leg over him. I no longer dare to jump stomach first on his back then swing my leg around. We're off like a ball thrown, my legs shaped hard against him.

The sun is up. It might be a dry warm day. You never know. Over the ridge I can see down to the stream. Pablo drops down the pitch with his legs stiff in front, and his rear humping to and fro, his ears pricking, his nose high, his breath heavy and wheezing. Then I see it. A mountain lion at the stream's edge, its head bent over the water. Pablo's nose is high so as to see the full distance. We come down a little. The mountain lion's head lifts, and for an instant I see it's brown. A little closer and it's reddish-brown with black stripes from mouth to eyes. The tip of the tail is black. A female. The head is small and round with a black spot over the eyes. Her belly is wide with babies. Mountain lions are solitary animals. She takes off running across the plain and pretty soon she's up over the ridge. She must be four feet long, maybe a hundred pounds.

I've never tasted the stream water. There might be a dead animal rotting in it upstream. There are parasites. You just never know. Some people drink it.

Edwina steps out of the bathroom brushing her hair.

Nuts. These knots.

No sense in all that brushing. Your hair's going to get messed up riding back over to my place. She raises her hand to spin the silver hoop in her ear, and when she sees me watching she leaves it alone. It's a good thing she's left that patent leather skirt in her bedroom. She's wearing short shorts. The insides of her legs are bare, and Pablo will sweat on them. She says this is all right. She doesn't own any jeans, man, she says. On her feet are tennis shoes.

She asks where did I get boots like that.

Town, I say.

Cost much?

Not if you wear them all the time.

You didn't want to pierce your ears?

Not really.

I climb onto Pablo using the second step of the porch, and Edwina does what I've just done. She's on tightly behind me and I can feel her small breasts in my back, her arms holding on around my waist. Her breasts aren't so small that she could walk down the railroad tracks without her shirt on and someone wouldn't notice. They seem to be the size of oranges, and they're alert.

Not so tight that I can't breathe.

Sorry.

We ride across the hills and down by the stream for a ways, and grasshoppers flip out and spit tobacco juice. We ride over the ridge to my mother's house.

Most vegetables should be grown in at least six hours of sunlight each day. In the back of the house we have a yard of grass fenced in, and a clothesline. There's a redwood picnic table and a black barbecue on three legs. Behind that is a plot of land as big as the lawned yard, and it makes an ell to the side of the house on the east where the sun will come up. The house will block the sun and put the plot into shade in the afternoon. That's where we'll plant the cabbage and lettuce. We won't have a fence around our garden. After the garden is planted, one of the dogs will be tied here to a leash on a post. Rebby or Pokey-Joe. He'll bark and snarl if an animal comes in to feed.

Our soil is full of clay. It bakes hard under the sun, sheds water and drains slowly, is slow to warm up all spring and even into the early summer. We add gypsum, sand, peat moss, and sheep manure. Edwina knows about some of this. Her mother has a garden in Michigan.

She talks almost all the time, though her words are slow. I think it takes some time for her to finish a thought in words.

You know you've got a wasp nest over there.

I look at the barn and see the cone hanging in a corner: I'll get it later.

I'm allergic to wasps. And bees. Anyway, when I was fifteen I started working at my old man's, and a week later, the day after I turned sixteen, I quit. It's a milling shop. Milling, drilling, boring. Boring. No kidding.

She works while she talks. She mixes the gypsum and peat mixture into the ground. She uses a hand spade: Had to ride to work with Dad every day, getting to know you, getting to know all about you for that silent twenty-minute Mercedes ride from our house to the shop.

Some of her words are punctuated with spade stabs. Her eyes on the ground: The old man's not what you call a great conversationalist.

What was your job?

Answering phones. Greeting customers. Made the coffee. Marbleized counter where the coffee urn was, and the hole puncher, the postage machine. Et cetera.

She sits on her haunches and looks over at me. I'm digging too, and I sit back for a minute. She shades her eyes with a hand: My desk was a couple feet—well, Dad's desk was behind me and up two steps, like on a platform, like he was a king or something, King Helmet, Helmet being his name.

Her eyes turn away from mine: I might slit my wrists if I had a name like that.

Why were you only there a week?

I left. Edgar was the main salesman. Old guy always broadcasting his sales goals. Drove the old man nuts 'cause Edgar could never make them.

She rubs her face and a piece of straw falls away: Like our goal here is to grow the largest number of veggies possible in the space available with the least amount of maintenance. Edgar had his sales goals.

Her fingernails are long. Red dirt is packed under them and around the ridge of cuticle. You lay out your seeds and seedlings so that when they grow, the taller ones won't block the shorter ones. I have a list in my mind about how we'll lay out the vegetables. Each vegetable is labeled spring, summer, or fall, but you need two thirds of your space for warm-weather crops. Spring has passed, but it's time now for the spring vegetables because of the cold ground in Wyoming. Every season we plant Roma VF plum tomatoes because they don't, as much, get root rot and wilt. I buy my seeds early and store them in the pantry where it's cool and dry. The soil's ready now. I take a handful and squeeze it. It isn't dusty or too solid and sticky. It's beautiful ready red soil that crumbles like Dutch apple pie topping.

Machine shop stinks like grease and oil. Coolant. The guys have awful BO. Well, she says in her slow humid talk, they work hard. I had a pot of coffee going in the office all the time to cancel out the smells.

She pauses and turns her hoop earring. Do you want to get those seedlings now?

I sowed the seeds in peat moss and perlite. I planted them in cut-back milk cartons covered with clear plastic bags.

They're out back in the shade, I tell her.

My gramps owns the place. He likes his coffee strong with sugar—but to hell with him. I don't much care for coffee. You?

The smell of it makes me sick, I say.

I put the cut-back milk cartons on the windowsill and when the plants came up I watered them with a mist of spray from a bottle. When they grew to one inch high and had two or four or six leaves, I put the seedlings each into their own cut-back milk cartons. I get up and clap the dirt off my hands and wipe them down my jeans. I see a front coming in. The clouds hang like dark blisters. I think they're called mammatus clouds.

You sweating or what out here in those pants? Edwina asks.

Julian comes from behind the barn where he's been putting together a tool shed out of two-by-fours and planks. He takes off his billed cap and wipes a sleeve over his forehead.

Not so much, I say.

There's a line on his bald head just before his forehead where the cap has left its mark. His lips are dry and lined, and there's stubble around his chin and lower cheeks. He looks like a tired old dog.

Rain coming, he says.

I'm thinking about whether I should get the tomatoes that have been growing in the back windows since March. I've been shaking them in their crates once a day for pollination. There are pepper seedlings. We'll have potatoes and cabbage, onions, carrots, beets, and maybe corn. I think of putting off the planting until the rain passes, even though it could rain tomorrow and the next day and the next. We have to be lucky in our planting, that the soil should be just right, that it should crumble just so between the fingers like pie crust. The rain sometimes comes out of nowhere. This front is moving slowly.

This is Edwina, I say.

Mucho gusto, he says.

Hello, she says.

Julian, I say.

Her white short shorts are mighty red-brown by now and he's looking first up from them as they are his focusing point, then down to the tips of her now bare and dark feet. She has beautiful slender legs.

You hear what it's supposed to do tomorrow? I ask.

Did not hear, Julian says.

The soil might be too wet in the morning. We might have to wait until noon.

Edwina and I walk into the house for something to drink. I tell her I'm not sure that Pablo and I can ride her back over to her aunt's house with the storm coming.

I'll call my aunt and ask her to come get me. She won't mind.

I tell her the storm might come on in the middle of our ride, and I'm not much a fan of lightning when I'm riding on the plain.

My mother isn't around. Maybe she's in her bedroom. Edwina and I go to my room. She sits on the rocking chair and I lie on my bed and close my eyes for a minute. Edwina leafs through my record albums.

Why do you like Dylan? she says.

I don't know.

You like his voice?

I like it because it doesn't have to be perfect.

He kind of moans.

That's all right with me. You didn't tell me why you left Detroit.

No, I didn't.

Do you want to?

Can I put one of these on?

Sure.

She chooses the Stones. She puts the needle on Mother's Little Helper and Mick starts in.

I saw them last year in Chicago, she says.

Wow, I say.

You know they got arrested for urinating in a public place.

Animals do it anywhere they like.

But what if everyone went around urinating all the time? In the city?

So tell me why you came here. I listen to the words of this song while she thinks. Mother's Little Helper has words about house-wives getting through the day. What it takes to get through the day.

You don't have any Kinks, Edwina says, running her finger across the vinyl top of my record player. The record player belongs to Clements. When he went away, I took it.

I've got James Brown.

Papa's Got a Brand New Bag. I'll put it on after this. I'm ashamed, in a way, she says. I had a pretty big fight with my old man. I said a lot of things I shouldn't have.

Antonio is in the kitchen clacking and rattling and grunting and pounding down his bread. A pot of soup has been simmering on the stove all afternoon. It smells like venison and doesn't send waves of nausea through me so much as other food.

Do you want to stay for supper?

I better call Aunt Tin.

Phone's in the kitchen. That's Antonio out there getting supper.

She comes back in three minutes and says she'll stay.

What kind of jewelry's in that jewelry box? she asks.

See for yourself.

She looks inside my jewelry box. It isn't too elegant. It's made of dark leather worn and marked and frayed at the corners.

It was my grandfather's, I tell her.

Not a thing, she exclaims.

Not a thing.

Why not?

I don't know. For me jewelry's—well, I don't know. Like men and their ties. What purpose does a necklace serve?

I think ties were used like napkins. Historically. In Detroit I saw a woman wearing a tie.

Not here, I say.

She spins the hoop in her ear and is silent.

I'm embarrassed. I think I've offended her. But no.

She says, You've got to get out more.

I laugh a little. Half a laugh. I don't need to see women in ties. I don't care what they wear in Detroit.

Have you been to the city?

Which one?

Any one.

Nowhere.

Nowhere?

Chicago. When I was a baby. Do you want to tell me why you left Detroit?

Don't you ever want to go to the city? Any city?

Sure, I say.

Her eyes tell me she thinks I'm strange. Maybe I am. No. I'm not.

What happened is, this guy comes in to apply for a sales job.

She starts rocking in the chair. Not small nervous rocks like my mother used to make when the chair was in her room.

He's a lot younger than Edgar, and I can see the light in my old man's eyes. I can hear his mind working at the prospect of replacing Edgar with this MBA in a seersucker suit.

I think of the song: Hush little darling, don't say a word, Papa's going to buy you a mockingbird. My father moved the rocking chair into my bedroom.

What did you say his company makes?

Bombs and stuff.

Bombs.

For the war. They make some parts for color TVs and a part for a typewriter. Gramps telling me every day about the pressures Dad has, and I tell him, not in these words exactly, to save his breath.

Papa's got a, Papa's got a, Papa's got a, Papa's got a. The needle's stuck.

This is scratched to hell, she says with her nose over the record. She bumps it with her finger.

About these records. I tell my mother that some kids at school gave them to me, but really, the money came from her. Tucked away in change from grocery shopping in town. I'm her slave for that, so she has to pay for some kind of pleasure, and I choose music.

Edwina stops rocking and leans forward with her elbows on her knees: My back's tight. Do you have any Mentholatum?

I don't think so.

The way my old man talks about his bombs not being nuclear and therefore acceptable. Sick bastard. She stares at me: You're tired, aren't you? I can see it.

I stand up and close the bedroom door. I lie down on the bed and put my hands behind my head, my arms butterflied.

What I am is pregnant, I say, and nobody knows but you.

The sun hits against the window like yellow arrows. Small fine particles of dust dance in the light. I'm staring at the dance and then at her as she watches it.

I think whatever you tell me about your fucked-up old man, it had better be good because I have here in this house one strange mother. I've got no father. He left when I was four. My brother likes to kill. He'll make a sport out of almost anything. They use piano wire over there.

I'm in the dark, Edwina says.

I don't think you're stupid.

I'm not.

I told you my brother's in Vietnam.

Is he one of those baby killers?

I don't know.

Your mom know about the baby?

Not yet. I don't want to marry the father.

How far along are you? Do you love him?

I unzip my jeans and split them down as far as the zipper goes and stand before her in my underpants.

I don't know, she says. I've never been pregnant.

Three months. A little more. I don't know.

You don't know if you love him? You going to keep it?

I am. Yes. I don't know if I love him.

I zip up my pants and lie down again. I roll to my side and face her.

Hey, man, she says, it's not the end of the world.

Of course not.

Who's the father?

A sheeper. I stop for a moment. I've spilled my history in twenty seconds. I've never done that before. But, I say, tell me the rest of what happened at your job.

Edgar went into the men's room and slit his throat with a motherfucking letter opener. I found him on the linoleum with a little blood around his face.

Dead?

Not then. A letter opener, for Christ's sake. Three days later he did a much better job with a razor. On his wrists.

Christ.

Then the door creaks slowly open. My mother's face is cut in thirds by the doorjamb and the door so that part of her nose and one of her eyes can be seen, and some of a smile. I'd like to keep the image, but the door is pushed all the way open. She stands there in her bra and panties. Her eye shadow is blue as a blackberry, and she has ratted and sprayed and divided her hair at the crown. The back part is mussed on purpose like a crow's nest.

Hello, hello! Isn't this nice! All girls! What a pleasure to have you here, young lady.

Mom, this is Edwina. She's staying with the Picardys.

Could you sit with us at supper?

Yes, thank you.

I'll be happy to drive you home afterward. You call Tin and tell her so. And tell her we say our prayers before supper. We always do.

Thank you, Mrs. Behr.

Come on, girls, wash up.

She closes the door quietly behind her.

Are we supposed to dress up? Edwina says.

You never know about her. But we're not going to.

I mean, is she drunk or something?

She doesn't usually have her wine till the ten P.M. news.

Is she a drunk?

Oh, she has one or two sometimes. No, I don't think so.

When you going to tell her?

I don't know.

Is she going to be mad?

She's a Jesus freak.

Christ, dressed like that with all these men running around?

The Lord is her shepherd. She shall not want. She does some crazy things sometimes.

Is she crazy?

I don't know. What's crazy?

Christ.

It's warm in the bedroom. I open the window. The breeze pushes in and blows the curtains, and they skip, then settle down. My mother's out there talking with Piraté. Her hair rises in the wind. It rises in back-combed clumps.

Why don't we get dressed? Edwina says.

What do you mean?

Come on. Where's your mom's room?

She doesn't like strangers in there.

I don't know why I follow her to my mother's bedroom, then to my mother's bedroom closet. It smells like Chanel No. 5 perfume.

Will she mind?

What are you thinking? She'll kill me.

You can blame it on me.

She'll hate you.

She takes two dresses from the closet and pinches one at the shoulders. She holds it in front of my shoulders. The dress is dark blue rayon with white stars on it. She wore this dress last year to the Fourth of July parade. Edwina walks into my mother's bathroom.

Forget it, I whisper. Come on.

I leave and hear her footsteps behind me on the hall floor. She holds the dresses over one arm and carries lipstick and eye pencil and a powder compact in her hands.

Mother's dress sleeves rest just below my elbows, and its hem lays upon my knees. My lips are weighted with her lipstick, my face is pale with powder, which Edwina put on for me. Our brows are penciled broad as caterpillars and our hair is ratted in unorganized clumps.

Edwina is slightly taller than my mother, but fifty or sixty pounds lighter, maybe more, and my mother's dress hangs on her.

Supper! my mother calls from the kitchen. I look at Edwina and she looks at me. I feel like we're about to jump off a bridge into a lake.

We go to the kitchen. Julian's smile makes the men turn. My mother's lips part, and her shoulders pull back. Edwina's smile fades, and I wipe mine off the planet, leaving red on my wrist.

¡Qué linda! Antonio says.

My mother hushes him. She stands and puts the napkin from her lap onto the table. Edwina, get your things, she says. Julian looks down, his smile gone.

I follow Edwina down the hall. In my bedroom her front teeth are over her lower lip, a slim smile on her face. My mother explodes.

What kind of joke is this?

It was my idea, says Edwina.

Do you mock me?

We don't mock you, Mrs. Behr. We wanted to dress up for dinner.

It's an uncomplicated lie. Still, she can lie.

Go wash the makeup off your face, young lady, she says, frowning at me.

In the bathroom I turn on the faucet and wait for the water to warm. I cup my hands and let water flow into them, and rinse my face over and over. I watch the small puddle of red and black before it whirlpools down the drain. I hear my mother's footsteps along the hallway as she walks into the kitchen. When I'm finished, I go into the bedroom. Edwina smiles, and I smile, and she leaves so that my mother can drive her home. I close my door. I'm not hungry. I'm empty in my stomach, but unhungry.

The sky to the northwest is full of thunderheads like a mound of ash. The wind scatters them easily, and you could push them along with one finger if you could stand on a ladder tall enough. And push the horses from the left part of the pasture into the easy shed so they're safe from the storm. You won't let anyone push you into thinking you're the devil's little girl. The air burns like a match, sulfurous with lightning. Here it comes, the storm, but it will be gone before too long, moving so fast, already away from the west. There in the west the sun is still four hours from setting, and hangs perched like a fish eye. Filaments of yellow light are strung down to the damp plain. That fast.

part Three

Most of the plants, before the vegetables arrive, will produce flowers. I pinch off the tips of the peppers so they'll come in anything but small. The berries and thick rinds are growing in. One cheap packet of seeds will give me two hundred plants. Too much for us. I planted only one tenth of the packet. They became seedlings, and now this, the flowers and berries and thick rinds. The tomatoes were started in March in the wooden crates, and laid up against the windows at the back of the house. Their flowers bear yellow five-parted nodding petals. As for lettuce, you can choose many varieties. In butterhead there's Bibb, buttercrunch, and dark green Boston. In crisphead there's iceberg. In leaf, the black-seeded Simpson and Red Sails. In romaine the Parris Island Cos. They're beautiful names, aren't they?

Edwina sets two apples under her shirt at her teats, and throws her shoulders back. She has very good posture anyway. The boy bagging our groceries is Matt Natelson, good-looking with crooked teeth and braceless. He has a system of keeping one hand close to the bag and quickly tossing canned goods and produce from one hand into that other hand. He misses with a grapefruit, though, because his eyes aren't on the food. Or maybe they are.

What are you looking at? Edwina says sharply to Matt.

In a low voice he says, Did you think I was looking at you? You think you're pretty much something, don't you? Edwina and I are standing hip to hip and he shifts his eyes to me. I like your neck-lace, Sophie, and your earrings.

Thank you, I say. Edwina gave them to me. This is Edwina. She's staying with Tin and Rudy Picardy. I don't have pierced ears. These are clip-ons.

He's the opposite of ugly. Looking at him makes me point my toe around stupidly.

Edwina tosses back her hair and glares at him.

I pay for the groceries and Edwina and I lift a bag each. Then he says in a low voice, his brown eyes on her hidden apples, Hey, are you going to pay for those, or are you just a thief?

She flicks her hair up in the back and we walk out. Then we go to the drugstore and leaf through magazines. She pulls the apples out of her shirt, hands me one and bites into the other.

I think he likes you, she says.

Who?

Who do you think?

That's just Matt. I've known him since we were in kinder-garten. He's only had two girlfriends, Mandy Fresquez and Billy Jean Rael. Those girls aren't anything like me. I'm not anything like them.

You want him to want you, you have to treat him like shit.

Who says I want him? I'm having a baby, remember? I don't even know if I want Demetrio.

Boys around here couldn't love a girl like this, she says about the model in the magazine. She's Russian. Look at those legs.

But they could love a girl like me. Is that what you're saying? A girl who acts like a boy half the time, with her big old horse and her boyfriend who lives in a tin camper, a girl who has shit on her boots?

I didn't say that. I see model-type girls in Detroit. But I don't see girls like you. Your hips aren't skinny like a boy's, though.

Of course not. I'm pregnant. Hips grow when you're pregnant.

You seem, she says, like you'd run into lightning if you could, just to spite it. Or open a bull's mouth and stick your head in. I bet all the boys around here are crazy about you, aren't they.

Don't be crazy.

Just remember, if you want any of them, treat them like shit.

Okay, Edwina. But I think you're full of shit.

Hey, did you say there's a line of whorehouses around here?

Down by the tracks.

I want to see them.

I don't want to go there.

Why not?

Because I don't.

You're not curious?

Edwina, those whores are where the sheepers go on weekends, most of them, drunk and whoring. If we go into one of those places just breathing the air we might catch the same diseases those sheepers get. Just listen to the hired hands around your place, the way they cough and wheeze. You never know. Anyway, what are we going to say if we walk in? Just looking around?

We could go to a bar and see if we'd get served.

I know all the bartenders in this town. This is Bluerock, population two thousand eighty-six. Everybody knows I'm not twenty-one. I can't drink. It's not good for the baby.

Don't you want to see things you haven't seen?

I think of what I haven't seen and would like to see. Waves crashing against rocks. Maybe even waves crashing surfer boys into them and hurting them just a little. The state fair where they have machinery hill and a million chickens in cages waiting to be judged. Tennessee Walkers come into the stadium and the announcer says, Walk on. The inside of a woman's tunnel to see if it's like my own.

Sure I want to see some things. Do you know much about flowers?

Not really.

I wonder if there's a rose without thorns. I heard that somebody invented a watermelon with no seeds.

You're weird, Sophie.

I know.

Hey, Soph, what's happening? comes a man's voice over my shoulder. I turn around. It's Jack, chewing bubble gum.

This is Edwina, I say, and he shakes her hand. I tell her he's our bus driver.

Was, he says. Waldham Window Washing now.

He hands me his business card.

I want to make the world something to behold, even to those who have to stay inside. When're we going for that hike?

Have you got time? I ask.

I go every weekend. I bring the kid in my backpack. He can almost walk now.

That's great. I'll call you. But I'm sad you won't be our bus driver next year. I blink and pinch my wrist to keep from crying. I'm too emotional. Way too emotional since the baby started growing.

You never know, he says, then tells Edwina, Nice to meet you, and walks away. He has a sway to the left. It's something you don't notice in a bus driver unless you see him out of his element.

The dullness of the moon brings out the garden. The night breeze barely flutters the clothesline and Rebby lies chained beneath it, his soft paws breathing the scent of grass and weeds. The beetles under the soil bulldoze tunnels and eat what they like. Snails, slugs, cutworms are creatures of the dirt. Everything dead rises from life and everything in life rises from the dead. To make a baby, the seed coating is broken into, and there you have it. The moon has settled softly into the garden. You might as well think of night as a beautiful time. You have no choice but to accept it. It'll come and come again no matter what you like.

If I have to leave after my baby is born, I wonder if I can live with my father. I'm angry that he's never contacted Clements or me since he left, and why he hasn't is one of the things I'll ask him. Someday I think he might want to see me.

The first time I called my grandmother I didn't ask her right away about my father. I wanted to know things about her life: How were her grandchildren, my cousins? Did she still take the bus to Niagara Falls in the summer? Did she still crochet hats and scarves?

My grandmother's always written to my father. Sometimes she gets a letter, but most of the time her letters are returned unopened with a red stamp across the front. Undeliverable. He almost never lives where there's a telephone. We rely on our telephone. I remember when my grandmother visited our house. I was four. It was summer, and she came with Uncle John. Their hair was black like my father's, and the print of my grandmother's dress had many daisies. I thought if she went outside, the bees would try to make honey from her dress. My father must hate Mother. He must hate her, and we, his children, are reminders of what he made with her. He must hate us.

How old was I? Three or four. What I remember about him are these things:

His hands were big and tough, and the skin across his knuckles cracked in the winter. He braided my hair and tied a blue ribbon at the bottom where the rubber band was. Our wiener dog was fat. His little pickle dragged over the ground when he waddled along. His name was Walter and he was Walter Wiggy Walk to my father. He was a house dog.

The muskmelon vines of my garden will reach ten feet across. Fruit hangs on the vine and its ripeness causes it to detach and fall to the ground. It's ready to harvest when the stem slips easily from the melon. Its ripeness is the pressure it needs to slip carefully away. The breeze barely ruffles the clothesline, and the night air smells of sheep and pollen like honey and flower lobes, flower lobes as ear-lobes that could take pearl earrings from pearls of the sea. One day I'll let salt water wet my ankles.

My father wore overalls and brown boots.

He shouted at one of the Mexican sheepherders. *¡Cabrón! ¡Cabrón!* The sheeper's saddle had made saddle sores on his horse, and my father didn't tolerate that. I rode in front of my father on his brown mare across the plain to the sheeper's camp. *¡Cabrón! ¡Cabrón!*

My father's hair was short and dark and his eyes were brown. The white scar under his chin was like an alphabet noodle. Were his hands really big and rough, or was that my belief as a little girl? I once came into the living room when he was sitting in the stuffed chair. He was under the brass lamp, lighting a match and holding its flame under a needle. I got close around his knees. There was no blood when he lifted out his sliver. He wiped Merthiolate where the sliver had been, and his skin turned pink.

Mother once told me the reason he left was a matter of irreconcilable differences. All ties severed. All ties were not always severed. Grandma Irene used to send Christmas and birthday gifts. Then only cards. Then nothing. I thought the gifts and cards had stopped coming because I'd done something bad. But I couldn't think of what I might have done. I asked if I could call her. You're forbidden, Mother said, then recited the story of Adam and Eve and the apple that changed life for man- and womankind forever. I think that story is just a story.

The fence blends together with the easy shed, and the pens blend with the barn. They stand out against the dull gray sky. I see no mushrooms along the dirt border of the grass. The moon would make them glow, even dull as the moon is tonight. Rebby stands out against the clothesline pole. He faces the garden. His tail thumps back and forth, and tiny whines chip the air. It's easy to escape from my bedroom.

I can smell the carrots of the garden, although they're really only roots trying to become carrots. I stop in my tracks when I see that my mother is lying face up, as if she's crept here on her hands and knees and has now rolled over and spread herself out in the garden. Her arms are wide open. Her bare dirt-covered feet are crossed at the ankles.

When I walk past Rebby, he takes after my ankles in his playful way. He doesn't nip, but tries to gum them. Go on. Sit. I whisper. He doesn't sit. He wants to play. *¡Siéntate!* He sits.

My mother lies unmoving, her head in the grass, her legs and feet over the seedlings. I fear she crushes them. The dirt makes a thin line down her shins, thicker at the thighs where her shift is pulled up, and a border of white panties shows. Above are soft

white thin clouds. Her hands are outstretched so that she looks cru-
cified on the plot. She moves, lifting a handful of dirt, letting it fall
onto her breasts and stomach. The dirt showers onto her shift.

Mom?

Her eyes are closed. Her chest is lifting and falling as if she
couldn't live by breathing so slowly.

Mom.

Hmm, she utters.

What are you doing?

Looking. Her eyes closed.

What are you looking at?

Waiting to see, she mumbles.

You're full of dirt, Mom.

Yes.

Do you want to get up?

I look to the garden and moon, and define this moment with
my eyes, and sigh. But what's crazy? What are the boundaries of
the actions of that word? I shouldn't wake one of the men to help
me. Am I the only one to have seen this, or has she done it in front
of them already? Looking for the Virgin? Is this what she does?
The garden and moon return my eye-definition.

I can make a bath for you, I say quietly. Come on. Come out of
the garden.

Come on. The water's hot. You like it hot. In the hallway's light I see
the stain of dirt on her feet and legs. The stain of grass on the back
of her yellow shift at the buttocks where she has the most weight. I
lift off her shirt and unhook her bra and pull down her panties.

We used to take baths together, she says stepping in and pulling
out. Too hot.

I run cold water. I run my hand in the water up and back to
mix the hot with the cold.

All right, I say.

She steps in. We used to take baths together when you were
only a baby. I used to put you on my chest.

Yes, I say. I don't tell her I have no memory of that.

I rub the washcloth with soap and take the washcloth to her back. She tips her head and looks up and moans softly. I wish you could take my shoulders off, clean them out, and put them back on, she says. They need oil. Or something. Then she laughs.

Is she drunk? I don't smell wine on her. She isn't drunk with wine. She crushed the seedlings in the garden. A fraction of the garden, lying there, the seedlings conquered with her leg weight. She took from them the dirt they needed, and showered her legs and shift with it.

You used to sleep in our bed. I got you and brought you to our bed, and your father went to the couch.

She almost never speaks of my father. I hang on the word for a moment, waiting to see if she'll give more. The water rolls from her shoulders as if her shoulders have been oiled. Her skin is white and beautiful and thick in flesh.

How old was I when you brought me to your bed?

With both hands I wash her neck. She reaches back and grasps my wrist and says she's so happy that I'm here for her.

A child. Three or four.

Why did Daddy go to the couch?

It wasn't right that you were in our bed with your father. He wanted no mistaking that. That it wasn't right.

I was just a little girl.

Yes. It would have been all right, I think. But he didn't think so.

Why did you bring me to your bed?

Hand me the razor. Honestly?

Yes. Honestly.

So your father would go to the couch.

She lifts her leg and rests her foot on the tub rim, and soaps her legs, and shaves.

Why?

I didn't want him in bed.

Why?

She doesn't answer.

I would whip the washcloth to her shoulder skin and make a red welt, then leave her alone in the bath. But I want to know more. I remember that he came in in the morning when there was no light through the windows, and put me in my bed. My mother was so angry. She said angry things. My bed was cold, and next to her I'd been warm.

She's trying to tell me that once we were close. That it doesn't matter how you come to it. It matters to me. I couldn't come to closeness through her bringing me there to put him out.

Then he left, I say.

Then he left, she says. Her shoulders round and the bumps in her neck come to the surface of her skin. I press my fingertips to the flesh between them. With both hands she lifts cupped water to her face. She's crying.

What were you doing out there, Mom? I'm not as calm as my voice. What were you doing in the garden?

Forgiveness.

Forgive what?

I don't remember the bed or her bringing me there. I remember my cold sheets when my father carried me to my room. Her navel was like a tiny acorn. Her belly was a pillow for my head.

Let me be, Sophie. Please. Thank you, but I'm through now and I want to go to bed.

I throw the washcloth on the floor. You'd better tell me!

Her head turns. Her eyes narrow. Or what?

The night air is warm. I know it is, but I'm cold. I close my bedroom window, lie down, and pull the blanket up to my chin. I'm too tired to take off my shorts and blouse and socks. I'll sleep in them and wake up, water the garden in them, ride Pablo in them. That's how lazy I am. I probably am not lazy, really.

But she spoke of my father. The bitch.

To get to sleep, sometimes I have to trick myself. Good thoughts need to enter my mind. Chances are, good thoughts will not only lead to sleep but to peaceful sleep. Good thoughts blend into pleasant dreams. There was a silver tub that hung from a nail on the side of the silver camper. Demetrio and I filled it with water from the underbarrel. We boiled water, and some we used cold, and it made a lukewarm bath. We couldn't sit in the tub, not even one of us. Too small. First Demetrio stood, and I with the sponge pressed warm water on him. It was May before the sun was hot enough to warm us on the plain, on our barrel-water-wet nude bodies. You need to forget any angry thoughts before going to bed, if you can. I was on my knees at the tub and Demetrio was standing shin-deep in water. He stooped to pick up a dusty rock, and wiped the dust across his leg. I washed it away. He bent to lift a handful of dirt, which he spread across his stomach, and when I washed it there he was streaked with mud. He curved his body and kissed my mouth, first gently, then with roughness. I cupped below his weathercock with my mouth and took in the seasonings of the plain and the sweat from his work and sun and horse. I call it a weathercock because it tells the climate of our tranquillity or non-tranquillity. The Sea of Tranquillity is a place on the moon. My feet, from dusty boots, put brown in the water. The place he touches first is my knee. He moves the sponge to wash my knee, and when he's finished he touches me there with one finger, blows on my knee to dry it, and moves to the other knee. When he's finished there, he moves to the place behind my knee. And the other. And squeezes the water at the back of my waist. Many times. I can no longer bear the pleasure. The bath is finished, I tell him, and we go inside the silver camper where it is warm and pleasant from the sun. The small chills from my wetness outdoors are absorbed in the sheets.

This morning Edwina and I drive to the veterinarian in Bluerock and buy Ivomec for the Picardys' sheep, who are infested with ticks and sucking lice. Then we buy two ice cream bars and drive forty miles east to the Platte River.

The sandy shore is crowded with people. I don't believe the sand is natural. I think it's been dumped here by truckloads. The rest of the shoreline is yellow dirt.

We park the truck in the parking lot, which is dry grass. We take our things and walk toward the river. The water's very clear. The river comes south from Casper through the Alcova Reservation, and runs into the Pathfinder Reservoir. It wanders down to the Seminoe Dam and through the reservation. We catch it south at the V where it branches off into the Medicine Bow River.

Edwina has hawk's eyes. She turns to me: Do I see what she's looking at? Two boys at the far end of the strip of beach. Our towels hang draped around our necks. She carries a paper bag with sandwiches and apples. I'm in charge of the thermos of lemonade.

Tin lets Edwina take the truck almost any time she wants. Before we can have the truck, Edwina needs to finish her chores. Most mornings she makes soup for dinner. Last week she made a fruit soup in the blender, and the ranch hands wouldn't eat it. They like meat and potatoes. We went to the library and checked out a soup cookbook. There were some recipes with macaroni and turnips and pumpkins. She had to make sure she added meat and potatoes to the recipes. She uses the cookbook partly, and partly her imagination. Cooking isn't hard, she says. It's like painting or writing a poem. But I haven't painted, save for the trim on the house. I've never written a poem.

There are all kinds of people here at the Platte: old men with snow-white bodies and hairless chests. Mothers with their children. Edwina wears her light blue short shorts that have been cut off from corduroy pants and are frayed up an inch at the bottom. Her hair is gathered at the top of her head and tied in a ponytail. It hangs down and keeps time with her swaying hips. Her legs and arms are very tan and her hair has bleached brightly in the sun. Her eyes pierce the light.

Boys are playing catch in the river and a dog on shore barks at them. The current in the river isn't strong. Small children squat in the sand and use little shovels to take sand from one mound to another. Teens in inner tubes drift downstream. A man stands in the river with a little girl. She wears an orange life preserver. He holds her while she kicks her small legs and splashes water over his face. His eyes are sun-pinched.

Edwina has to wash clothes for six ranch hands. One of them, a fat sweaty one, has his eye on her, she's told me. When he winks at her in the yard, she puts up her middle finger. From time to time we pick up supplies for their sheep: Curatrem for liver flukes, sheep dip for ticks, Tramisol for stomach worms, and antibiotics.

We're almost at the end of the beach. The boys' transistor radio is on, and the rock-and-roll is full of static. I can see that they're around seventeen or eighteen. Edwina spreads her towel. I spread mine. She slowly and carefully unzips her shorts, moves her hips to get out of them, and lets them drop to the towel. She straightens up and lifts off her T-shirt, and drops it to the sand. She's wearing a yellow-and-white polka-dot bikini, and I can see a fine red rash where she's shaved her pubic hair at the sides and top.

I sit down to take off my clothes. In my house you have to take what you can get. My mother buys my clothes because I have no allowance. In the past year and a half I've managed to steal about forty dollars in weekly lunch money and change from errands I've run for her. I'm saving it for emergencies. It's tucked in an envelope in the barn between two bales of hay. My bathing suit's dark green and one-piece. It's made of synthetic material that stretches in all directions. It holds my stomach in as much as it can be held in at three and a half months along. My stomach is a potbelly, as if I've eaten too big a meal only moments before. Say, two plates of ribs, slaw, four pieces of toast, and two servings of ice cream with bananas and fudge. I'll get much bigger. Then the baby will come out. If my baby is a boy I'll name him James after my grandfather. A girl? Her name will be Frances after no one. I'm aware that I look like an idiot next to Edwina, and that these boys must think we're two opposite girls finding friendship. It's remarkable what two handsome boys not from around Bluerock will do to you, and what kind of hole they'll put you in without knowing they're putting you into it.

Their hair has been buzz cut. Maybe they're high school football stars and homecoming-king types. I'm viewed by the kids at my school as unordinary. Not extraordinary. A strange duck. I'll never be a homecoming queen unless they vote me in as a joke. Flaws can be inside or outside the body. Maybe the boys are in college. They surely aren't in Vietnam.

I'm not an ugly toad, but who'd want a pregnant girl when they could have a nonpregnant girl like Edwina? If they viewed my stomach as a little pot of flesh, and if they viewed my new cleavage beautiful, still, there's something about Edwina's head raised so high and her mouth so full and promising, and the way she unzipped her shorts. I'd like to take down my one-piece straps, pull the green shiny suit to my waist, and walk chest-naked along this stretch. I'd like my breasts and back to brown in the sun. But the Platte River isn't France.

When we spread our towels, someone caught someone's eye. It would seem to me that it usually starts with that. I don't think I caught anyone's eye. The boys are equally handsome. One of them has a jutting chin and blond hair and slits for eyes. He wears an allergy chain around his neck. The other boy wears sunglasses. The bows are across his perfect short sideburns. His legs are longer and thicker than his friend's and his teeth are very white and straight. He's not smiling. He's only looking into the bright sunlight, and his saber-teeth are exposed as he squints. My experience of boys is limited in the broad sense of numbers, especially outside of Bluerock. I won't judge them too quickly. These boys are foreigners to me. There's something both frightening and desirable in that. Edwina gives her earring a spin.

The boy with the allergy chain says hello, and Edwina says hello back. You know how it goes. Pretty soon they move their towels next to ours, and the allergy chain boy is spreading suntan lotion along the length of her legs. The other one on the far side, whose eyes I can't see for the sunglasses, faces into the Platte as if he's focused on the tiny whirlpools the current creates. What an interesting thing the tiny whirlpools are. Maybe he's a math or science wizard busy calculating a new whirlpool formula.

They are Kyle and Horace. Kyle has the allergy chain.

Before you know it Edwina and Kyle are in the river embracing. As they get to the middle, and his head and shoulders are still above water where hers would be under, she wraps her legs around his waist. He carries her farther into the deep. They bob and suck water drops and sun off each other's faces.

They told us they're from Casper. Kyle is in his freshman year of college on a football scholarship. Horace works at his father's hardware store. The royal blue convertible Ford Mustang in the parking lot is Horace's. They've come down from Casper and stopped here on their way to Denver, where Horace's grandmother lives.

I take out a cheese sandwich and offer half to Horace.

No thanks.

Family name? I ask.

He gives me a sideways glance: What?

Is Horace a family name?

My grandfather's.

I nod: It's unusual.

Yeah, he says looking down, not toward me.

A dozen mallards fly in and land below us, softly upon the river. They're quacking, the females, and the males *rab-rab-rab*.

Do you sell wire fencing at your hardware store?

Used to. Didn't sell enough of it. People who need that go to the specialty store. Ranching supplies.

Did you sell any woven wire fencing?

You a wire expert or something?

I don't much like woven wire, but in places we use it. On the bottom half of our fence.

What weight?

Nine. On the top and bottom. Eleven on the stay.

You put it up?

I help sometimes.

You stretch it?

I know how.

He makes a half-impressed face, although it's not my intention to dazzle him this way. I feel a little foolish watching Edwina and

Kyle go at it out there with us sitting on our towels and nothing to stare at but them and the whirlpools. Maybe Horace feels the same way. He lies back on his towel and I lie back on mine, my hands clasped behind my head, and my arms butterflied. Yeah. I really dazzle him. I sit up for a minute and have a drink of lemonade from the thermos. Another dozen ducks have flown in, and rock easily on the water. Edwina and Kyle are close to the other side of the river. The river isn't too wide. They're near the ducks.

Horace lies front side down. His face is turned downriver toward Edwina and Kyle. Whatever revs your motor.

I don't hesitate. I lift the straps off my suit. I pull the top half down to my waist. The sun feels pleasant on my breasts. Is his face turned away because he's repelled by me?

A red-cheeked and penny-nosed girl of six or seven running ahead of her mother stops and stares at me. I stare back. Her mother comes along and looks at me. She takes her daughter's hand and moves ahead. Mama, can I take my bathing suit down? Hush, the mother says. I lie down. In a moment I'm thinking of Demetrio.

This will stay on, he said bending to my ear. His hand on my breast, his tongue circling my ear.

His *huevos* were fragile and I took care when handling them. I cupped them.

¿A quién quieres más? he asked.

For three months I rode to him with hunger and we ate together at the small table in his silver camper. We ate bread and jam and drank black coffee, and went to the bed and lay together. His dark eyes and lashes, and the notch between his brows, sweat dripping from his chin, onto my breasts, all along as he moved onto my stomach and thighs.

What was this place between my legs? I looked at it in the hand mirror in my bedroom. A torn red grapefruit. A small seed in its pod. Parting the lips there lay the mouth of the tunnel that took him in.

I was so grateful to him that I brought gifts: fresh warm applesauce that Antonio had made. I skipped my last class to buy cologne at the drugstore. A brush of boar bristles. A jar of expensive black boot polish.

The flat of his hand brushed lightly across my breasts, teasing.

He closed his eyes tightly, as if in pain. A line of perspiration over his lip. His body ripe from the day's work. Salty and the faint scent of horse on him. The muscles in his arms and back taut, and his lips murmuring. Words in Spanish I didn't understand. His tongue clucking, lips pursed, inches from my face, as if in a tight kiss, yet we were not kissing. A gentle collapse, his eyes closed tightly.

If there was no moon, I rode home before dark. If there was a moon, I rode home by it. I touched the cleft of his chin and kissed him good-bye, and looked into his shiny eyes. My mother would be watching television or she might be in bed. She always asked where I'd been. If not that night, she asked the next morning. Where was I? Riding, I told her. Thinking by the stream. I watch the catfish in the pond. Why do you keep asking? What else would I be doing?

When Pablo and I moved across the plain toward home, my hips moved to his canter, and the motion wasn't unlike the way I moved with Demetrio. Pablo has never aroused me, though.

What do I know of Demetrio, aside from his fingertips across my back, and the exact location of his finger on the seed in the pod? He dreams of yellow-eyed wolves and of taking me to Guadalajara to meet his mother and seven brothers and sisters. He grains his horse well and asks Antonio to save meat bones for his dogs.

He says he loves me. Once at the sheep camp when I couldn't tell him I loved him, he shook me until my brain rattled. I left at a gallop on Pablo's back, and didn't see him for two days until he rode over the hills to my house and stood in the yard, and waited for me to come out. He stood with his hat rolling around in his hand: *Lo siento,* and would I come back and eat with him, and lie with him.

I can see that they're still out there necking. I wave.

Hey, Sophie! Edwina calls.

Hey, Sophie! Kyle calls.

What—oh they want me to come into the water. Not yet. Not yet. The sun is so nice on my chest. Horace sits up. He looks over my breasts, then into my eyes.

You're going to burn, he says, staring at my breasts.

I lift the suit from my waist and pull the straps over my shoulders.

It looks like you might of already. You might could use some lotion. He holds up a bottle of Coppertone.

I'll pass, but thanks anyway.

His hands wring, his knuckles crack. I don't know if the knuckle cracks prompt him to crack something in his neck. He arches his neck to one shoulder, and I hear the crack. He stands and walks toward the water, and when the water is up to his waist he dives in. He swims upstream. I think Edwina and Kyle must be getting waterlogged. The skin of their fingers puffy, finger rings defined. I lie on my stomach and the sun beats on my back.

I have serious eyes and a heart that pities the suffering of others, and I'm made of flesh that Demetrio's held tightly in his arms and explored with his hands. What more am I than that to him? Can he really love me? When I said I might find a way to Climax, Colorado, the whole of his face lit up. I didn't lie to him. I wanted to find a way. But I didn't want to wholeheartedly. I think of the sadness I caused and hate myself for it. I tried to make myself fall in love with him. Why couldn't I? He's a good man, but somehow I think we don't understand one another. When I tell him, Listen to the rabbit eating the grass, he looks sideways and tight-eyed at me. Also it's this: When I can be certain of my future, there will be love. Love seems to live for the future. I have love for my unborn baby, and that seems enough for now. My passion for Demetrio is a part of love, but the passion is more a pleasure than the whole of love.

Child's laughter pulls me from Demetrio. I want to know what brings on such peals and high-pitched giggles. I sit up. Near the river's edge stands a girl maybe two years old in a pink bathing suit with ruffles around the bottom. Her fat legs take her to the water, then back her away as she watches two boys play ball waist-deep in the river.

A woman calls out to her. Her mother? Katie Glencoe. Katie Glencoe. Don't go in the water.

It must be something for Katie to see the boys in the river. Their legs are invisible and the water reflects their chests and faces, and every now and then a person floats by in an inner tube.

The mother finally gives in to the squealing and lifts the daughter into her arms. She walks out near the boys and dips the little girl in to her waist. The girl's mouth forms an O and she giggles as if stunned maybe by the cold, by the moving water. She giggles and squeals.

Child's laughter pulls me away from Katie Glencoe. No, it's not the laughter of a child. It's Edwina's. I've never heard her laugh like this. I look downriver. They are nearly at the far bank. She splashes through knee-deep water. It's muddy there. She has a hard time pulling her legs up and moving forward. Kyle's chasing her. He catches her. She isn't laughing now. He's dragging her back to the middle.

I told you I can't swim!

He says something and I can't hear what it is.

He has her by the waist. Both arms around her waist. This isn't tenderness. He walks backward toward the middle, and she's being dragged there.

She wriggles out of his grasp. She goes for the yellow dirt shore.

He runs and catches her again, and takes hold of her around the shoulders. And the neck. I can't see her face. They move to the deep.

Let me go! Son of a bitch!

Then he lets her go. But she's floating downriver. She goes under. I get to my feet and walk to the edge of the river. Where is she? I run downriver and the ducks on shore scatter. For a minute I don't see her. Kyle's swimming downriver. Then he stops and stands and looks. He lifts a hand above his eyes.

Edwina! he calls.

I run into the water as fast as I can until my legs can't come up easily for the weight of the water. Then I swim. The current helps me downriver. She isn't too far away. Twenty feet. She's moving toward shore. Swimming a dog paddle. Good. Good. Then he's there on top of her. With both hands he pushes her head under. He's so intent on what he's doing that he does not see me. Then I'm on top of him. I take him from behind. Both hands over his eyes, and I use my fingers to dig into his eyes. He screams. He wheels around, and I'm beneath the water and kicking away downriver. I see her legs and arms in her dog paddle. She moves toward shore. If he comes at me again I'll dig my fingers into his eyes again.

I reach her and come up for air, and we're side by side. She's breathing hard. Her eyes are like corks. In a minute we hit up against the mud, and stand, and wade through. The mud sucks my feet. Edwina falls and I take her around the waist and bring her up. We walk to shore and sit down. Two men and a woman from the beach are swimming toward us. One man walks along shore toward Kyle and Horace.

Edwina's crying. Fucker. Fucker.

Upriver Horace stands next to Kyle. They're near the sandy shore. I can't hear their words. An old man walks up to them and talks to them. The one who's been walking finally reaches them and there are demanding words. What was going on over there? Who do you think you are?

The woman and man reach us.

What's happening down here? the woman asks, standing, her ankles all muddy as she comes onto shore. The man is waist-deep in the river as if the woman should meet us. I tell her a little of what happened. Then the man comes to shore. The woman tells him what I've told her.

Are you all right now? the man asks Edwina.

Yeah, Edwina says.

Are you sure?

I'll be better tomorrow. I'm a little embarrassed, frankly. Thanks for stopping by.

All right then, Helen, the man says to the woman.

Thank you, I say.

The man raises his hand and the two walk up shore, then slip into the river and swim across.

Up where the boys are, Horace's hands are on his hips. Then his arms cross over his chest.

He said let's go over there and have a good time, Edwina says. When I wouldn't, he called me a prick tease.

The boys pick up their towels and radio. We watch them walk up the beach.

Forget about it.

Easy for you to say.

They're leaving now, I tell her.

The ducks have flown off. Katie Glencoe is sitting on shore with her mother. The dog's barking.

Why don't we get back across now.

I can't swim.

You dog-paddled.

She looks at me. I think she's going to cry again, and I don't know what to do. Drying mud coats her legs and feet. The blue Ford Mustang leaves the parking lot.

An empty beer can lies in the dirt by a spent round fire of charred wood. I wonder if a man and woman in love lay by the fire. My biology book is full of interesting facts. It says that if a person's pituitary gland is damaged, it's thought that person will not have the capacity to love. A tumor on the pituitary gland could cause the inability to love, couldn't it? I've rubbed my hand over Pablo's back and down his legs to his hooves in search of tumors, but the tumor he had was deep inside and couldn't have been found by the hand. I run my fingers across my scalp. Where's the pituitary gland? I've forgotten. I pick up the beer can and take it to the river and fill it with water. The mud sucks my feet. I bring the can back to Edwina and pour it on her leg. I rub the mud away. Thank you, she says. I take the beer can back to the river and fill it again. I pour it on her ankle and rub the mud away. This I do six times until the mud is gone from her legs and feet.

Thank you, she says. Thank you. Her eyes are closed.

Her legs are so beautiful. For a moment I want to touch them and feel their softness, but I don't think it would be right. She'd think I'm strange.

I'll get the truck, I say. It'll take me some time to go up and over the bridge.

I don't want to stay by myself.

Then we've got to swim.

She ponders.

It's narrower downriver. Not far. Do you want to walk downriver a ways, then cross over?

No. All right, she says in a voice full of failure, I'll wait for you to get the truck.

I have to go to the bridge and come back down.

How long?

Five, ten. They're gone.

I'm not worried. I shouldn't have stayed out there so long with him.

I'm not worried about their coming back. I'm worried that she thinks she did something wrong. She gave too much, she says. Maybe she made him promises. I wish I had a gun. I'd like to shoot out their tires. We could have found ourselves in dire straits. He could have taken her to shore by the cluster of milky eyebane in the weeds. In the lavender flowers.

I swim back to the other side and take the keys from her shorts' pocket. There's a glob of spittle on the windshield. Nice. I check the tires. No, they're not slashed. I put the truck in gear and the wheels roll through the dry grass, onto the gravel road, then to the blacktop. In a mile I cross the bridge. I ease down the bank and drive along the plain in line with the river. In the absence of a road I make one, the grass and weeds behind me flattened. Bumpy. Sage and rocks.

When I pull up behind her, she doesn't turn around. She doesn't move. I get out of the truck and she raises a hand in the air, and I stop. There's a snake. It's dark. Five feet long and thick around the middle. It's only a bull snake.

It's not poisonous, I call to her.

I walk closer and the snake S's off into the eyebane and lavender flowers.

You drive, she says.

If we get caught.

Will you please?

I took in a mighty amount of sun and my back is on fire so that I have to sit forward in the seat. We have but a few sips of lemonade left. I pass the thermos to Edwina, she drinks, and passes it back to me.

What did you do with them? I ask.

We're talking about the ducklings her father got for her sister and her for Easter when she was five.

Kept them in a cardboard box in the kitchen—the kind a refrigerator comes in, cut in half. Those little baby fluff balls peeped all day and night. My sister and I went into the kitchen while my parents were asleep, and let them out so they could run around.

They grew up, then, I say.

We let them go long before that. My aunt lived out in the country and she had this scummy old pond on her property. Our old man drove us out there and we let them go, and they were so happy, you know, quacking away, swimming out to the middle. Their little fluff tails going like mad. Snapping turtle drags one of them under, and my sister and I start screaming bloody murder. My aunt runs up to the house and brings back a half-blown-up raft, and she's blowing it up a little and paddling and kicking and blowing it up some more. Gets out to the middle. Snapper comes up for another one and my sister and I are screaming on shore and my old man's yelling at us to shut up. Anyway, Aunt Meg's got a rock with her and she fires it on that snapper. Then we went home.

She sighs and I think I see her tremble a little. Sometimes too much sun will make a person tremble.

To me it was violent. You?

I stop and think. I say, There's quite a bit going on on a ranch.

I saw a dog get hit by a car once, she says.

My mother has a tendency toward violence, I say.

She ever smack you around?

She has.

My old man used to whack me with a crocodile belt.

Now when she gets mad she goes into her bedroom and prays. That started about three years ago.

I turn on the radio and the only station we can get is country. Kitty Wells is singing making believe I never lost you.

We talk about kissing.

But when you kiss, Edwina says, and you're mouth to mouth, sight and smell don't really matter. If you think of kissing in its purest form. Taste and touch matter. When I was out there and the river was around my legs and hips—I didn't know about his past, nothing about his future. But I knew something more than before we went swimming. Life seemed good, you know, and then that had to happen.

I tell her I'm sorry that it happened that way. I sense she doesn't want to talk about it. I tell her I think kissing involves every sense. You're lost in the kiss and shouldn't be in the frame of mind to question what senses you use. A kiss involves all the senses. Kisses are like snowflakes. Can you imagine how many billions of kiss equations there have been since the beginning of time?

She tells me she's never slept with a boy. That her mother drilled into her the honest principles principle. Edwina, her mother said: Does a boy have honest principles? Edwina had not been sure about any of the boys she'd kissed, and there were many.

You might want to abandon that principle so you can find out, I suggest.

How are you sure of love? she says.

I think: My mother's bitter because my father left. I don't know how long their love lasted, and why it failed. She bears a lot of weight running the ranch on her own, and I know this, and she bears weight eager for Clements to come home from the war.

How are you sure? she asks again.

Hank Williams on the radio sings about grief coming tomorrow, but we can have a good time tonight if we want to. The road is as smooth as a bedspread.

I'm no expert on love, I say.

What were you doing with your top down?

Catching sun.

Did you like him?

I didn't know him.

Did you want to make it with him?

I was catching some sun on my teats. That's all.

You didn't want him to take you back to his car?

I don't know about having sex with a baby growing inside. I don't know if it could hurt the baby. There's nobody I want to have sex with, other than Demetrio. Is there something wrong with naked teats?

Against the law.

So is driving a truck without a driver's license. Why did he do that to you?

I took it in my hand for a while. But I didn't deserve what he did.

I know you didn't. Sure. Sorry. I'm tired.

I'll drive.

I like to drive. I wish I could drive into Idaho and up into California. Have you been to the ocean?

Every Christmas we go to Hawaii. Maybe you could go with us sometime. My brother brought his girlfriend last year.

The baby and all. I can't leave it with my mother. I wouldn't want to.

There's a lot to a baby, she says. Diapers and baby food and clothes. Have you thought about that?

That's what teats are for. Baby food.

Babies turn into kids. Kids turn into teenagers.

Now there was a thought. I'm only a teenager. My baby. Already to be thought of at that age. It's not impossible to think of that. My son's voice changing. Or if a girl, my daughter's menstruation coming and going like the moon.

We're silent for a long time, long enough that I go into my thoughts. I go deeply as in a dream. It isn't hard to drive the truck here. The surface is straight and flat. I keep my eyes open for deer and antelope, but in the daylight they rarely jump in front of cars. It's the beams from the eyes of the car that do it to them.

Edwina falls asleep. Her head just above the temple gently taps the window. Her mouth is barely open.

Love is full of push and pull. I believe my mother and father pushed and pulled, and finally my father was pulled from the house through the screen door, and drawn into his truck. He was pushed by a wind down the circular road to the blacktop. I'm not saying he didn't know what he was doing. He knew most surely that he was leaving. There was push and pull between them. The question is why.

Demetrio said to me in half Spanish, half English: Sometimes I don't sleep. I wait for you to come to me in the night, and you don't.

I can't, I said. Sometimes my mother's watching. I can't always come.

If we could go to Guadalajara. Do you dream at night, Sophie?

Like everyone, yes.

What do you dream?

I can't recall.

I thank God for my dreams.

What's God? Define it.

My dreams take me out of my hell. I know there is a God because I know there is a hell. You see how I live, Sophie? In a tin camper.

You can't define God, then shut up. I'm not blind. I see how you live.

Do you know how hot it gets in the summer in a tin camper?

You're away in the summer. In the mountains.

I leave in six days, Sophie.

Do you think I don't count the days?

How can you say there is no God? Who do you think made the plains? Where do you think all of this comes from? The sun and moon? All day long and sometimes at night I talk with four-legged creatures, and in the morning and late in the afternoon I speak with a kettle of bubbling water. I am happy to rise into my dreams for the sake of company.

But you chose your work.

I made a mistake coming here. You know, someone told me Wyoming ranching was money and blond women and big open space. A kid's stupid idea of a dream. Foolish. Were it not for you. That was the lucky thing. That was luck.

What people are in your dreams?

Ghosts, thieves, street urchins. I am glad to speak to them, and they are glad to speak to me. I want to make a life with you. *Te quiero.*

I can't leave the ranch.

We can make a family. Look at your hair. Like soft, folded black velvet. I told you my grandmother makes velvet capes for the rich women. She lives near the beet fields. We can live with her.

I can't leave Pablo.

Then he shook me until my brain rattled. I screamed, Stop it! And when he did: Never do that again!

Please, Sophie.

Shut up! Never do that again!

Then good-bye, Sophie. I won't see you before I leave for the mountains. Good-bye.

But he came in two days, stood outside the house, and waited until I came out. *Lo siento,* he said. Will you follow me on your horse?

I placed my hand on his rough chin and drew myself into the warm breath of coffee and sweet bread, and whistled for Pablo.

Antonio left us the fourth week of June, but not for good. He went back to Pamplona to see his wife and five children. He hadn't seen them for four years. Summer is a good time for him to leave our ranch, as the weather is lazy and there isn't so much to do with half the sheep in Climax, Colorado. I can't know his thoughts, but it seems to me he does fine without his family. The men don't discuss their personal lives with me.

The weather is warm and I spend many evenings outside on the front steps, my buttocks cool through my nightshirt or pants on the chilled cement. The wind blows almost steadily. It dries the soil and drives the sand and tumbleweeds. At twilight there is, in one moment, the uncut sky, and the next moment there are stars. One, two. The dippers and animals of the sky are like thin knife cuts across a blackboard. They're lost and then they arrive. Freshly cut.

I'm lying in my bed, stomach down and face to the wall, when my covers are thrown off. I turn my head. Mother is there with a mug of steaming coffee in her hand. A warm mug of coffee should give comfort, but it doesn't, not to me. It makes me want to vomit. All smells and tastes are different now from nonpregnant years.

Rise and shine, lazy girl! she shouts happily.

Who's lazy? I think. I'm so sleepy I can't mouth off to her. She's lazy too. She watches television until fuzz fills the screen. There's a purpose to my sleep and a purpose to her watching television, and we should have that right. We shouldn't complain to each other. When she wakes me like this, I'd like to pull the TV aerial down from the roof. During lightning storms I wish lightning would strike the aerial on the roof and send it to the ground, but she'd only have one of the men put up another.

What on earth is she wearing? A flower-power dress. Pink and orange and yellow. Daisies in these colors, and the hem is risen to a foot above her knees. On her feet she's wearing sandals. Her toenails are neon orange.

Wash your face and brush your teeth, and meet me in the kitchen, and she's gone.

I've been waiting for the right moment to tell her about the baby. I mocked braces and disobeyed Pastor Fabila and his church when the moment called for it, but now I have to defy her with this baby and the sex that made it.

Our kitchen is an ugly thing. It's plain and without modern conveniences. It'd be nice to have a dishwasher, and I believe we can afford it, but Mother doesn't think of such things. She goes along with the same fence and the same prayers like scratched records. The porcelain sink is stained with yellow.

Mother only saw my backside as I lay unclothed facing the wall. The muscles coming down from the sides of my back have thickened. I might tell her about the baby when she's looking over the tomatoes and beets and carrots in the garden. She likes to work the soil, watch the growth, predict the weather. It's only been three weeks since we planted, and not much has happened, but in time it will. Everything happens in time. Sometimes she stands in the garden for a long time, or stoops or kneels there, working the soil. Then sun comes down on her face, and her eyes blaze. She looks beautiful.

I walk slow-moving into the kitchen.

Whose shirt is that? Clements'?

I got it out of his closet.

Mind you don't ruin his things.

Should I ask his permission or something? Shoot. He doesn't care.

A dozen eggs in their carton are in a bowl on the counter. She cracks them one-handedly into a stainless steel bowl. Her face is shiny from oil or cold cream. Her hair's pulled back from the forehead and hooked with an ivory barrette.

Grate some cheese for me, will you? On a plate.

I'm going out for mushrooms. If we're having scrambled eggs.

The horses are at the far end. They lift their heads and walk over. They come together, their heads bobbing slightly as they walk. I don't want them to walk to me, but of course they will. There are three puffball mushrooms near the loafing shed, and I don't want them following me there and hoofing them.

I fork some hay and they trail me to the east side of the corral by the gate. There's some nettling among them when I lay the hay into the pasture. I have to pitch another hay block and divide it in half. They bow to the hay, their tails swinging. Tootie, the bay mare, trembles a little.

It's always a great temptation to smash a puffball with the flat of my foot. There are three puffballs here and they're giants. I saw them by the loafing shed yesterday. They're more than a foot around. Their skin is smooth as kid leather. They're creamy and huge and round. Mushrooms are mysterious. They appear suddenly. They're like the beetles and moles. Busy underground. Out of sight. Growing. You shouldn't pick any old mushrooms and eat them. You can die as quickly from a poisonous mushroom as you can from deadly snakebite. Or you can have a stomachache, vomit, cramp up, have face and neck flush. Your hands can tingle and a metal taste can come into the mouth. You can sweat and your vision can blur. You can cry. Julian ate a poison mushroom once. He plucked it from the ground in our pasture and dusted off the dirt, and split it open to be sure there were no worms. Then he ate it. He offered some to me. No thanks. We took him to the hospital.

I pull only one puffball up from the ground. There's plenty of mushroom for our eggs in one huge puffball. We'll eat the reproductive part of the mushroom. The spores.

When I come back in I ask her if she wants me to make toast.

Bread's in the bread box. Three days old. You'll have to make some more this afternoon.

Shoot, I don't know the first thing about bread.

I know it's the shits that Antonio's gone, but hey, little girl, we have to pitch in.

I don't even know how to start. I'm not a little girl, Mom, so knock it off, all right?

You're my little girl. You'll always be my little girl, like it or not.

Well, I don't. Like being called a little girl.

You never watched Antonio make bread?

I never much cared.

Open your eyes, young lady.

My eyes are wide open, Mom.

Mother puts her cigarette out in her coffee in the mug. I don't like the hiss of the lighted end as it whispers out.

That's uncivil.

What do you mean?

Rude.

What do you mean rude? It's my coffee. My smoke. I think I can do what I like with it.

The hissing smell of coffee makes me sick. When I have the baby I'll like the smell of coffee again. But never the hissing.

Don't be odd, Sophie. You're an oddball sometimes, you know it? Where's the dill? Have you seen the dill?

Maybe I'm plain tired of hearing the hissing of the cigarette in your coffee.

A moment before, she was enjoying her coffee. Then she put her cigarette out and it hissed. I'm odder to her than I am to me. I wonder if every person thinks that: I'm not odd, but that person is.

I wish I didn't smoke, she says.

Why don't you stop?

The thought terrifies me. She laughs a little. It's not just the withdrawal, sweetheart, from the nicotine. If we all knew exactly what terrified us, we'd have the answers to everything, wouldn't we.

She lights another one and pulls deeply, but exhales the smoke without inhaling into her lungs. I could try to quit, she says. I could try. The smoke curls out of her mouth, not thin as it would if it came from her lungs.

Piraté's dog, Sharpa, is dull gray through the screen door. His stump tail is like a ticking clock. My mother opens the screen door and invites him in. He's unsure at first. I can't recall whether he's ever been in the house. He spends the hot days of the summer under the trailer. He steps carefully as if the floor will cave in beneath him. He sniffs the floor and around my mother's feet. He trots into the kitchen, his nose in the air. My mother kneels next to him and folds her arms around his middle. She buries her nose and mouth and forehead into Sharpa's fur. The dog licks her hand. She buries one cheek, then the other. I think she smells within him all the beautiful things of the plain: sage, red dirt, buffalo grass, willow bark from by the stream, the red sumac he wandered into. Her cheek in his fur and her eyes lightly closed and a pleasant smile up like a new moon. Her eyes flash open and flutter twice like green leaves. Her cheek is still upon his bouquet. Do you like to cook, Sophie?

It's all right.

Should we go to the mountains this summer and camp?

We've never been to the ocean.

She lays the other cheek on Sharpa's fur, turning away from me. She says nothing. I don't care. Yes, I do. In truth I don't want to hurt my mother right now. But I don't want to go camping with her. She might look for the Virgin Mary in the tree. She would talk about Clements and his brave ambition. We would hike along a trail, and she would point out the names of things: redheaded woodpecker, blue spruce, cumulus clouds. She would mention the moon.

And I'd say, In the full moon darkness is visible. The moon rises at the rim of the sky. The horizon pales and the sky is lighted dull yellow, almost green.

A red squirrel, Sophie. Look. Blue grouse. See? The male. Twinflowers. Such a pretty pink. There're seven hundred trees native to North America.

Sharpa whines at my mother's feet. Come, Sharpa. She opens the screen door. Go on now. Thatta boy.

Julian and Piraté come in like ducks flying home for the spring. It's unclear to me what cue ducks have when they leave the north and return to it, and how they make their way, but the smell drifting through the open door and windows is the men's cue. Sausage and coffee travel a long way on a light wind.

They wash their hands and faces in the kitchen sink, and dry them, and their faces are rosy from the weather and the rough towel when they sit down. Their weather-wrinkles without the coating of dirt are plainly exposed.

They have no manners. They scoop steaming eggs onto their plates and advance toward their heaps with poised forks. They glance questioningly at one another as if we have laced their eggs with a poison. Carefully Julian lifts the fork to his mouth. He's more careful than Piraté because he may know the brown flecks are mushrooms. I've seen Piraté single-handedly eat a dozen chopped uncooked lamb balls with raw onions for breakfast. He digs in.

Puffballs, I say to Julian. No poison.

Good, he says. Ah.

The food is warm and tender. Sticky and salty. It's comforting.

Better than the runny eggs Antonio makes. It occurs to me that I'm
no longer as sick as the previous week. The absence of nausea has
come about gradually. The thought of most food now isn't unpleas-
ant. I eat as if I've been fasting for days. I'm at the end of my fif-
teenth week. Warm is a certain taste as cold is a certain taste. The
depth of the scrambled eggs is warm.

For a moment while we were cooking, I thought I could tell
her about the baby. I saw in her eyes some pleasure that we were in
the kitchen together. Some togetherness can be better than no
togetherness, and maybe it's the lack of this that makes her so bitter. I see a thread of hope that I might be able to tell her about the
baby. That there's a way in by spending more time doing things
together. We haven't been friends for so long. I can't remember
when that started. Our not being friends.

After lunch the wind has drawn together, and pushes the dirt and
tumbleweeds. It dries the soil and stirs thin clouds. I saddle Pablo.

Piraté walks toward his trailer and shoots a hateful look at me.
He says something in Spanish, and I don't understand the words.
He pats his stomach twice and smiles. A sneering smile. He has no
proof.

Pablo's tail is matted with straw and I pull some of the straw
out.

I kick him good and pretty soon we come to the stream. He
walks lightly along the edge. He has his drink here and eats the
green grasses. We go along pleasantly so that I can feel the ease at
which he works. We're soon halfway to Tin Picardy's house. The
sparkle along the bank and above it some comes from feldspar. The
moon's land is full of feldspar, and sometimes at night when I've
been riding home by the moon or can see it from my bedroom window, I think how beautiful it would be to run my fingers across
moon rock. Who has Piraté told? The other men? Not my mother.

I lift off my saddle and Piraté walks out of the trailer, the red beret
off his head. He's wearing a different shirt, green and blue plaid. I

washed it last Saturday morning. If you spill bleach on a plaid shirt, it will spread into stars. I think he needs a few stars on his plaid shirts.

The smile.

Prove it, *cabrón,* I say.

He comes closer but is still six feet to the south, and his smile drops. He looks as if he wants to fight anything. I'd like to fight him.

Prove it, I say again.

When I ride up to Tin's, I find Edwina on the porch with a brown cat on her lap. She tells me Tin left a few hours ago to see her boy in Fort Collins. She made soup, and why don't we put some lemon in our hair, she says, the sun will bleach out our hair while we're riding. I need to try and understand a horse, she says.

We cut two lemons in quarters, squeeze them into our hair, and comb it through. The wind is heavy now. It dries the soil. My garden will need to be watered heavily today.

I'm not crazy for horses like you, she says, but I'm here and so are these horses, and I might not get the chance again.

You never rode a horse when you were a kid? Not at a county fair?

Watched some English jumpers at the state fair last summer. Some weirdo and his wife sat down next to me in the stands. Started asking me questions about where did I live and would I like to come to their horse farm and learn to ride an Appaloosa. The man put his hand on my leg. Creep. I don't know shit about horses. You must think I'm ignorant.

I don't think you're ignorant.

We go to the barn where there's a little tack room. Everything hangs on hooks against the wall: bridles, hackamores, martingales, a snaffle with full cheek bars. There are three saddles on the saddle trees and they're shiny and well worn.

The girth is made of mohair, I show her. You can wash it and dry it and it won't harden.

She touches it.

Do you know anything about her horses?

Fed them a couple of times.

She's got one out there. A nice mare. Red one. Do you know which one I'm talking about? Tin rides her sometimes. Why don't we see if we can get her and saddle her up.

Her name's April, Edwina says.

I take the hackamore down from the wall and we walk out of there into the bright light and the warm wind where the air isn't so stifling and dusty. We get some carrots from the kitchen, which is fragrant with pepper, simmering chicken, and vegetables. We walk over to the pasture. I can't see the horses.

She gets behind me on Pablo, her hipbones up against the back of the saddle, and we ride into the pasture and see them, a dozen or so on the other side, standing under a grove of poplar trees whose domed tops make a nice shade. The horses' ears prick forward. They stir, and one of them whickers. Edwina climbs off, and I dismount with the hackamore behind my back. They aren't the kind that come toward us when they see carrots, but I think they're going to stay put because they're curious. One of them has lifted his neck, and his nostrils milk the air. We're almost within touching distance. The red one seems indifferent toward carrots, but she's easy to catch. She has a bald face and stockings on her rear legs. Edwina and I ride Pablo. I hold the reins in one hand while April trots along. In a minute we reach the gate. I tie April and Pablo to the fence and go back inside the barn with Edwina, and ask her to grab that blanket. I take the saddle off the tree.

You think you should be doing that? she asks.

I do it with Pablo's.

Why don't you let me carry it.

It might be good for her. Her arms are scrawny. They could use some muscle.

That's a heavy motherfucker, she says.

You want help?

Let me do it.

I slip the blanket over April. This is a slightly swaybacked horse. She has bloated herself in the belly and I give her a little knee. When she lets out, I tighten the girth. Edwina settles in, and April's head comes up. I adjust the stirrups. There's no tremble to the horse and no dancing about, only a little shifting. The creaking of saddle leather is so nice.

I don't know how you wear long pants in this weather, Edwina says.

I smile. I don't know about wearing shorts on a horse. And tennis shoes.

She cracks her knuckles. Then carefully, as if the reins will burn the palms of her hands, she takes them up between her fingers.

I tell her this isn't an impossible thing we're doing here. We're not breaking horses. This one is broke and not too awfully young.

I get on Pablo. April follows us at a slow walk like a quiet child might follow its mother around the house, every now and again pulling at her apron strings. April nuzzles up against Pablo's rear quarters. Pablo snorts a little and lifts his head. We walk around the house and up and down the drive and along the pasture fence. Edwina doesn't need to worry. This isn't barrel racing or chasing down sheep. The other horses are curious.

She wants to know why horses shit so much.

Their gut only holds three or four gallons of food, I say. They eat all day long.

Three or four gallons seems like a lot to me.

A cow holds forty gallons, I tell her.

Her eyebrows shift. I don't know if she cares one way or the other about a cow's insides.

We ride quietly for a while, and I sense she's becoming more comfortable with April. Her legs have relaxed. She slumps a little in the saddle.

She talks about her father and says he's mean-natured. Maybe my father was mean-natured. Edwina progresses to the trotting stage and reins her horse to the right and left, and Pablo and I trot on. Edwina pulls back on the reins and April stops on a dime. That's good. My hair is stiff from the lemon and it's attracting flies.

I went into one of those whorehouses, she says.

What'd you do there?

Just went in and looked.

Are the girls all lined up half naked?

I only saw two. A skinny one with glasses. I don't think she's a whore. I think she works behind the desk. And a big woman with teats down to here, she probably is one. You think they make a lot of money?

A living, I guess.

I asked that big-teated woman. She was friendly as hell. She said she makes two or three hundred on a good night, and she wanted to know if I was asking nosy questions because I wanted to join up. That's what she said, join up. But I said no. I left. Some greasy Mexican came out of one of the rooms.

Don't say that.

What?

Greasy Mexican.

But he was greasy and he was a Mexican.

Okay, but don't say that.

Touchy, touchy. Okay, sorry. I know your boyfriend's Mexican, but he's not greasy, is he?

Just don't say it.

I—look, okay, I shouldn't have. My old man says it. I should know better than to repeat anything that motherfucker says. Who's your best friend?

I don't have one. I laugh. Pablo, I guess.

Mine's Mary Loretto. Her old man sent her away to a fancy summer boarding school in Vermont. We fight a lot because we're too much the same. Sometimes in school we'd show up for class and die because we'd bought the same shoes, or the same shirt. You know what? I don't talk to her like I talk to you.

How do you mean?

Sometimes you and I sit around and don't say anything, and it's fine.

Yeah.

We take the saddle off April and lay it over the saddle tree. We brush April down and put her out to pasture. I tell Edwina she might want to wax the threads on the buckles of the girth with beeswax so they won't rot. In the pasture April lowers her head and walks along grazing. She doesn't seem to care, for the time being, about finding the others.

We go into the house and take turns washing our hair under the bathtub faucet. I mean to ask how she got that bump on her nose, but it might offend her. Maybe her father has a bump on his nose and she inherited it. I'd like to see pictures of my father to see what I inherited from him. I mean to tell Edwina that she might try to make up with her father. But that isn't my business. I don't know the extent of their disagreements. Maybe he's wholly evil. I don't think any person is wholly evil. I could be wrong.

The kitchen smells beautiful with chicken soup simmering in a stainless steel kettle. The flame is low.

Mind if I sample? I ask.

She's already taking down two bowls.

We go outdoors and sit on the porch swing. I blow on my soup and sip from my spoon. It's too hot to sit outside and eat soup, but as my brow breaks out in a sweat I know that this is some of the best I've ever tasted.

How did you learn to cook?

Watching our housekeeper, Carmen. She did everything. I loved her.

She left?

Died of cancer. Last year.

All the good ones die, I say. I don't know this for sure. Nicklow wasn't such a good man, but I think he did some good. He made spanakopitta for the neighboring ranch hands every Easter. My mother always makes ham and scalloped potatoes on Easter.

If there's a heaven, she's there, Edwina says.

I don't believe in God.

You have to!

That's crazy!

Are you tired?

Not too.

Do the hormones make you sad?

Do I look sad?

Your eyes. Today they kind of droop.

A chain saw whines and a hammer's strike echoes. Those sounds fill me with emptiness.

I tell Edwina I'd like to make a collect call to my grandmother in Chicago. I explain that I can't do it from my house, that I'm forbidden to do so, and although I've committed greater sins I'd like not to have to battle my mother over a phone call. I try to choose my battles wisely.

Go ahead, Edwina says. She nods. Really, go ahead.

My grandmother's voice holds a trace of Polish.

Sophie, I wish you would have called sooner.

I ask her how she is and how Uncle John is. Uncle John's fine. How are you, she wants to know, and is your mother well, and is everything all right?

Nothing's wrong, I say.

Good. Good. I wanted to talk with you. I got a letter from your father. He's in Pinnacle Butte, Colorado. Do you know where that is?

No.

Uncle John went to see him three weeks ago. I sent along a box of cookies and a nice new white shirt and three pairs of wool socks. Your uncle didn't stay but one night. There was rotting food and no toilet. They had an argument, then a fistfight. Your uncle had a black eye.

What did they fight about?

I don't know. I told your uncle to tell your father, Come home, Joey, and live here. I can give you a little to live on, not much, but enough to get you by until you find work. You don't have to work right away. Come home and rest. Go out. See your old friends.

Where did you say he lives?

The mountains. Beautiful there, your uncle says. Your father isn't the same man as when you were a little girl, Sophie.

I never knew him too well to begin with.

You were so young when he left. Oh, I wish you would have called sooner.

Sorry. Me too.

My mother said my grandmother hired a lawyer to take the ranch for the divorce agreement. My mother lies and says her prayers. Everything is good with Jesus's redemption. I want to see my grandmother, but it seems impossible. Pablo. The baby. The ranch. All that way to Chicago.

Does he have a telephone?

Mercy no.

Do you have his address?

General delivery. Where are you calling from?

My friend Edwina's house. Her aunt's.

Your friend Edwina. That's nice. Do you know how much I miss you? I love you. Remember that every day. I love you with all my heart.

I love you too.

After we hang up I find Edwina in the barn in the tack room staring at the saddles and bridles. Her arms crossed over her chest.

This is very confusing, she says.

Not after a while.

How's your grandma?

She told me my father's living in the mountains.

Do you want to call him?

He doesn't have a phone. He never does. I don't think he has any electricity either, and maybe no running water. I guess he shits by the trees.

Where?

Pinnacle Butte, Colorado.

Maybe I could drive you there in the truck.

Yeah, maybe.

Tin and Rudy's bedroom is long and narrow. It looks like a builder's mistake. The bookcase is heavy with stacks of *American Rifleman* and *National Geographic* magazines. A set of old encyclopedias. We look up Colorado and see a map of towns and cities, but we can't find Pinnacle Butte. A can of Glade air spray stands on the dresser next to the phone. That's what makes the room smell so sweet. Too sweet.

Look at this, Edwina says, pulling a map from a stack of papers on the top shelf.

I unfold the yellow map and spread it. A corner breaks and falls away like a brittle leaf.

Oh, Jesus. Is it valuable?

I don't think so, she says.

I'm sorry.

Forget it. It's only an old map. It doesn't even say of what.

We could start the bread dough, I say.

But it has to stay warm and covered on the stove. And you wanted to go home.

I'm tired.

You could sleep here, she says.

Could you ride over with me?

We'll have to start the dough at your place. It needs to stay really quiet and warm.

Like a baby inside, I think, quiet and warm. I fold the map. I crush the corner in my hand and put the pieces into my pocket. It's just a piece of dead paper, I say. It came from a dead tree.

Hell with it, she says.

Living things rise from dead things, and the dead things rise from the living things.

Whatever you say, she says. Should we saddle up?

My mother, you know. She'll be there.

Your old lady's one cracker shy of a box.

Everyone is, I say. I'm embarrassed that she knows this about my mother.

Sometimes I want to strangle my old man, she says.

We're all a little weird from time to time, I say. I hesitate but ask in a moment of courage: What do you think of me?

She thinks for a minute. I think you're unconquerable.

What do you mean?

What I say.

I want to kiss her, but she might get the wrong idea.

•   •   •

We've planned on her riding behind me on Pablo, her pelvic bones against the saddle rim, but now she wants to ride April. I say I'm not sure if the old girl is up for a four-mile round trip but Edwina says this will be good for both of them.

We walk into the pasture and find April grazing close to the gate.

Trotting unsettles my body.

I remind Edwina to use her stirrups. Stand up a little and you won't bounce so hard. Edwina stands all the way up and April's ears shift back. Edwina opens her mouth and sings *ah* in a low voice for a long time. She sits down and bounces on April's back, takes a breath, and blows out *ah ah ah*. I'm not so unhappy here, she says. It's not as big a disaster as it was when I first came.

It's not a cosmic catastrophe, I say.

The stream shimmers in many dotted lines. The horses bow their heads and drink. It's nice to hear them sucking water. The afternoon sun pitches. I think we should be going. I lift my reins and we move on. A meadowlark sings in the distance. I never tire of the beautiful song. A piece of straw lodges in Pablo's mane. I pluck it out, roll it between my fingers, and lift my fingers to my nose. I know the perfume.

Down the hard-packed road to our house, Pablo's rear humps back and forth. He jumps, his ears prick up and back, and he sniggers. It's not usual for him to jump like this. April's head is up. Her nostrils drain and pull air, and she lopes sideways. Edwina's face is not confident. Don't do this. She pulls back on the reins and April skitters crosswise toward us, running broadside into Pablo. Then I see the mountain lion to the right, running through the sage. She's narrow in the stomach. Her teats hang low. She carries a lamb in her mouth, its neck bloody and limp and swaying as she lopes. Edwina cries out, and her cry sends chills through my back. Pablo starts to sidestep and I pull him in and hug him with my thighs, but in a split second he grows wild, rearing up and prancing, his front hooves clipping. I look over to see if Edwina is all right, my head and chest and stomach leaning into Pablo's neck. He rears up again and we fall together.

In the darkness I dream. I'm in labor. The end of the pushing. When the baby slides from my womb, it's more of a rabbit or a kangaroo than a human being. It has black fur and sits perched on its long thick kangaroo tail. I stare into its face. It has my exact face, my dark brown eyes and lips like tiny severed grapefruit.

When I wake up, I find myself in a strange dark room. I squeeze my left hand and realize it's bound in a cast. Caught in a sling. Pain. Throbbing and searing at once. I pinch my hand and slow the hand-blood for a moment and know that I'm in the real world and not dreaming.

I see a tall man and plump woman in the hallway, people I've never seen. The man's mouth turns up at the corners in a smile. The plump woman in white from hat to shoes lifts a hand to her mouth and nods. I squeeze my hand again and pinch the skin at my knuckles. There's pain. Pain in the arm and pain where I pinch. It's true. I'm awake.

I move to sit up. My muscles ache. My bones feel as if they're held together by nails. My lower back and neck throb. With my free hand I pat my face and head. I have two eyes and a mouth and my hair is matted. There's a spot at the base of my head. It's ridged. Painful. A shocking, burning pain from the one arm. Are the bones so shattered that some will work their way into my body like worms? Will the bone bits enter my lungs and clog my breath? Will they puncture my baby? My heart? There's a tube line in my vein attached to a small clear bottle of liquid on a silver rack.

I remember the mountain lion and Edwina's horse. Edwina. Is she all right? And what of Pablo?

Both hands go to my stomach, my fingers apart. If the baby were not there, would my stomach still be round like this? I touch my breasts. They have the bruised pain. It's a relief. I poke firmly around my stomach and feel the hardness inside. Then, something in my vagina. No, in the place where urine comes out. I pull it and the quick dull pain makes me cry. What is this? A bag of yellow liquid at the end of another line.

The nurse outside the door rushes in and the tall, pale man with crew cut hair follows. White white white. What is he? A man-nurse? The woman leans in close.

Hello, Sophie. Welcome back. How do you feel? Can you tell me your last name?

Behr.

When were you born?

How long have I been here?

Do you know what year it is? Her breath is like radishes. One hand on my underwrist checking my pulse, and her eyes on mine. The light comes on in the room. The man did that.

I moan. My arm. My arm.

Call Dr. Glauser, will you? the nurse spits at the man as if he should have known to do this already. As if he is an idiot.

Within minutes Dr. Glauser enters. He's in his seventies, his hairline ebbed, his body thin, his shoulders sagging slightly. His eyes are large and blue and wet, gray eyebrows full of chaos.

Lie back, will you? How do you feel?

Not so great.

Are you having pain in your arm?

Yes.

His hand comes forward as if it's going to move my arm. I pull back.

You've managed to land yourself a compound fracture. I'm sorry about that.

How long have I been here?

Two days.

Dr. Glauser brought me into this world and somehow, although I can't remember that event, I think it must be stored in my brain as the first blurred other-eyes and warm hands in a cold room.

Could I have some water? How long do I have to be in this cast?

Time and patience.

Time and patience, I repeat with gloom. That's no answer.

The nurse pours me a glass from the water pitcher at my bed-side, and I drink greedily. It's cold and good. I dip my fingers into the cup and dab the cool water across my forehead.

You've pulled out your catheter, Dr. Glauser says.

I take another drink of water and taste chlorine. It's almost sweet. There was a mountain lion with the lamb dead in its mouth. Hooves clicked and there was a scream. What was the purpose of our ride? To go to my house and make bread.

Who brought me here?

Your mother, naturally.

My friend—is she okay?

What's her name?

Edwina.

She's left messages. Half a dozen, at least.

Why was that in there to begin with? I mean the catheter.

You were unconscious for two days after your spill.

Pablo. Is he all right?

I don't know. I assume. Your mother will be here within the hour. It's Sunday. We've phoned the church to get a message to her. Service is over at noon. Sophie. There are a few things I'd like to address before your mother gets here. There'll be plenty to address, as it is, after she arrives.

Tears fall from my eyes, and I put my hands over my wet lashes and hot cheeks. I know what he wants to ask. He lifts my hand.

Are you pregnant?

I want to shout. What's wrong with having a baby? The only thing wrong is that a mother makes it wrong. She might beat me and throw me into church. Here. You take care of her. The slut. The whore. She might break every other bone and rebreak my arm. You don't know, Dr. Glauser. Sex isn't evil. But I say nothing.

He gazes upon me with sympathy: Sophie. This is no small issue. Please tell me.

No. I'm not.

His shoulders lift and fall. His smile is pained: You are, are you not?

I think, I can't fool the man who brought me into the world. I tell him yes.

I think you're four months along. Am I right?

I'm not sure.

I don't want to say any more about my baby. I'm thinking that's between my baby and me.

He waits for another answer. I shrug.

Very well. Are you in pain anywhere else, other than your arm?

My head. Back here. I touch the spot. My back.

Yes, you're stiff from the fall.

The man-nurse walks in and pushes a thermometer under my tongue. It's an invasion into my private opening and I want to reject invasions. Dr. Glauser stands.

I'll be back, he says. Rest up.

I have been resting, I think. Now I want to go home.

I have to stare at the man-nurse tapping two fingers on his knee. I look to the windows, but the shades are drawn. I lift his wrist and look at his watch. Eleven-ten.

Dr. Glauser returns and comes to my side. He smells of ammonia. He pats my forearm with his warm veiny hands and leaves. Is he so busy that he can't stay with me for a time? If he'd sit by my bed, his hands patting me, those hands that brought me out of my mother's tunnel. Should I hate him or love him for that?

I think most girls would be happy to know their mother will come within the hour. My baby is inside, and they know the baby is inside, and I am unpeaceful. The man-nurse lifts the shades, then leaves. Too much light in this room. My mother will be here after church, stinking of Chanel No. 5 and full to the eyes with spirituality.

I lie on my side facing the hallway and see too much light through the thin skin of my closed eyelids. Preserve the eyes.

I listen carefully. A breath. My breath. Scuffling feet and patients calling for nurses, and doctors calling for nurses. Between them they relate funny things and muffle laughs behind cupped hands. There's an air of gossip, and the rattle of medicine trays. There are nurse's aides in pink-and-white-striped dresses that swish against knees in the sweet breeze they create going in and out of rooms. Mother will be on her way. To comfort myself, I think of hours into the future, of the peaceful time after my mother leaves. My eyes half close. My muscles aren't strong. The worst part about falling asleep is that I'll wake up to a bad mistake that has left me inferior. It will feel unreal at first, as if I've only dreamed it. I'll have to take the first breaths of my waking up and think: It's real.

Have my bowels forgotten to move? Have I been sweating? I wear a sterile smell. What's the look on my face? I don't like to be unconscious and know nothing of those days, as if those days never were. If I die on my seventy-ninth birthday, I'll have to think that I died on my seventy-ninth minus two days of unconsciousness. But calm, calm.

I must have sensed someone in the room and now I'm awake. Have I been asleep a minute or an hour or a day? My mother isn't here. Dr. Glauser is. I wasn't airlifted to Denver, he tells me, because they waited to see if I'd regain consciousness.

What time is it? I ask.

Noon. I hope your mother got the message.

I ask him more about my accident.

I'll be back, he says holding up a finger. Let me call the church again.

I walk to the cream shades and pull them down, but they snap up. The cloud tops are dull pink, and it looks as though rain could fall from the dark gray underclouds and the tops would stay pink.

He comes back to tell me there's been an error in the message-giving. That my mother has gone with Aunt Alice to Calley's Dough-nuts. Now they're on their way here. Six blocks away. Dr. Glauser tells me the rules of my broken arm. No lifting, even with the good arm. I could offset my balance and fall on the broken arm. What crap. No riding until the arm heals. To hell with that, I think.

Does Dr. Glauser know what it means to try and keep me from riding Pablo? What does he know? Blue-eyed babies and rashes and flus and ingrown toenails. Are they two blocks away now?

I can go home from the hospital this afternoon if everything checks out in the physical exam. My mother should be here in seconds. Can I read an eye chart and how well does my brain work? This is what they want to know. I don't know what to expect from the exam, and it makes me uneasy. Will they glue electric sticks onto my scalp? Will they strike my funny bone? Settle a needle into my navel?

These seconds move like a hot and tired animal, and I sit and watch the dull grass of the lawn made dull by gray clouds. The cars and trucks come and go on the side street. I think about whether or not I'll have to make an apology to my mother. She'll manage to scare the shame into me. I set my mind and tell myself she won't.

I pull in my lips like a fish and kiss the air. Kissing the seconds good-bye.

My mother stands stiffly in the doorway and Aunt Alice rushes to my bed. She touches me on the forehead and on my shoulder. Poor baby. Poor baby. My vision. Does dizziness come from a virus germ? I'm the poor baby. Not my baby. Is this what she means?

My mother wears her long khaki skirt with her brown lizard belt and silver buckle. And a white cotton blouse with a ruffle down the front. Conservative. She wears no makeup, save for the blood lips. Her eye whites are dappled with red. She comes to my bed and touches me at the side of my neck, her hand curved into the base of my skull. Touching me there as if I'm an interesting large rock. I look into the whole of her face. It's twisted and dimpled like a pared orange peel. I think I'm going to be sick.

Suddenly she stands and takes one step back as if I'm poison, as if she won't be able to control herself if she stays too close in the doorway. Her straight body is a safe distance away.

Her head cocked to the side, her hands wringing so that I know she's struggling to be calm. She bears false calmness. Her eyes flash. Sophie. Dear. *How do you propose to feed a baby?*

I bare my teats.

How do you propose to clothe it?

I place the sheet from my bed into my mouth, and tear it with my teeth. It rips down the center.

Do you want to tell me who the father is?

Another doctor enters the room. I know him only by sight from Dr. Glauser's office where he also practices. Dr. Meegan is his name, or so it says on the door of their clinic. He has slightly graying hair, and thick black glasses too big for his long thin face. I've seen Dr. Glauser for tonsillitis and chicken pox, and I'm unfamiliar with Dr. Meegan's ways. When you don't know, you can't trust. Dr. Glauser was here only minutes ago. Where has he gone?

Good morning, he says.

He's within two feet of my face, and puts out his hand, his elbow resting on his hip. He thinks I know his name. Never think like that. I'll trust you better if you make an effort to be my friend.

He draws the curtain around my bed while Mother and Aunt Alice wait on the other side. He parts my hospital gown and makes it open at my back, listening to my heart and lungs. He feels around my neck and under the arms. He motions for me to lie down, lifts my gown, and pushes against the gown lightly, right to left, in a horseshoe upon my stomach. He lifts my gown to my neck. I pull it down. My breath is frozen.

Please, he says.

Let the doctor do his job, my mother says quietly.

He lifts the gown carefully and looks upon my naked breasts. His brow pleated. I pull the gown down. He has no right. My breaths are shallow and quick. He has no right to look at me as if I'm a sideshow freak. My swollen breasts and brown nipples and swollen belly. I think I'm going to be sick. A circle of lightness in my stomach. I'm cold.

He leaves and I lie quietly on my bed behind the curtain and pull the covers to my chin. They're out there whispering, the three of them. My blanket is some kind of protection. Am I stupid? Protection? She's only hit me once in two years. I told her to fuck off when she tried to make me clean the sheepers' truck. Cleanliness is godliness. Sheep shit dried dusty on the floor. Piraté's cigarette butts spilling over the ashtray and old food behind the seat. Pennies and dimes under the seat.

Aunt Alice opens the curtain. My mother's body is large and stiff as a saluting soldier. Her fingers knotting.

Try and stay calm, Aunt Alice says. We'll get through this.

I wish I could believe her. The degree of pull on my bile is at eight. When it reaches ten it will come up.

Let's don't think about the baby right now. Let's think about getting you better.

I'm keeping my baby, I say loudly.

Mother lights a cigarette.

My hands tingle and my face heats. I'm sweating cold now and my head swims in hoops. The degree of pull on my bile is nine. My mouth fills with its own juice. I have a point of no return and the bile comes up and showers the blanket. I scream gutturally at the pain in my arm as I retch. Aunt Alice folds down the bedding and my round stomach rises through the dotted print of the hospital gown.

I have the urge to cradle my bad arm. I don't believe the cast will keep the bones from splitting into kindling and clogging my veins.

A nurse enters with linens over her arms. I leave the bed and walk to the chair. My left knee pains me and I touch a crusty cut the size of a stamp. I need to go to the bathroom.

My face in the mirror is dappled with red, and tight with small flecks of dry skin. What drugs were in the bottle on the silver rack? Would the drugs hurt my baby? I keep a tight grip on my gown at the thighs.

As I leave the bathroom Dr. Meegan steps into my room and we face each other. I need to give you a pelvic examination. Have you had one before?

I shake my head.

A nurse brings supplies. These items are laid on a white cloth on the tray. A piece of glass, a spray bottle, and a silver metal duckbill.

I'll need to insert a speculum into your vagina. It won't be painful. A little uncomfortable. I need to feel your uterus, Sophie. I won't hurt you. This I promise. Do you know that word, vagina?

Does he think I'm so stupid?

Relax. I won't hurt you. I do promise.

He tells me that it will not hurt. What does he know about my pain? What good is his promise?

He motions for me to slide to the end of the bed so that my feet are at opposite ends. He adjusts my feet, legs apart. I pull my knees in so they touch at the inside. He brings them apart with gentle hands and raises and lowers his hand as if to ask me to relax, as if to ask me to trust him.

He says, Let your knees out. Take a deep breath. Relax your stomach.

He pulls thin rubber gloves over his hands and takes the metal duckbill from the tray. Cold metal touches the lips between my legs. He shouldn't try to force his way in. I withdraw, pulling in my knees, and he removes the cold metal. I can smell the burning cigarette and see the smoke as it rises over the curtain.

Open your knees, won't you?

I look away. He's trying to walk me through this humiliation. One hand patting my stomach as if this will loosen the muscles that I make stiff. The muscles hold me together and keep me from crying out a kind of primitive sound. I want to call Edwina and have her come get me.

My tunnel has known one man and I don't want this metal duckbill inside. I slide back to the pillow and straighten my legs on the bed and cross them at the knees. What can he see by opening me here? Did my great-great grandmother have such a pelvic test? Did Indian mothers?

He throws up his hands and surrenders. He shakes his head and asks me to sit up. He taps my knee with a rubber mallet and sends my leg forward.

I must take an eye examination and perform some feats of coordination. I must submit to more blood tests and urine tests.

Somewhere within those fluids they'll see that my baby is growing inside. What more can they tell? That my baby is normal? That its feet are not webbed? What if my baby is born with something unfixable? A faulty brain. A hole in its heart. An arm with no hand.

The jeans that Mother has brought for me to wear home are too small. I have to wear them half unzipped, and the tails of the blouse out. We gather my things: toothbrush, toothpaste, shampoo, and hairbrush that Mother must have brought when I was unconscious. She throws them into a paper bag.

At the nurses' desk Mother signs the papers to release me, and we walk out the side door. Stiff like a candle she steps ahead of me out to the parking lot and Aunt Alice's station wagon. We get in with Aunt Alice behind the wheel, Mother next to me by the window. I'm ready for the silent thirty-two-mile ride home. On Barton Street, women from the penitentiary in green suits plant blue and yellow flowers at the edge of the sidewalk.

My mother angles herself to look at me. Who? she asks.

I turn to stare out my window.

She takes my arm roughly and I throw it off.

She holds me by the shoulders and forces me to face her: Who's the father?

It's important for her to know who the father is so she can punish. She's not a stupid woman. She'll come to the right conclusion in time. Maybe I could be pregnant by Jack the bus driver, the postman, a boy I met at the river.

Her lips are the color of newly drawn blood and they're pursed and thin. Her knowledge of my pregnancy overrides everything. The problem is that she'll have to take revenge on someone. It's too big a thing for her to only pray on it. She'll have to take some kind of revenge.

There is more to silence than the absence of sound. There is a kind of energy that fills the car.

Could she think I let the ram loose on Piraté out of revenge because he got me pregnant? I'd rather sleep with a goat.

At Pilot and County Road D we stop at the four-way and she looks at me. Aunt Alice whistles Mac the Knife. She's a terrible whistler. I focus on the semi coming toward us, coming down from Wicks' land maybe. The semi's cargo is sheep. I see them through the slats. Sheep stacked on shelves. Mother mumbles the Lord's name. She doesn't favor the trail of dust from the side road coating the car. She doesn't favor the slow semi. I know what she's thinking. Couldn't he have been polite enough to let us go first? Couldn't he have been thinking of someone other than himself?

The road is flat for the next eight miles until the hill after the start of DeWolf's land. I can almost see to the hill and I figure in my mind one, two, three miles passed. Aunt Alice slows down so there are five or six car lengths of room between the semi and us. A cautious driver. Unlike my mother she drives under the speed limit. Ahead and to the left a black cow grazes. She's found greener pastures where that part of the fence has been down, down since I can remember. DeWolf is old now, and some say he's gone senile. He has a few cows and I've heard he makes cheese from his goats' milk. The grasses in this pasture are overgrown with purple flowers, and the cow has come to the edge over the broken flat fence and stepped into the grass of the green ditch. Then it wanders onto the blacktop, and at that moment I feel my mother's body tighten. The truck's rear suddenly grows large as we close in, as it stops, and I'm thrown forward by the sudden brake of our car.

Sweet Jesus, my mother screams, he's hit her.

We swerve to the right and stop on the shoulder. The truck has stopped many feet after its impact. The driver backs up, his elbow resting on the window base. He gets out, a stocky man with an orange mustache.

He removes his duckbill cap and wipes his brow. His hair is thick and wavy and orange. He walks over to the east side of the road where the cow lies on her side. He walks back to us standing near his semi. I leave them and look to the cow. A Black Angus. She's been thrown into the standing part of the fence and lies there, quivering.

Damn fellow supposed to mend his fence. Damn fellow. This ain't the first time I seen one here.

The driver moves his truck to the shoulder. The cow's tendons are glistening and there's crimson red at her broken bones. From the neck, blood arcs in beats, maybe they're heart pumps, and leaves bright red on the grass. I hope the brain is dead. The arc of blood from its neck stops. Her eyes glassed over. Good. She's dead. Body and soul.

Aunt Alice and Mother and the truck driver stand talking at the middle of the semi. Bleating sheep. Shut up! They fear everything! Aunt Alice and the driver walk toward the cow, and the driver pulls his orange chin stubble as if milking a teat. If they'd keep these fences mended, damn fellow, none of this would happen. His hands shake as he lights a cigarette and holds the pack out for Aunt Alice. Ain't the first time I seen a cow break out of there. Damn fellow and his fence.

In the winter there's no fence line at all. The snow covers it. DeWolf only keeps a few cows and goats at his place. In winter they huddle around the feed lot, safe.

My mother watches the cow. The crows will hover in. Turkey buzzards. Gathering flies.

Who'll tell DeWolf? I ask.

The truck driver frowns and looks at me. His hand comes up and strokes his chin. I got a schedule, he says, and with the heat and those sheep.

My mother kneels down to lay a hand on the cow's black back. Only a cow, thank God, she says.

Aunt Alice points southeast toward DeWolf's place. Up there, she says. Half a mile.

She was just a cow, my mother says. A poor, pitiful cow.

The driver steps into his truck and drives up the blacktop half a mile to DeWolf's drive. He turns in and rises over the hill. My mother strokes the dead cow's face. Then she looks up to heaven. Her eye beams are trying to find her Lord. Can she ask for the cow to be made whole again? I never hear of miracles in the here and now like they happened in Bible times.

Aunt Alice bends over and says something to Mother, but my mother doesn't respond. She stands and walks over to the downed fence and into the grasses. The freakish little things of the ground are scurrying out of her way. The prairie voles, deer mice, pocket gophers with incisor teeth tools and strong forefeet and big curved claws. She lifts her arms, palms to the sky, looking down. Aunt Alice goes after her. The sky is clear and blue. If heaven is a place with no sun or moon or water, what are its rhythms?

We pull through our gate and round the drive. Aunt Alice parks the truck. Oh, there are the horses in the pasture. Pablo canters along the fence.

No riding until that cast comes off, my mother says.

To hell, I think, with you.

The men look content when they drink coffee and eat cookies. Fig cookies today. For a minute the men stare. Then Julian comes to me. I press myself into his arms as if they'll absorb me and I'll become invisible. From the living room Mother glances at us. Is it Julian who made the baby? No, no, I glare at her. Leave him out of it.

The night air smells like rain. The moon is gone and I've lost track how it lies in its monthly schedule. The moon is above the clouds, hiding.

Pablo and I are in the open grasses, his nose nuzzling my neck and grain-full back pockets and the stickiness of my underarms. In my imagination I hear old Samurai crying and the scared voices of Indians covered by rock slides, and mothers and their children eating goats' eyes in a tent somewhere in the desert. I hear Tin Picardy talking about her constipation, and Jack the bus driver cooing to his baby boy in the bathtub. No more grain for my horse. Eaten. He stands elegantly in the dark, glowing white even without the light of the moon. I think I should call Edwina and ask her to come over tomorrow.

When I wake up it's nearly four o'clock. My bedroom window is open and the curtains are quiet. A thin sheet of gray hangs overhead, and small dark clouds gather in the west. I wish rain would fall and break the heat.

Edwina comes into my room! What a great thing to see her! At least my mother hasn't sent her away. I think she won't allow those things that give me happiness. I wonder how clear I've made my pleasures. I wonder if she'll know what to take away.

Edwina's voice moves fast as she tells me about the day I fell off Pablo. She rode the rest of the hill and came into the yard and found Mother. Pablo stood next to me, unmoving. My mother drove me to the hospital. Edwina brought Pablo to the barn and unsaddled him and put him out to pasture. Then she rode home on her horse.

In the hospital Edwina came to my bed but I was unconscious. Does she know? Edwina asks.

Yes.

If she prays, do you think she'll get over it?

It might lessen the anger.

What about the pastor? Is she going to drag you to him?

She might bring him here.

Then?

I don't know.

What can she do?

Send me to a home for unwed mothers. I don't know. Look at me. Weak. This arm. I'm inferior.

Not to me.

What do you think of me?

I think you'll go on.

What do you mean?

You'll be okay.

She presses her fingers into my aching neck and shoulders, and the pinch of rusty nails that holds my bones together fall away. I want to use her safe shoulder as a pillow. I want to tell her about my mother's strange habits. There have been so many. I could tell her the story about Clements and our calico, but I'm tired.

She's driven over in Tin's truck and she has to go back now for supper. If I need her, she says, I should call her. She'll come, no matter what.

When I wake up it's almost eleven o'clock. A sunny day. My stomach feels hollow with hunger and I have a huge thirst. My nightshirt is stained with raspberry jam. In bare feet I walk into the kitchen and find Mother sitting at the table with Julian, drinking coffee. Morning, I say. They say that back. His face is dusty and there's a line on his forehead where the rim of his hat was. Mother's feet are kicked up on the vinyl of the kitchen chair, her sheepskin slippers shiny-bottomed, hair combed back from her face, nose and forehead glossy with oil, and a pink glaze over her lips. Her upper and lower eyelids are lined in black pencil. When she pulls on the stubbed cigarette, her face gathers inward as if her body will be drawn into the cigarette. Julian steps outside. When he turns to look through the screen door, he waves at me and settles his hat on his head. I feel pitied and empty and sad.

While I'm eating a piece of toast with jam, Piraté comes in, eyes blinking. I wonder if my mother told him the news about the baby. He'll brag to his comrades, I knew, I told you. Big deal. He and my mother talk in low voices, her eyes shift to me, and she and Piraté step outside. In a moment she walks in and takes her gardening gloves from the tin pail by the screen door. Then, as if she's forgotten something, she puts them back. She walks down the hallway to her bedroom. I pour a bowl of cornflakes and add milk, and slice a green apple in half. We don't have orange juice, but there's a lemon. I cut it in half and squeeze it into a glass of ice water.

I need to write Demetrio a letter about my accident.

Mother has boxes of sand-colored matches. I cut them in half and glue the rectangles together until I have a shape of beautiful stationery. On my bed the leftover pieces, the white-tipped matches, are like soldiers standing at attention.

I write that everything is fine except for my arm. I want to tell him about the baby, but I don't in the letter. I want to see you, I write. Also, I'm unsure about my mother, who grows stranger every day. There's a difference between my mother and me, isn't there? Please tell me how I'm different. The garden's coming in.

I haven't been to the garden for five days. You shouldn't work in a garden every day, except in cases of long heat when the plants need to be watered. If you go into the garden every other day, you can look forward to the garden changing. I wish it would rain. At my window I'm getting ready to pull the curtains so I can dress, and I see Mother walking through the yard with stiffness and quickness. She has Pablo by a lead, attached to the halter over his broad white face. That's my horse, not yours. Maybe he's thrown a shoe. If something's wrong, why didn't she tell me?

She drops the lead and walks away from him. He bows his head and eats the overgrown green grass in the yard. I can hear through the open window the grass coming up by his teeth.

Pablo, I call.

He lifts his head. From the corner of my eye I see Piraté step out of the barn carrying a rifle. Now what? As he moves to his right I can't see him, and I put my head out the window. He raises the rifle.

Pablo isn't twenty feet from me. I scream. I scream. I leap out the window and fall into the dirt, my face in the dirt where the rain comes off the eaves, my hand tearing at the edge of the grass and my arm searing so that my shoulder and neck are on fire. I pull myself up then, but Pablo's body is laid out. Behind us the rifle is held at Piraté's side. Blood drains from Pablo's neck.

I don't know how loud my scream is. I don't know how far it reaches. I'm screaming and I can't stop. His brown eyes are glass. My arms go around his quiet neck, and the air from his nostrils is quiet and faint. A pool of blood forms. My arm is covered with it. It's warm. I have to call a vet. I'll have to leave you, Pablo, and call someone. If I leave, will you die? I can't leave. I press my face into his warm mane.

The smallest rising and falling, the smallest movements stop. I put my hand under his nostrils. Nothing. I run my fingers through his mane, touch his ears, and the place between them which he loved me to rub. I quiet my face in his hair, his skin, his warmth. I roll over and lie on the grass next to him, and face the sky.

I run for the truck as it rounds the drive. The back of Piraté's filthy beret. I'm screaming after the truck and my eyes burn from the dust. But it pulls away. I scream Julian's name.

When I turn and walk back toward Pablo, my mother's standing near my bedroom window. She's stiff against the house, as if she's holding it up. Her hands are unsteady and seal her mouth, and her eyes dart right and left. Her makeup has run from her eyes, and the black is smeared under them. A piece of hair hangs over one eye. She looks afraid and lost.

Julian walks toward us from the barn with slow steps. Shaking his head and walking toward us, his eyes on Pablo. His tongue makes clicking noises.

My mother's hands come away from her mouth and there's a thin line of drool.

Oh, Willy, he says. This is bad. Very bad.

I fall on Julian. I cling with one arm to his neck and shoulders, and beg him to bury Pablo, not to pour gasoline and light him on fire. Please, oh, please. Julian smooths my hair. Mother is gone.

I wander to the pasture and wait by the loafing shed. The horses come from the far side and mill about and whicker. They want to eat. Julian is driving the backhoe with the engine smoking oil. He ties Pablo's back legs to the rope attached to the tractor. He pulls him slowly across the lawn and more slowly across the gravel. I open the pasture gate. The horses stare for a minute, then gallop off.

On the far side, the engine stops smoking and Julian steps down. He has not stopped shaking his head. Maybe he knew of this plan. Maybe they talked about it, but he wouldn't have any part. He misjudged them. Crows hover in cottonwoods like rows of black umbrellas.

If he's not buried, buzzards will come and crows will pick his bones clean. Inside the womb of the earth he'll rot in the land. It's all right if the worms have him. The freakish little things of the underground. If we don't bury him way down, the coyotes will get him. Coyotes bring killing and sadness. They're evil.

Julian takes the ropes from Pablo's back legs. He drives the backhoe along the fence. He stops and lowers the backhoe. When the tractor stops I hear the crows caw. Then the motor starts again and the shovel goes into the ground. The day is hot and clear.

Julian pulls off his hat and wipes his brow and chin with his shirtsleeve. Poor Pablo. How does my mother look at me? Evil, sinful, a sexed, lazy girl. I try to view myself as she views me, but I can't. I hate her. I think of all the harm I can bring to Piraté.

Each dig raises earth that spills over the shovel's sides. He unloads the dirt in front of the grave. I stare at him working, and at Pablo's lifeless body, and at the crow-umbrellas and at the hot blue sky. The pit's shaped now, but it needs to be deeper. If I had a shotgun, I'd scatter the crows. They sit crafty and looming and shifty like a black curtain.

If I find my father, and if he won't let me stay with him, I can live with my grandmother. I'm a brown-eyed black-haired girl with a baby in her stomach. I can work in a house. Clean the house and make soup. I can paint walls and fences. I can care for horses and gardens, and bleach clothing until it's so white it hurts your eyes.

A billowing cloud splits like a cell dividing, making baby clouds. I haven't felt the kick of my baby. Does my baby suffer in the heat? I won't sit in the shade under the crows who want to pick my horse clean. They won't have the chance. Julian has soaked his shirt through and finally he takes it off and works in the thin sleeveless undershirt made gray with his sweat.

At last he walks to me where I sit against the fence. He says, Come on, Sophie. Come, dear one.

The grave is deep and long. Pablo will be eaten by the freakish little things and shat from their bodies and he'll settle into the earth.

Julian is shiny with sweat. He knots the rope around Pablo's heels. He climbs onto the backhoe and my horse is pulled inch by inch through the pasture's grass. His rump rises as the backhoe pulls the rope. Pablo's head is sliding, one eye in the dirt. He dan-

gles above the grave, swaying. The side dragged over ground is pit-
ted with rock. Oh. It's hard to breathe.

Pablo hangs nose down over the hole. The swinging gets bigger so that Pablo is going back and forth like a child pumping a
swing. It's too much. I sob from my heart as I can't remember. My
eyes burn. I go to Julian and ask him to stop, and he lowers his eyes
and nods. My horse hanging like this is too much to bear.

Put him in the best way you can, but do it now, I tell him. We
need to be done with this.

The swinging starts again.

How will we cover it? I shout over the motor.

I don't know, he says.

With stones.

I can bring some in the truck. If that is what you want.

Thank you.

Then I leave.

My feet whisper as I walk through the pasture. The whisper
runs through my toes and the arch of my feet, and up my shin and
across my knees. It reaches my teats, my throat, my tongue and
eyes. I don't know the words.

Mother walks out of the house wearing a mini dress. Her shirt-
sleeves are rolled up and her eyes don't have black liner. She walks
fast to me and throws her arms around my neck.

Don't touch me!

I feel the bile rising. I run into the house, to the bathroom, and
am sick. My arm throbs and feels as if it breaks like candy brittle
and makes slivers in my blood.

She stands at the bathroom door with a washcloth and tries to
wipe my face. I push her away and go into the kitchen and pick up
the telephone. She grabs the phone from me. She's weeping, her
body's heaving, and she screams like a chicken. The Lord giveth and
the Lord taketh away. The Lord giveth and the Lord taketh away.

I take the phone again and call Edwina. Oh, please. The phone
rings and rings. Finally she picks it up. I shout, Come now, come,
my horse is dead, come as soon as you can.

My mother sinks to the floor, her arms strangling my knees, and I'm suffocating in her grip and shouting, Edwina, come now. Over and over. Mother hugs my knees and rocks, and stares ahead, her lips moving. Christ our Lord, Father our Redeemer. I try to push her away with my hand. Pablo's dead, come now, come now. I kick my mother in the stomach. Hard. She falls back. She touches the place where I kicked her.

Come now, Edwina, come now.

My mother walks to the couch and shoves a cigarette in her mouth with hand flutters like a hurt moth. The match burns down and she throws it into the ashtray. She lights another.

Sophie. Soph. Let's not get overly dramatic about a horse. We've got a ranch to run. A horse, for heaven's sake. I was thinking of buying some peacocks, that raising peacocks would be good.

Come now, Edwina. My horse is dead.

In the dark my heart bumps against my ribs and makes a song with the bleating lambs. Rebby sits up, but he's tied to the clothesline. I whisper, Rebby, good boy. His rear end waggles. He doesn't bark.

The money comes from the envelope between straw bales. I go back into bed and think of killing Piraté and of the consequences. Pablo and Piraté and my mother are three apples tossed by a grinning juggler. Have I gone as crazy as my mother? Do we both belong in a nuthouse and would we be forced to share a room? Killing, killing.

Piraté knows how to do it. He's done it hundreds of times to pregnant ewes whose lamb-bearing lives were spent, and whose lives were less important than lambs'. Killing sheep is the way of a working ranch. I know Piraté is paid by my mother to do his job. But the others don't show so much satisfaction in killing as Piraté. His cursing and smiles. But meat and wool equal money. I have a roof over my head. A shiny green swimsuit. Bread and jam. Lamb chops for lunch. Am I a pretender if I stay? Slicing throats is part of the work.

Why don't I slice my mother's throat? I'm afraid. Isn't there a drop of my mother's blood that loves me?

I rode to Demetrio's silver camper and lay with him. In March my nipples tingled and a baby was growing. Why did I take a chance? I knew a baby might be made. What does a baby bring? Diapers, crying, nights with no sleep, worry over colic, my watchful eye made more watchful with the baby: Where I go, the baby goes. The anger of my mother.

What about birth defects? A slow mind? A crazy baby? Does craziness skip a generation? What about kidnappers, hit and run, river drowning?

But there's learning and teaching: walking, riding a horse, singing, reading. Laughing. Here's a luna moth. This is a puffball mushroom. See? You can smash it with your foot if you want. That's a magpie. It will eat the food out of Sharpa's bowl.

The true selfish reasons for having a baby: to see its likeness to Demetrio and me. A woman, not a child, has a baby. I'll have my own family. My rules will be different from the rules my mother makes.

If I slice Piraté's throat, I need to do it well and go away. I can't go to my father. They'll find me there. Where can a girl hide forever?

I've borrowed sugar from their trailer, and last winter I stole two apples for Pablo and me from the bowl on their table. The door is never locked. My eyes adapt well to the dark because I haven't been in the light.

The trailer is dark, save for a dull yellow glow of night-light by the couch. The knife stayed very sharp since Clem went to Vietnam. You must wonder what kind of person I am. One thing the Bible says is an eye for an eye. I believe in that if I have to believe in something the Bible says. Demetrio held a knife to the trucker's throat on the day of Nicklow's funeral. Hand to hand. Steal a lamb and we'll cut your hands. I have no shame, only direction.

The knife's handle is wooden and bleached from sinkfuls of salted water. Clements put catfish into the water. The handle is bleached from the salt.

There's Piraté. He's asleep on his back. Snoring. Covers to his waist. Bare-chested. A clean white chest and neck. I could put him out with a stab through the heart. But a slice across the neck. I've seen him take a ewe from behind, thrust her head back with the heel of his hand, and jerk her head up by the wool. His knife wasn't sharp enough or his aim was off so she screamed and fell on her knees. Blood ran out of her until he sliced her again and called her *puta* for not dying faster. When sheep scream it's a bad sound. The cut needs to be clean and deep across the throat.

There is the smell of old sweat and dirty clothes and sheep shit. There are his boots. His pants. He thinks he'll step into them at dawn. His chest rising and falling. The small stinking bed whose sheets I wash. The pink-white scar on his head shines even in the dark. It will be so easy. His chin is raised by the soft pillow. What does he dream?

I have a flutter in my stomach as if daddy longlegs spiders are running in my gut, hundreds. I put a hand on my stomach. The flutter comes again. Is it too early for me to feel my baby's kicks? Wait. I should take dreams away from a person? I'm not a coward, but this isn't right.

I'm pulled from behind by a rough hand over my mouth, another around my waist, and dragged with force, as if my body is a broom. It's Julian who throws the knife to the floor. Outside, he forces me to the ground at the front end of the trailer. Sharpa's tongue strokes my hand. Julian sits next to me and holds me there with force. I don't fight him. I sit against the head of the trailer, my back in the gap below the frame where Sharpa hides in the day from the sun. I crawl into the space like a dog. My hand goes into his water bowl.

Julian pulls me by one leg and drags me from the space. My fingers are curved like claws, as if I can latch on to the earth. He pulls, and my nails fill with dirt. I kiss him tenderly on the earlobe and say good-bye.

I open the back door and whisper Rebby's name. I say, Good boy, Rebby, before I close the door. I take one of Clements' jackets from the closet. Edwina is parked down the drive. Yesterday she said, The motor will be off.

We'll drive south and stop along the way to get a map. My

clothes are in a green duffel bag. I think it used to be my father's. I found it in the basement with a raccoon hat and a cracked mirror.

Edwina raises her hand.

Let's get out of here, I say.

I close the door and crack the window.

Did you sleep okay? she says.

No.

She turns on the inside light. I have this, she says, and holds up four twenty-dollar bills.

I hold up my envelope and tell her it's not much but we can buy food. If my father tells us to go away, we can sleep in the truck. In two or three hours, Tin and Rudy will know that Edwina has gone with their truck. By then we'll almost be in Colorado. She backs out of the drive, into the tall grass. She shifts into first, then second.

part *Four*

*I*N THE REARVIEW mirror I see the three-quarter moon, an ax blade over the house. The television aerial and the windows of the house and trailer are black. I feel everything and nothing.

Maybe Pablo could have lived thirty more years. Both of us would be forty-five then. If I could see where my life would be then. Pablo didn't die fast. For those seconds that he suffered, I bear grief like a hot iron in my chest.

He had a shaggy mane like straw, wet eyes crusted in their corners, manure in his hooves. The muscle of his back and thighs trembled slightly as I ran the flat of my hand over him.

Someone will find out where we're going. The choices are my grandmother's, Edwina's parents, or my father's. We can't live forever out of a truck and take baths from the faucets of gasoline stations. How far can we go on this small amount of money? Tin and Rudy are good people. I wish we didn't have to take their truck.

We bump along the dirt road and turn right onto the highway. Pablo could sense anything. Burning *ovejas*. An eagle perched before it flew from its nest. Bad water from the stream. A mountain lion. Did he sense death? Could he have run fast and far enough from it? Would they have found him wherever he was?

The fence and land are black. Barely a moon. I open the window. When I was four years old I rode Pablo bareback and clung to him with my thighs. I turned him by his mane.

In the time between saying good-bye to Julian and Edwina coming for me, I made hot water for tea. In kettle-steam my memories of Pablo swirled and rose. I couldn't stand those memories. I took the kettle off the flame and watched it for a while. I thought how in an hour's time I'd leave this place. Then I was afraid my mother would walk into the kitchen. But prayers bring sleep for sinners. Sin is forgiven, the conscience cleared before dawn.

The bumping of the truck and the hum of the motor, my face against the cool window, and this silence, are drugs that lead me into sleep.

The sky is pale yellow as old newspaper. Edwina's left foot is on the seat and her knee is up. She holds the wheel with one hand and with the other she taps a finger to Patsy Cline's voice.

You okay?

I nod. Tired. Really tired.

I think of who's awake now: my mother, the sheepers, Tin and Rudy. My mother's awake. I feel sick. I need something to eat or I'll vomit. Eating takes the nausea away, but there's nothing to eat or drink. I'm not so brave. If I start to cry, I wonder when I'd stop. I imagine I'm pulled through Pablo's soft flesh, and as I meet his spine he whickers, and I cling to his ribs into sleep.

A redheaded boy pumps gas into the truck, and Edwina pays, returning with a map in hand. She unfolds it. She no longer wears pink on her nails, but her plain nails are stained anyway. As if they're red-faded stained. Climax, Colorado, looks to be about three hours away, she says. Pinnacle Butte maybe five or six.

In my mother's eyes Demetrio will be the one who fathered my child, and he'll be fired. He'll smooth the roped muscles in my neck with the stroke of his hummed song. His lips will touch sweetly as moth wings on my ear. The song he learned from his grandmother is old and sad and calm. He'll go to Guadalajara. But I need to think of myself right now, of the baby, of the next few hours.

I take out my notepad and start a letter. Dear Clements, a bad thing happened. But my thoughts take me away. What do I expect when I meet my father? I think he'll explain that a misunderstanding made him leave.

I write to Clements about the baby. When I tear the page from my notebook, I fold it three times and put it in my pocket until I can mail it.

If, in the future, I married, would my father have stepped forward in the nick of time to walk me up the aisle? If I hadn't seen him since I was four? I'm not sure I go in for formal weddings: church weddings. But if I did. Would my father show up and walk me down the aisle?

I tell myself, Think of nothing but a slow stream of maple syrup from a bottle. The beautiful rough elbows of Demetrio. A fire crackling in the fireplace. Not popcorn, but a fire snapping at logs. Count sheep. No, that's stupid. Think of stars bumping against black, like blood through a throat vein. Think of nothing.

Conifers and conifers and the remains of an old mining site. What if my mother tried to suffocate my father with a pillow? Maybe he jumped to life as she smothered his face, then burst out the door.

Thinking like this is as ugly as a snake's darting tongue.

What could have been so irreconcilable? Before the Masterson sisters turned on me for my supposed ugliness or because they found out I was an abandoned, I had a sleep-over in their bedroom attic. I thought by morning my feet might be frostbitten, the toenails blue with cold. I heard the Masterson sisters' parents, in thick German accents, fighting downstairs. Mrs. Masterson hated Mr. Masterson's fat warthog mother and Mr. Masterson said Mrs. Masterson spent too much money on bread and sausage. Mrs. Masterson called Mr. Masterson a lazy so-and-so and told him to get a better-paying job. The Masterson sisters slept through, but I kept my ear to the floor and shivered until I think it could have been my chattering teeth that woke the girls. What's worse—an abandoned girl or a girl whose parents wake up at dawn and curse each other from floor to ceiling? I held my feet and rubbed them between my palms, thinking I was the lucky one.

•   •   •

While we wait, Edwina and I eat sandwiches we bought at a drugstore counter fifty miles back. A man wearing a hard hat with the
words Opus Construction on his truck drives into the clearing and
turns around. He waves to us on the way out.

In the distance there is a sound of bells like a small choir
singing. It's a hollow sound, but quick and nice. Our sheep are to
the right, on the green of a mountain. Moving like a billowed
cloud. Two dogs tucking them up and Demetrio on his horse at the
back. Blue sky dusts his shoulders. Here's what I see: a white wave,
dogs tucking, and a man on his horse.

I've been to this place half a dozen times with Mother, to pick
up Piraté. It takes time for the sheep to eat their way down. The silver camper is here at the edge of the woods.

Edwina tells me her father has forbidden her to ride on the back
of the boy-from-school's Harley, but she does because the vibrations
feel good. She also enjoys putting her hands around the boy's waist
and shouting in his ear. In his basement he gives her shotguns of mar-
ijuana. His mouth to her mouth. Grass, she says, makes her so para-
noid that she once went to sleep in her closet. Her mother found her
there in the morning and said she needed to go to a head shrinker.

She offers me a stick of Doublemint gum.

No thanks.

You don't have to tell him if you don't want to. What if he
wants to marry you?

Maybe I will.

You'd marry him?

Why not?

I don't know. I don't know him, she says, staring down.

The breeze draws across the yellow dirt in a sad angling sigh.
Sheeps' bleats aren't low. There they come, sifting out of gray
conifer trunks, dogs loping at edges. Demetrio's yellow-brimmed
hat low on his head.

Eight months ago I sat cross-ankled in a blue skirt, black boots,
blouse, and plaid vest, on the front steps, doing homework. Because
we had not bought him groceries yet, he came down from the sil-

ver camper on his horse. He came down four nights in a row for supper, but the first night when he came down the hill and reined his horse to the corral, I was already thinking. My heart was near to bursting through my spine and flying off with sparrows. In the winter he moved to the trailer next to our house. I watched him as he walked to the pens. I watched the way he held his fork at supper, how the coffee steamed his eyes, how his eyes opened slowly from his cup. In the spring he went back to the camper on the plain, and I cried for a week.

Now he's here. His scratched and stained leather-chapped leg lifts over the saddle, and dusty-booted feet drop to yellow dirt. I kiss him on the mouth. His eyes are bloodshot and puffy.

Dios mío, what happened, Sophie?

I kiss him again on the mouth.

What happened to your arm? Something is bad, even more than this arm, he says, taking off his hat. He runs a hand through matted hair damp at the forehead, and dusty. He looks toward Edwina standing against the truck. Her hands are buried in her shorts' pockets.

You haven't met Edwina. She brought me here.

Que vision you are, Sophie. Then to Edwina: *Mucho gusto conocerle.* He walks fast to her and shakes her hand. You speak Spanish?

German. Sorry. My father's a Nazi. He made me take German.

Demetrio strides back to me and guides my body into his arms. He kisses my forehead and eyelid crescents. He steps back and stares me up and down. You look different, he says. I think you have been eating more. Good! But this arm.

In the sun his forehead shines as if it has been rubbed with gasoline. He and I walk into the pines. I think it's a whippoorwill in the tree. Its voice is like water.

First let me tell you that yesterday my mother had Piraté shoot Pablo, and he died.

Ah me.

I tried to kill Piraté last night.

You tried to kill Piraté?

Julian found me in his bedroom and took the knife away. I was going to slit his throat.

He swallows. How was your arm broken?

I don't tell him right away. If I do, I'll have to tell him about the baby. Why I kept the baby from him. I ask if he'll help me take off my shirt.

He looks around. But no, Sophie.

But yes, I say. Please.

The pain. I don't wear a bra. I tell him, Look here, my belly's full with a baby.

Oh, he says. Then he says nothing for a long time. He holds my right breast and pulls close. He pulls back then. He's wondering if the baby is his.

It's yours, I tell him.

He puts a hand on my belly as if trying to cup its roundness, and when he can't, he moves the hand to all the places on my belly.

Since March, I say.

And you did not tell me? he shouts.

I tell him about the hospital.

You did not tell me? He stands and kicks dirt. Then he quiets. You have much pain?

Yes. Yes. I blurt out, I thought in time I'd know. I thought in time love took you in or pushed you out. I still don't know.

I can't look at him. I'm ashamed and afraid. But then I look. I don't know if he's going to slap me. He pulls the shirt over my shoulders and buttons it. Ouch, I say. *Lo siento,* he says.

I'm going to live with my father, I tell him.

You are going to live with me. We are going to Guadalajara where we should have gone three months ago.

I can't go with you to Guadalajara.

Why not?

Because.

That isn't an answer.

Because I don't know how I love you.

My family is there and they will—

No.

What a long time a few minutes are when you're staring at a robin cocking its head to the ground. It brings up a worm. I was with Demetrio for the first time last February. I rode to him. I went there to spite my mother. To see and feel and taste him. Now we sit here watching a bird fly off with a worm.

In the night Demetrio groans with disfavor. He says, Edwina is fine there. Let her sleep. She is surely asleep.

How do you know?

In two hours she can fall asleep.

I don't like it that she's out there alone. What if she's afraid?

She has only to call out. Go out to the truck and tap on the window. Ask how she is. Do you want me to go? He throws the sheet to his waist. His body's heat hits me everywhere, even though we're only touching feet. He throws the sheet away from the bed and curls up to me.

For two hours we have talked. No more talking.

We could make a bed for her on the floor by the stove.

His finger to my lips. Sshh. His eyelash on my nose. Say the word.

Pestaña.

That is a beautiful Spanish word.

Creo que sí, I tell him.

You are a beautiful little bird.

His hand comes to my thigh and a finger traces eights to my knee. When I touch his chest he moans with pleasure. There's something else he likes. I push my finger into the back seam of his ear.

Careful, I say as he rises over me.

Will it hurt the baby?

I'm thinking of my arm. I think the baby will feel it's being rocked.

Do you think it is a boy or girl? he asks.

Do we have to talk about that now?

What do you want? A boy or a girl?

A whole baby. Put it in, I plead.

It doesn't go easily at first.

Have you ever spread your arms so you're in a cross and your lover stretches his arms over yours, and your hands meet and lock? My body pushes down, and he takes himself farther in.

What are you thinking? he asks, lighting a candle on the narrow ledge.

About Pablo first, then seeds. About Pablo—sometimes I feel his minutes before he died. His eyes were like nickels of fear.

Now, Demetrio says, he is in a place where snow never comes, and the wind is at his back.

He's in the ground! The best I can hope for is that his soul is released!

Demetrio hums the Mexican lullaby that tells me everything will be all right. I'm safe. Before I fall asleep I'll think Pablo's name a hundred times.

Edwina's waiting, I tell him.

Then I will follow you.

Do you think you're the only one in misery?

I look up to the sky because I can't gaze into his black eyes every second. They eat me. Clouds pass. Where are they going? I want to go, too. No, keep me in Demetrio's arms. Our hands lock as if we're going to throw each other to the ground, but I'm drawn to him.

Good-bye until I write you.

I do not want letters. I know what love is, Sophie, and you are a fool because you do not. You are a fool, Sophie.

Stop thinking of everything but an earthworm moving through the soil in lullaby rhythm. The ranch is dead.

In Little Spring a river runs along the right. A man in green waders stands hip-deep fishing. We pass a salmon hatchery, or so the sign reads. Jagged mountains rise. Blue-green pine trees. Peaks to the north are brown and barren.

I have a silly idea of my father's house. The bathtub has bear claws and I can fit my body into its hot water up to my chin. His couch is stuffed with feathers and his bed has a down comforter. Silly ideas. He's a smart man, according to my grandmother, but what mother would call her son stupid? There are many kinds of smart. Maybe he's the kind of man who knows the answers: what kind of mud do you use to put out the fire of a rash; when you see a horse's ghost do you call out to it or let it run?

In the corral near a house to the right, sitting back from the road, is a buffalo. I shade my eyes with a hand. A white buffalo. I wonder if its eyes are red as the eyes of an albino cat. We had a white cat with red eyes. She was deaf.

And why should I think my father has such qualities and taste to know, for example, that he should buy soft kidskin over cowhide? Because his senses are strong and he cares about feel and color? An avocado not too hard and not too ripe. Does he read books, unlike my mother who reads magazines and watches television? My mother said books cost too much money and take too much time to read. In our house I couldn't open many books and smell their pages. My books borrowed from the library were read and returned. That was better than nothing. But why do I think I'll walk into my father's house and find books on his shelves?

Do you read books? I ask Edwina. Or magazines?

Both. I don't like *Seventeen.* Do you?

I've never read it. What's the first book you ever read by yourself?

The Brothers Grimm.

Not *See Spot Run?*

Nope. I'd like one Grimm's fairy tale of my own.

What fairy tale do you want to happen?

For my old man to have a stroke and my mother has to take care of him, but she kind of says, well, I've done my duty all these years, and she lets him go, you know, doesn't shave him, lets him reek. And his toenails get all black and fall off and there's fungus behind his ears like potato sprouts. And pretty soon he shrivels up like an old balloon and my mother flushes him down the toilet. That's a fairy tale.

You'd feel awful if your old man had a stroke.

No, I wouldn't.

In Pinnacle Butte the main street is graveled and lined with small framed and scalloped houses along the street. There's a bar called the Salty Bread. People on bicycles. At the end of Main Street wooded evergreens rise into mountains. It's the end of the road.

The post office is smaller than ours in Bluerock, and there's a smell of spice. The room is gloomy with darkness. A woman with long hair talks and smiles with a bearded man behind the counter. He hands her a sheet of stamps, then takes the stamps from her and puts them in an envelope, and hands them back. He touches her wrist.

I ask the man if I can buy an envelope. Clements' address is in my memory. I buy a stamp and put my letter in, seal the rim, and hand it to the man. The man draws a map on a piece of yellow paper. Unpaved road. A path through the woods. A cabin.

Do you know him? I ask.

I see him around, the man says. I hunt on that property. That's Deminoux's place.

Where do you see him?

You got something against him? the man asks.

I'm his daughter.

I see. Well, every now and then he'll come down. That's the way with most of them. They come to town to get rid of their cabin fever.

What do you mean?

Can mean all kinds of things, but mainly they have a good time.

My hand is at an angle against my forehead so I can shade the sun. My thumb on my temple. I tell Edwina I have to think. Could we stay by the truck a minute while I think.

Relax, she says.

That's impossible.

Come on. Let's go.

The sun is an hour to the south of noon when we drive off Main, onto the unpaved road. I pull a strand of my hair to my mouth and taste it. I used to bury my face in Pablo's mane when the wind was strong.

The road dead-ends where the pine and spruce start. I don't think it would be right to show up at my father's door with our luggage. We leave it in the truck. The air is sharp and sweet with evergreens.

Edwina leads. I watch the back of her hips as we walk. The path is narrow, and winds through conifers where my father might walk when he travels to town. I watch Edwina's backside. Her hips are narrower than mine. I've watched people walk and have seen them move from the ankles or from the knees, but I haven't seen such a beautiful sway in any person other than Edwina. Her walk comes from the hips. Hips are chairs for babies, shelves for grocery bags, places where lovemaking starts and ends. I don't walk like Edwina.

The path is overgrown with short grasses, shrubs, and ferns that crowd in from the sides. It's cool through the trees. The going is slow and the path in places is steep and harsh.

In a blink we come out of the woods into a narrow meadow, walk across it by the path, and travel across the fall line. The meadow is thick with yellow flowers. And blue and white columbine. There are pink flowers. I think they call them fireweed. An avalanche might have come through and pulled everything down. Maybe a fire. I wonder how my father makes his way out in the winter.

My hands are cold with nervousness. I'm struck with the thought that my father has no idea I'm coming. He might laugh and send me away. He might have a woman, and she might not like a father's attention to his daughter. It's not polite for me to show up like this, but I can't think of politeness now.

Sunlight comes through aspen leaves that switch about in the breeze like shimmering coins. They have the brightness and puz-zle of a mosaic. I'm carrying ten pounds more than I would have carried four months ago. Thin air wears me down. I'm building a small moving house inside. At our ranch, on top of the high flat land, I could see antelope and cows on the far plain. Here in the mountains there are so many places to hide.

We rest sitting on the ground in the trees where it's shady and cool. Edwina pulls in her legs and tucks her knees under her chin. Sweat glistens on her forehead and she's taken on the color of blood in her cheeks. I don't feel red in my cheeks, but white. I've been going too fast up this path. My shirt is damp with sweat that I can't smell. I wonder if when you can't smell your sweat, others can. It makes me tense that my father might smell my bad sweat. I'd like to walk through these woods without feeling tangled in my neck and back. The odor of the forest is sweet, and the sharpness comes and goes.

The path opens into a clearing and a small cabin sits to the left. Dark logs rise to a low roof. We step up to the door and a dog barks. I feel a thousand darting beetles in my stomach. I run the back of my hand over my forehead. Light brown caulking is wedged between the logs. A fly hums along the lower half of the window. I knock.

I draw back from the window when the barking dog inside lays its front paws on the sill. Over the dog's head, on the mattress, is a man lying face away. He's wearing his clothes, but is barefoot.

Maybe my father's dead. Maybe the dog has been shitting inside, and it needs food and water. What if my father left, and this is a man who took the cabin for himself?

I lift the wooden handle, then push with the underside of my hand and drive it up. The dog pushes its snout out and I see there are no fangs. Its nose lifts and pulls air. It runs out. He's male and looks to be part shepherd. His thick gray tail is curved up in a quarter moon. He's like every dog, sniffing around my feet and private parts, then does the same to Edwina. He runs into the path and finds a rock, and drops it at my feet. I throw it to get rid of him, and Edwina and I walk into the cabin.

It smells in here, but not of death, and it doesn't smell of rotting food and shit. It's not a bad smell.

The man is on the bed like a winding plant, thin and viney. He breathes with even lightness. His mouth is open. He wears a green shirt and olive green pants. We could be thieves. Life is so safe in his dreams. He doesn't know that Sophie stands at his bed, and that her heart is thorned. Wake up, Father. I want to know where you've been for eleven years. Wake up.

I touch his shoulder. Nothing. I move his shoulders, and he shifts and raises his head. He turns and blinks his eyes. The eyes. A ridge in the brow. Why doesn't he sit up and recognize me?

I'm Sophie.

He sits up and glares.

I don't remember the mole on his cheek. His eyes press on Edwina, then on me. He stands and goes to the kitchen sink, and draws water from the silver pump. Brings water to his face and wipes himself with plaid shirttails. He's not so tall as I remember. His hair is black and glossy as a wet stone, and hangs a foot down his back in a ponytail.

This is Edwina. She's Tin and Rudy Picardy's niece. Do you remember them?

He doesn't say anything.

He used to carry me around the yard on his shoulders, holding my ankles so I wouldn't kick him, giddy-up, as if he should canter and whinny. Sitting above the world on his shoulders, I put my hands over his eyes. Who turned out the lights? he'd shout in false alarm.

He comes to me, stopping before he pulls me softly to him. He lays his hands on my head. His breath is soft on my forehead. Oh, I have a tear on my cheek. Not my tear. If I start, I won't be able to stop. We look at each other, and we look lost. His breath is like apples.

He lifts his chin. There's the scar, like an alphabet noodle in the bracelet of sun down his face.

You're fifteen now.

Almost sixteen.

I know your birthday. September tenth.

Twelfth, I say. I'm having a baby. I'm in my fourth month.

You're going to have a baby. What happened to your arm?

Do you remember Pablo?

Yes. He smiles.

I tell him everything about Pablo, and some things about the men on the ranch, and about Mother. I tell him I've been talking to Grandma Irene on the telephone, and he tells me he knows that because she writes to him.

But you didn't write to us, I say.

I did.

Then Edwina comes in from outside and stops at the door. She turns around and goes back out.

You know Clements is in the war.

Your grandmother writes. He looks out the window and doesn't answer. I know a lot from your grandmother's letters. You could've written me.

You could've written us.

I did. Many times. Your mother. You know. She's tough.

Tough, I think. I don't care. What kind of father are you?

Afternoon shadows stretch across the slatted floor. We're eating apples and cheese.

When do you go to town? What do you do for work?

I plant trees and cut them down. A little of both. You're tired. You should sleep.

Okay, where?

On the bed.

I lie back on the soft mattress. I think, You're here, and this is all you can do for now.

When I wake up, my father is at the sink washing dishes, his back to me. His black hair is straight. My bare feet touch the cool floor. He turns and looks at me without a smile or frown.

How do you feel?

Tired. Fine. Better.

Do you have morning sickness?

I tell him, It's not only morning sickness. Doesn't he remember that morning sickness can last all day and night? Maybe my mother wasn't sick when she was pregnant. But in the last few weeks most of it's gone away. I think my emotions are in my stomach, and that sometimes I get sick not from the baby but from my emotions. I wonder what he thinks about babies? Are they like cabbage seeds planted and watered and sunned? Am I a grown cabbage? I ask, Where's Edwina?

He lets the dog in. The dog's name is Knight. I see that my father's brought the luggage from the truck. Do you know what that means, he says, emotions in my neck? Pain in the neck. Pain in the neck. A smile. Your friend's outside.

When he pumps the silver handle, water flows. He cups his hands, bends over the sink, and brings the water to his face. He spits from his mouth and wipes it with shirttails, running both hands through his hair. He shakes his head as if he'll free demons.

Could I have some water? I ask.

It's the altitude, he says. It'll dehydrate you.

I've been really thirsty since I got pregnant.

Does he remember the ewes during lambing? Their thirst?

He pumps again and fills a tin cup with water. The cold water tastes like metal.

I walk outside and find Edwina reading *The Great Gatsby*. Lying on her stomach in the middle of the weedy yard, legs bent at the knees, feet in the air, the late sun on her back. Trees' shadows fall around her. A tepee of sun over her body. She takes the water gratefully. I lift the book from her fingers. I tell her I've read Steinbeck's *Red Pony* and London's *Call of the Wild*. Has she read *Call of the Wild*? No, she says. You should, I say. Then I read about Jay Gatsby and his love for Daisy Buchanan.

He had passed visibly through two states and was entering upon a third. After his embarrassment and his unreasoning joy he was consumed with wonder at her presence. He had been full of the idea so long, dreamed it right through to the end, waited with his teeth set, so to speak, at an inconceivable pitch of intensity. Now, in the reaction, he was running down like an overwound clock.

My father walks out to us. I recognize his walk in Clements. His steps are forwardlike from the knees, and his shoulders are round. Clements would know his walk in our father as I know my eyes in his. The first second I saw his eyes I thought, There they are. My eyes. Only mirrors. His hand is on his mouth. The lines around his eyes pleat up. He's by that aspen, watching me.

For supper we have boiled millet, carrots, sliced apples, and coffee with powdered milk. It's not so bad. He won't let us help with dishes. He lights a kerosene lamp and the room goes yellow. He makes himself a cot of coats and blankets on the floor next to the wall across from the fireplace.

He pulls a deck of cards from a kitchen drawer. I want to join him and Edwina in a game of gin, but I'm sinking again into sleep. She sits cross-legged, her back against the wall, her cards like a fan. His back is to me. I can see the red and black patterns of the cards. My eyes darken with drowsiness.

When I wake up in the middle of the night, Edwina's lying curled up next to me. Her face is toward the log wall. The dog sits by the door looking up at my father who, in the dark, is a silhouette. He pulls boots over his feet. Then he and the dog leave.

Outside, the air is sharp with pine and I hear the ticking of brown crickets. With bare feet I stand on a bed of tree needles and bend to pick one up. The needle has a flat, pointed tip. I hear an owl. Are its glass eyes fixed? Owls are bad. They can take a cat or mouse and fly away. Those poor victims will swing in the air. I'm in my T-shirt, slapping mosquitoes from my legs. I wish I could use both hands.

The dog's curled up on the stone hearth, although the fireplace is fireless. Maybe the spot is a reminder of warmth. A habit. Where does my father go in these woods in the dead of night that can be pleasurable or interesting or of the nature of survival? Maybe hunting? He didn't take a gun.

I'm afraid to bathe in the stream. That its coldness might sneak through my skin and shock the baby out of my tunnel. My last bath was at the ranch. That morning. I know where the stream is. Edwina's there now. I saw seven cans of beer bobbing in the slow current of the shallow near side. They bobbed in a metal cage tied by a rope to an evergreen. That's my father's stash.

I bathe at the sink sitting on the counter. I sponge over my ankle. The kids at school used to say I didn't bathe. That I had dirt on my ankle. It's only a birthmark. Stupid kids.

I put on Clements' jeans and shirt, and sit outside on the log turned up, the smooth circles of its age. The dog comes to me and lies at my feet. What is a knight? A knight in shining armor. Night is a time when stars come out. There's an earthstar mushroom. Purple-brown and powdery in leaf litter. Leaves are beautiful. You can see life in their veins. This mushroom has stars. You can wish on any night star. You don't have to travel there.

I'm not just a girl knocked up. Bun in the oven. In a delicate way. Great with child. In the family fashion. I was loved when we made the baby.

My father and Edwina step out of the woods together. They walk to a cluster of plants where there is some rhubarb. My father picks a stalk and hands it to Edwina. She tears a bite from the top and winces, maybe from its sourness. It needs to be dipped in sugar.

His elbow is propped against an aspen. The flat of his hand holds his head at an angle. Edwina wears her short shorts frayed at the bottom, and she stands with bare and tan legs and bare feet, her naked stomach, the navel showing, her thin waist. Her breasts are covered by the polka-dot bathing suit. He chews rhubarb and her chin is lifted toward him. He reaches toward her and snaps something from her hair.

It's a crazy feeling I have watching. They must know I'm here, but it's as if they're alone. Then my father looks at me and smiles.

His eyes go down. Does he want Edwina? Does she want him? I'm not thinking right. I'm just tired.

How was the river? I ask Edwina.

Cold, she says, pitching her eyes to mine, then to the pine-tops. There's a magpie hopping around up there. It's huge with a pointed black and white tail.

She asks if I want to help her pick rhubarb. Cooked rhubarb is good for the intestine. It makes things move. She falls to her knees in an awkward way and tears up the rhubarb. She hands stalks to me and I shake dirt from them. I hold them like an odd wedding bouquet.

The truck's stolen, you little fools, he says.

I don't think I like that word. Fools. Weak light falls through the front window. My father says the stolen truck has to go back to Tin and Rudy.

Borrowed, Edwina reminds.

My father says I should see a doctor.

There haven't always been doctors, I say. Babies come out. They're born.

Sometimes they need a doctor's help.

I'll take my chances, I say.

Your arm.

It's not ready. In a couple of months.

He shakes his head as if I'm crazy.

In the night Edwina and I meet in the mattress center. Her arm's over mine and her feet are between my calves. Those toenails. Painted tomato red.

Outside, trees keep the moon's light away. Where's my father? When I shift my eyes to the right, there are only pines and aspens. Back in the cabin I lie on top of the bed's wool blanket and close my eyes.

I'm awakened by Knight's rough tongue licking my face. Edwina's already awake and sitting frozen at the foot of the bed, the side of her face yellow from the kerosene lamp. My father is excited and doglike. He feels around the floor as if he's lost something. Edwina's shoulders are hunched up. I move to go to my father, and Edwina lifts her hand to stop me.

His fingers are apart and sweeping the floor. I fall to my knees and look at him, his face shadowed. I smell whiskey. His hair hangs in his face. He sits back and covers his ears with his hands, shaking his head and screaming.

She moves fast. From his coat pocket she pulls out the truck keys. As she yanks me out the door I see my father crawling like a baby to his cot, and curling up his knees to his chest.

I'm wearing the T-shirt. My cast is underneath it, and my underwear. My feet and legs are bare. My neck. My arm. Mosquitoes come. The moon is hushed in vapor-thin clouds. By the time we reach the meadow, the moon falls out of the clouds and purple flowers sit like throned small velvet-caped kings. The walk is downhill, and we go urgently. Edwina is barefoot and in a T-shirt to her thighs.

He tried to strangle me, she says. He's crazy.

What are you talking about?

He tried to kill me.

Sshh. My legs carry me unsteadily as if my knees will buckle if I step on an unsmooth stone.

The truck isn't parked in the place where we parked it. It's on the shoulder of the gravel road on slanted ground, its front bumper caved in. The metal of it shines in the dim moonlight. Edwina runs her hand over the damage. The damage is as wide as a telephone pole.

Look at this shit, she says. Man. Look at this. The moon barely lights dark half moons under her eyes.

We get into the truck and Edwina locks her door. She reaches across me, locks mine, and starts the motor. The gas tank shows a quarter full. She turns on the heat.

He tried to kill me. The motherfucker.

She settles back into the seat and crosses her arms over her chest, then reaches forward and turns off the motor. Within minutes the truck cools. I want to urge that we push ourselves together for warmth, but she must want no part of me.

What a bastard, she says.

I peer ahead, as if my father will step out of the woods and make an explanation.

What should we do?

What do you think? Get our stuff and get out of here. I can drive you to your grandmother's. At least he didn't total the thing.

I don't know, I say.

What do you mean you don't know? That bastard.

We don't talk for a while and our silence is broken by my yawn. Then Edwina yawns. She lies across the seat and rests her head in my lap. She pulls up her legs, her cheek and temple on my thighs. My feet are cold. I lift her head and she moves back against the seat to give me room to lie in front of her. We are joined, my back to her front, and I feel her cool breath on my neck. I wedge my feet between her calves. Her arms wrap me. Her fingers are like ribbons.

I'd like to tell her I love her for not shunning me. It's uncommon that I can tell someone I love them, and my mind-list of those who love me can be counted on the four hooves of a horse. Demetrio, my grandmother, my baby, the wish for my father that he'll love me.

He stuck his hands around my throat. He called me Willy.

I'm sorry, I say. I'm sorry.

One of her hands lies at the center of my belly, on my bare skin. If she presses hard she'll feel the gymnastics of my baby quick and alert in my warm water and familiar with its lifeline, as a bat flying for mosquitoes in its black sky. Edwina brings her hand to my waist and rests it on my hipbone. Her body unstiffens and grows full on my back and legs. Our breathing cycles in and out. I'm drowsy with sadness and slip like the moon behind clouds into sleep. But my sleep is thin.

•   •   •

Sun's rays slope through evergreens. Edwina lifts her hair where it's fallen warm around my neck, wreathing me. Her arm is across my ribs. My fingers slip between hers and connect at the web, as if we'll pray grace together, the prayer half mine and half hers. Here is the church and here is the steeple, open the door and see all the people. A six-year-old's game in Sunday school. I turn my body and face her so that we're shin to shin. The marks on her neck are purpling up.

We need to go back, I say.

I'm inclined to stay here, she says.

He was drunk.

Yeah, well, maybe he still is.

We need to get our stuff.

I'm going to hit him up for some cash. It'll be up to you to do something if he jumps me.

Like what?

Like get a log and hit him over the head, for Christ's sake.

Hit him over the head? Kill him, you mean?

We can't kill him.

I touch the mark on her neck and she pulls back.

Don't, she says. Don't touch me like that.

I don't know if she pulls back because the bruise hurts, or because she hates me to touch her. But our bodies touched in the night. We held hands. All right.

Edwina pulls a finger across the crushed truck metal and tilts her head in one direction and another.

Where are we going to get this fixed? Does he have any cash?

I don't know. My family's crazy, I say, and throw down my hands.

It's not much of an offering, telling her my family's crazy. I've heard that when you think the world is crazy, it's you who are. I want to tell her again that I'm sorry, but a thousand apologies would be an understatement.

·   ·   ·

The cabin window is absent of glare. My father is unclothed at the kitchen sink. His calves are raised and squarish. He bends over the sink to rinse his soapy hair. Where does he think we've been? Were we ghosts that fell into his drunken dreams? Drunkenness isn't the worst crime. But maybe he makes such a habit of it that Clements and I were ghosts too, or never real.

My father rubs his hair with a towel. He pets the dog and turns around. His chest has some hair, but there's not a blanket of it. His penis rests over one egg more than the other. He sees me and his face softens. He looks down, embarrassed, brings the towel to his waist, and covers himself. He opens the door. The cut at his eye is a red oval. His face is rearranged with his cut eye.

Couldn't be helped, my father says with misery.

Where do you think we were all night? I ask quietly.

Were you in the truck? Did I do something?

Did you do something? Edwina says stepping forward. You tried to kill me.

That's dramatic, he says.

Your hands were so tight around my throat I couldn't even scream for her to pull you off. She lifts her chin. See this? Do you know what you did to my uncle's truck? You crashed it. Man. Shit. She kicks the floor.

My father stalks to the mattress and pulls from beneath it a handful of bills. As if no one would look there first if they wanted to rob him.

Edwina counts the money. I don't think this is enough, she says.

Trying for patience, I think, he bows his head. His chest rises and falls. He walks back to the mattress and gets more money. I wonder if he came down the path looking for us.

Are you okay, Soph? he asks.

Not really.

The baby?

I guess.

He takes his pants from a hook in the logs. Please, he says, lifting them, and we turn our backs. I drank too much whiskey, he says. He sighs. And the mushrooms. He nods to the jar on the shelf.

So he ate mushrooms. He confesses his actions as if he were a bad boy of ten.

Psychedelic mushrooms, he says, lifting the jar. Hallucinogenic. Man, I had a bad trip.

His eye cut seems to draw his face shorter on one side, like the wood floor by the back door is warped, and angles the cabin there. My father doesn't look like he belongs to the mountains or to the woods, but to this small space. He hibernates here and tends to his flights as if they're cures to make him brave. He looks enclosed, as if he's in a capsule. As if he's a pupae with no hope of metamorphosing. His eyes are puffed and red.

The three of us sit staring. Finally, I get up and walk outdoors to the edge of the woods, and think maybe I should go to my grandmother's. But a grandmother isn't a father.

Thirst. Greedy water drinking. Doesn't he have a fly swatter? Edwina stands on the front lawn. Her arms crossed over her chest, one hip cocked a little higher than the other. The way her toe is pointed into the ground reminds me of the way the horses stand sometimes for hours.

We walk together toward the stream. When the path narrows I lead. We sit on the bank. We could wade to the other side, the stream narrow and shallow, but why take the trouble? We're here in the shade. Our shoes are off, and I'm sliding my feet over dark green moss.

You can't stay here, she says.

Why not?

He's unpredictable.

So he drank himself under and did some mushrooms.

I think you're in trouble if you stay.

I'm in no trouble.

What if you go into labor early? What if something goes wrong with the baby, and you're still here, and have to get into town fast?

Indian women squatted in the woods.

Don't be stupid, she says, and the words slap me on the cheek.

Even when my mother said it, Sophie, you stupid idiot, I never thought I was stupid. But somehow when she says it.

He'll get used to me.

Your old man's right on one account. You need to see a doctor.

A baby grows, a baby grows, a baby grows. Without a doctor. Can you believe it, Edwina? A baby grows all by itself, attached to me on the inside, by a cord. It doesn't need instructions. It grows.

This is no place for you.

Are you so practical yourself? You sit there high and mighty. All your life you sat down at supper, your old man there at the table your whole life.

Lots of kids go without fathers.

I scoff.

Sure, my old man, he comes home and plops his fat ass down at the kitchen table and pulls up his *Wall Street Journal.* After my mother clears the dishes and I'm over at the sink scrubbing my ass off, he's on the phone calling gun dealers so he can buy more guns for his million-dollar collection. He has a few martinis and walks his fat ass up to bed so he can get up the next morning and do it all over again. It wasn't so great, but at least he didn't try to kill me. Your old man, Sophie, had his hands around my throat. I thought, maybe he's mad 'cause I was reading, wasting his fuel. But nobody almost strangles somebody over that.

He didn't want to kill you.

Could've fooled me. You think it's safe for you and the baby? Soph. I'll take you straight to Chicago. Fuck the bus.

But I'm staying.

You can't see the situation for what it is. Why do you want to stay?

I can feel why, but I don't know that I can say it. Okay, if I stay, my father can't slip through my fingers and be gone forever. Almost strangling Edwina. That was bad. I'll tell my father, You can never do that again. I'll leave if you do. He might laugh. Be my guest, Sophie. Did I invite you here?

I'm sorry your old man wrecked Tin and Rudy's truck, but I'm not sorry I brought you here. I'll be sorry if you stay. You're not staying, are you?

I am.

I ask Edwina to help me tie my right shoelace. She does. My foot tightens in the shoe.

My father is in the front yard. His back is sunlit, and he faces two men in blue uniforms. Sun-glint on their badges draws my eyes there. The tall lanky one is about my father's age. He has a flat nose and wears a gun in a holster. The other one is younger. Almost teenage-looking.

Maybe they're going to arrest my father for hit and run. What if he hit a person and that person's hipbone made the dent? What if he killed somebody? I'm not so stupid. They might be here for Edwina.

The flat-nosed sheriff speaks. Hello there. Edwina?

That's me, she says in a gloomy voice.

My stomach gets a sharp feeling.

He's come to tell her that Uncle Rudy is on a plane to the Mesa City airport. At the airport he'll put Edwina on a plane to Detroit, and drive the truck back to Bluerock.

That's just great, she says.

In the cabin I put a kettle of water on the stove to boil for tea. My father will object to my stoking the stove so early in the day. Why doesn't he split the wood so it's thin, and can be arranged better in the stove? Why why why?

Then my father's knees are there. I look up. I light the match under the newspaper and blow on it.

The way he stands. I've seen it in Clements. It's their stubborn look. Legs apart. Feet rooted to the spot.

Better if you go too, he says quietly.

I feel my chin quiver, and put my fingers there to make it stop.

But where will I go? But but but. I sound like a baby. I am. A baby with a baby.

Your grandmother would want you. I know she would.

Edwina comes in and looks at us. She takes her T-shirt from the line, a pair of socks from the floor by the bed, and her book where it lays open-faced and down on the floor. Her book looks like it was thrown. She moves fast, as if leaving is a business that has to be finished now, with no emotion. Oh, please don't leave without emotion.

My father says, It has less to do with me than it does with you. I say nothing. I think: Bastard.

There are certain things I can't provide. One is a car so we can go to town in case of emergency. I can't afford a car right now.

I will not cry, I will not cry. I pinch the skin at my knuckles and look down to see if I've drawn blood.

I don't care about a car, I say, and I don't care if you don't want me. I'm not leaving. If you want those sheriffs to drag me away in handcuffs, then go ahead.

He walks outside and I close the door.

I'm on the edge of the bed and Edwina's by the door with her things. She's crying. I don't want her to leave without talking. She's thinking of the trouble she's in.

You're in a lot of trouble, I say.

It's not like I robbed a bank. Fuck it.

I think I'm going to cry again. I think, Fuck it. I tell her, I never met anyone like you. Everything I want to say seems babyish. I'm here now because of her. I've never seen such narrow beautiful hips and legs as hers. I know that people not from Bluerock comb their hair in a different way, get away with patent leather skirts, go to rock concerts and outdoor movies, and Hawaii, buy their shoes in department stores. Not in Bilky's bins. They can still know a lot about gardening, and nothing about horses, but want to learn.

She whispers in my ear, and I feel her breath and full lips. Stay safe. Stay warm. I love you.

I'm grateful, I tell her. I'm so grateful.

What a thing to say. She wipes over her eyes with a paper towel, then wipes mine, picks up her suitcase, and opens the door. My love for her isn't like any other love. It's unlike Demetrio love, Pablo love, Grandmother love, and baby love. But I don't say it.

Be careful, I say.

Why? You think I'm going to get myself in trouble?

Deep. If you aren't careful.

I'll take your advice for later.

When later?

Later.

My father lies on his blankets on the floor and reads his book, *Modern Man in Search of a Soul.* The book is tilted into the final minutes of daylight. I'm at the kitchen sink wringing water out of Clements' yellow shirt.

Is that book about the search for man's soul? I ask. Does it mean a woman's soul too? I want to say, Do you stop and think of meaning? What you see is what you get? X equals X? Why equals why? Do you wonder what it means to go away and never come back?

It's always the silence I hate. On the ranch there's the wind's rush, a crow's caw, and the distant bleating of lambs. The afraid, stupid, sweet *borregas.*

This kind of shading hushes everything. I should hush my mouth. I, the trespasser, should hush. I know what he's thinking. Why is she here? I'm stiff and achy in the knuckles and wrists, I care so much what he thinks.

It must mean both man and woman, I say.

No movement from my father's gray-lit mouth.

I hang the yellow shirt over the laundry line and wash another. A Bluerock Rodeo Days T-shirt. Clements tried to bull-ride then, and nearly got himself gored. I put my mind on the clenching and wringing of the material so I don't have to look at my father.

He rubs the kerosene wick between his fingers, and lights the end. The room glows yellow. There are edges all around. There is the edge of the hearth and the window l-edge. One blue-black fly edges across the glass. The edge of my father's book. An edge to my words.

I say, Sometimes I used to think of you and where you might have gone. I thought you could be living in a forest, or on a beach, watching whales, or drinking cactus juice in the desert, making snakeskin wallets from the rattlers you murdered. I thought you might be taking the train back and forth across the United States and into Canada, that strangers fed you and let you bathe in their homes. You lived off the generosity of strangers. Once I thought you were picked up by space aliens and they made tests by pushing needles through your navel. And they poked a needle through your brain and sucked out all your memory. That's why you forgot about us.

My father closes his book. He sits up, his back against the wall, his legs crossed Indian style. That's all.

Night settles in quickly.
But who owns this cabin?
Stefan Deminoux.
Who's he?
He owns a restaurant in town. I barter with him. Rabbits and venison. It's a French restaurant called Avec Lapin. People come from hundreds of miles to eat there.
What does the name mean? I ask.
It means with rabbit.

He sleeps late in the mornings. He's vigorous at night. By vigorous, I mean he goes out in the middle of the night and comes in before dawn's rays that break into our cabin crease after crease.

My father doesn't like it when I use his baking soda to brush my teeth. Baking soda is for cookies, he says. He's defined which area of the woods I should use for my private needs. He says I don't eat enough fruit and grains.
I throw away the sling on my arm. The cast stands alone.
One night I ask, Why don't you build an outdoor privy?
Because I don't need to, he says.
Some nights we dance the box waltz. He has a bad off-key voice, but it's deep. Mr. Sandman and Only the Lonely. Bye Bye

Love, you ain't nothin' but a hound dog. Our shadows follow and lead us in the yellow of the kerosene lamp.

He says, Clements was brave to sign up with the army and defend his country.

If that's what you call brave.

I'm not saying war is right, my father says, but what would you think if he ran off to Canada, or pretended he was crazy, or what if he said he was a homosexual? There must be some good in the boy. Isn't there?

He can lift a ewe into a truck. He made B's in school, except for English. He has beautiful, straight teeth.

Edwina's letter arrives in a card with a picture of wildflowers in a meadow. Inside are the words: You're like a breath of fresh air.

It's not an interesting card, but the letter's long. I have a hard time reading her small handwriting. Who taught you the cursive? I'll ask in my next letter. Her last paragraph: Being grounded isn't so bad because I sneak out every night and meet Max. Did I tell you his Harley was built in Florida, and it has wolves painted on the engine? Don't feel guilty about me being grounded because of Uncle Rudy's truck. Uncle Rudy was cool about it, it was just Dad. He can sit on a corncob and spin. What if I got on Max's Harley, we rode to Vegas, and got married? Don't flip, I'm not going to do that. But wouldn't you love to hear my old man then?

There's also a letter from Demetrio. He wasn't fired from the ranch. He quit and went back to Guadalajara. I'm coming back for you as soon as I can, he writes. I write, Wait, wait.

For the last four days my father has been working for the forest service. I'm alone in the cabin with my protector, Knight.

As the sun sets, he walks in and throws his pack on the floor, then collapses on his cot.

Tell me everything you did, I say.

Planted seedling pine, he says, his mouth half in the clothes pillow.

All in San Luis?

The San Luis Valley, he says.

Every day he's worn the dark green pants filthy with dirt, and lace-up boots with steel toes. He smells of old sweat, like canned soup.

How are you? he asks.

Fine.

He reaches into his pack and pulls out a small jar. He uses his knuckles to put the ointment over the lower part of his back.

When my father was away I slipped out at night. I went to the meadow and looked up and found the star Arcturus. It was bright, reddish, to the west. In the day I sunbathed without clothes, and walked through the forest that way too.

While he was away, the catcher-box stayed unset and I didn't have to look at the rabbits standing on their hind legs, reaching to get out. I didn't have to listen to them grunting in the box.

Watch and you'll learn, my father says.

The rabbit's head is hit with the back of an ax and the rabbit dies. Then it's tied to a wire between two trees in the backyard. With the knife my father makes a short slash in line with the back-bone. The insides are removed. He cuts across the middle of the back and pulls both ways. The legs are lifted out of the pelt.

Watch now.

I don't want to learn.

I crave meat. I like it best when it's skewered and roasted in the fireplace. But I can't get away from thinking of the rabbit before my father tapped it on the head. Tonight we eat skewered rabbit. My father asks, What do you want, a boy or girl?

A whole baby.

You must know if you want a boy or a girl.

I think it's a boy.

Why?

I don't know. It's a feeling. That's all.

• • •

How does a girl begin to know her father after he's been gone eleven years?

We start at the back of the cabin at a thicket of mountain alder. The bark is red-brown with small pressed scales at the surface. The leaves are purple. I close my eyes and feel the bark. In the damp soil by the trunk, five-foot-long fronds come up from the underground in clusters like wand bouquets. I pull the fern up by the base and touch the buds dangling from the bottom.

Eat, my father says.

The taste is like raw cabbage.

He points to a plant with two leaves. Kidney-shaped, thin, long-stalked. This is wild ginger, Soph. Good for your nausea.

My nausea isn't so bad, I say.

But the plant's not so good now. We'll wait till spring to pick it fresh. Snow on the mountain. That's the name of the plant. Don't touch! It can make blisters on your hands.

The bushy mountain maple in thicket form stands as a weak and bent shrub. My father on all fours crawls to the shady side and finds oyster mushrooms. They're ivory smooth. Their stems are short and thick. The gills spongy. I draw up my shirttails and make a basket. My father plucks them from the ground and puts them into my basket. I think my father's body odor smells less like earthworms and more like mushrooms. His odor clings to him no matter if he bathed yesterday or a week ago. Maybe friends or intruders shun him because of his odor, or maybe they take to his odor and are friendly with him. His odor is his weeding-out process.

Near the path is a rock of talc that I scrape with my thumbnail. The powder sifts away. I don't know how to make talcum powder from it, but even if I did, I only have this one small rock. If I were a tailor I could use it for marking cloth. Maybe someday I'll crave it as a mineral my body needs. Or I might draw with it against a black rock, or on the logs of the cabin.

My father comes in with leaves on skinny erect stems. He holds them out and I smell. It's like wintergreen. I want to bury my face in them, make tea from them, sleep with them under my pillow. My father turns the mushrooms in the stove with a knife so their undersides will dry. We'll eat them in the winter, he says. We need to pick some each day now, and dry them like this.

Sometimes I lie awake at night and think how I can get back to the ranch. I can't think my mother will run off, a screaming woman across the plain, and never come back. She's too strong in the lungs and blood to die. Would a banker make me a loan to buy the ranch from her? What a laugh.

She used to say she wanted to move to town. Sell out and buy an L-shaped house on a corner lot, plant geraniums along the driveway, and walk to the grocery store. Maybe when Clements comes home he can push her in that direction. Clements almost always wants to know what's in it for him. Maybe we could sell some acres to buy her one of those houses on a corner lot in town.

In this bed I listen to my soul-pump beat away. I worry that I'm becoming soul-less. How will my soul sleep tonight with these thoughts swarming like blue-black flies on a heap of dead meat? The sour rotting smell of it. I think of killing her. How I might do it. But if I do, I'm no better than a heap of sour-stinking dead meat.

On a picture postcard of Gold Peak, the mountain north of town: Dear E, I'm writing this at midnight. My father's gone out, who knows where. It makes me crazy. When he comes back, will he throw stones? Cook bacon and eggs and say, I love you, Sophie, do you love me? Hang me upside down from a tree? Ask me to help give Knight a bath? He gave me money to buy boots. He's generous with money, but not with words. You can't have everything, but sometimes I want to pry his mouth open with a stick and tell him to make sounds. Love, S.

There are ways into my father's heart. He smiles when I cook, and even if my cooking is burnt or mushy, he eats quietly and smiles between bites. He hums as he ties flies. We have pancakes once a week, rolled around olive-oiled mushrooms and potatoes. Let me tell you about our stove. When my father bakes bread, he browns the loaf by changing it from one side, then to the other, so it bakes evenly. The fire's built in the firebox at the left side of the stove under the cooking top. Beneath the firebox is an iron grate. The ashes fall into the box. The soot rises into the flue and later falls into the flue tray under the oven. I clean the ash box and soot once a week.

The cooking surface has six eyes. They're round openings with iron lids. When I fry trout or rabbit, I use the back eye to brown them, then move the pan to one of the cooler front eyes to cook the fish through. Sometimes I want to heat water fast, and I take off the back stove eye and put the pan over the flames in the firebox.

The main challenge with the stove is keeping the temperature constant. If it's too hot, I open the door or put a pan of cold water on one of the racks. I burned the corn muffins, and my father complained. But he doesn't complain too much about my cooking.

What's my daily bread? My food? What gives me strength to stay? I'm not suffering too much, and if I am, I should try to be strong. Other people have it worse. Heroin babies in Spanish Harlem. Fire-burned houses sending families to live on the street. Mothers and fathers and sisters and brothers of dead warboys. My father has said twice, It's good to have you here. Those are words like ice chips over a blistered heart.

When he slapped my face for calling him a son of a bitch and told me to think of the meaning, the literal meaning, that I was calling his mother a bitch, I went to the floor and hugged his knees. He stood stiffly against my chest. He deserved to be called something. Words led to words. He was stone-cold sober when he said, Dreams? Why, you're a kid with no pot to piss in. Knocked up by a Mexican dumbbell. Then I said it to him, the son of a bitch thing, and he slapped me.

He has the same high arch in his feet that I have. The other day there was a pebble in my sneaker and I snapped my foot forward so the pebble would roll into the space my arch makes. I think my father must do this too. I think this is my daily bread. That he's my father and I'm here with him.

This mid-August early morning the woods grow gray. Rumbling clouds close up over the clearing of our yard. The sky splits with a gray-blue light and sheets of thick cold rain fall. The woods fill with thunder. Rain darkens tree trunks and hits slanted against the width of leaves, knocking pine cones to the ground as if they're ripe apples. A flash of lightning bleaches the clearing in front of the cabin and everything is, for a half second, frozen. The whole day I stay in. I sit on the bed or lie on it and read *Modern Man in Search of a Soul*. I write Demetrio a letter and address it to Guadalajara. I sweep the floor.

My father reads on his cot. His face is turned to the side, and from time to time his eyes watch the fire.

In my sleep I dream about losing a front tooth. I fight going to the dentist, but every time I open my mouth the wind comes in and a whistle escapes, causing people to stare. I finally see Dr. Mercury. He tells me I'm scheduled for my court date in a week. Court date! What court date? Many people, he says, lose their teeth through fights, and fights must be controlled. His nurse is a skinny, poorly postured old thing: And what did you do to deserve this, little girl? I beg, Give me a new tooth. I'm not a little girl, you bitch.

When I wake up from this misery, my father's gone. I step onto the cold floor. The fire's eased away, but its coals glow. I put four logs on them. I wait for the flames to lick and rise, then pull the screen across.

The rain's stopped and the air is full of sharp forest broth from ferns and rhubarb. I pull my father's wool socks over my feet. I wonder if these are the socks Grandma Irene sent with Uncle Johnny. I pull off his brown sweater, full of holes, and slip it over my head and cast. There's a moth hole over the place where my ovary is.

Here's what my father said: When screech owls sound like women crying, there'll be an early winter. If there's thicker than usual fur on the bottom of a rabbit's foot, watch out for snow. If you see lots of spiders and black bugs on the windows, get your sweaters out.

I laughed. His jaw shifted from side to side. What do you mean that's crazy? he said. In the first place you're no expert. In late August if worms come up, then go back into the ground, it'll snow in a week.

But where does he go at this hour of the night?

The grass is full of rain, and my feet get damp and heavy. Maybe he fishes for trout, then lets them go. He brings nothing home from these outings. There's one good thing about wet wool socks. They don't itch as much as dry ones. But cold feet chill my inner thighs, spine, shoulders, and chin.

The night crowds the trees and pulls them together. Without darkness there are no dreams. Without dreams we'd stand like brittle dead limbs and break in two.

I wonder what my father thinks is good about the night.

Branches stand out against the starless gray sky. If you have pain, it will be absorbed by darkness. Any pain drifts to the stream, and to a river, then a bigger river. When it gets to the ocean, it vanishes. It's not so much my eyes, but my feet that lead me. When I get to the stream I see water moving over rocks. A silver-white shimmer settles into the forest and I make my way upstream in the pale light.

I haven't come this far north in the woods. Far off, a cluster of rocks sits along the butte. They're maybe only part of the mountaintop, weathered into a castle of circular walls. If this is a castle, there isn't enough light to see if people are standing watch. Pablo could have taken me easily to this place. The fucking bitch, my mother.

An owl flies to a limb. I once saw an owl hunting chipmunks. They hunt rabbits. I'm the darkest thing in these woods. I don't have to be a beam of light. It's not my job to whiten the night. That's the moon's job. Why can't my father sleep at night?

Then I see him. On all fours, moving away through the brush. I don't know if he's seen me. I crouch behind sumac and watch as he pulls himself up a big aspen, grabs on to a branch, and lifts himself. Branches break away but when one does he takes another. Then, like a J, he rests in the branch.

I take my stiff, dry clothes from the wooden chair in front of the stove. The chair is like me sitting. The pants I wore last night slipped over the chair legs, the shirt buttoned over the chair back, and wet socks dried over glass jars in front of the legs. Shoes like my ears over the chair top. All dried to a perfect chair form.

My father lumbers into the woods and gathers the wood. A fire isn't automatic. The ranch house has electrical heat that's from someplace I don't exactly know. As if when my mother turns up the heat there's a magician in the basement who gets the signal and waves a wand. If you don't chop wood so you can strike the match, you might forget where heat comes from. My father does belong to the mountains and the woods.

You have a scar on your left knee. There. Why don't you tell me about it.

Why do you suppose we have eyelashes? I ask, avoiding this question.

They keep out insects. And dirt. You don't mind if I have a beer, do you? As if I should ask your permission! He pulls up the tab, flicks it into the wastebasket, and tips his head back. When he swallows, his Adam's apple bumps up and down. Eyelashes protect the eye. Do you know the colors of the spectrum?

ROYGBIV.

Which color has the longest wavelength?

Red, I say.

The shortest?

Violet.

Very bright little girl you are.

I'm not a little girl.

Colors are the variations in the electromagnetic spectrum.

How do you know all this? Why do you care about things like that?

When I was in the war I trained to be a pilot but my eyes were less than perfect. Perfect in my mother's eyes. Nevertheless, the Air Force ended up training me in mechanics.

When were you in the war?

'Forty-three to 'forty-five.

You were just a kid.

Papa signed my papers. Your grandmother almost killed him.

You were born in 'twenty-six. I found your birth certificate downstairs in a raccoon hat.

Funny place for a birth certificate. October the eleventh. Chicago, Illinois. Playground for the Mafia. Irishmen, Italians, Sicilians, Slavs. Western Electric hired thousands of them. Mafia doings in that neighborhood. Scarface Al Capone, alias Alphonzo Brown, on the throne since 'twenty-two. Scarface Al. A razor gash on the side of his face. Are you going to tell me about that scar on your knee?

I didn't know you were going to be a pilot.

I have my pilot's license. Did. Do you know the pilots of the Second World War wore red goggles before they went out on their night missions? Red's the extreme of the visual spectrum. The longer wavelength. The red helped their rods. As in cones and rods. Did you know? Now, why don't you tell me the story behind that scar on your knee.

This scar, I say, stretching out my leg. I think, All I have to do is touch it as I would a worm, and watch it wriggle to life. This scar, I say, touching it. It's a small scar. See? The scar came in a beautiful way. It's still pink. A little.

It was deep, he says.

The deer at the ranch, I tell him, were standing on their hind legs to get at the crab apples. They were chewing the bark. I don't know why the antelope weren't. Only the deer. Mother told Demetrio to put chicken wire there.

Listen, Sophie, Demetrio said, I will collect the deer droppings and make a tea. I will paint the bark with it. The deer will stay away. Your mother will be happy, but more importantly, the tea must be painted on after every rain. After every rain I will have to pass your house on my way to this chore. You can meet me at the trees.

But I told him my mother wouldn't go for that. She wants her crab apple trees fixed for years, not days. Chicken wire. That was the way, as she told him in the first place. Don't argue with her. You don't have to come to me. I'll come to you.

We wrapped the trunks three times with wire. It had rained the night before, and the trees were pink. Their perfume made us drunk. He picked an apple, crushed it between his fingers, and painted my face with the juice. He traced his painting with the tip of his tongue. When I was on the ground, my knee went into the head of a twisted nail, old and rusted. It went into my knee and Demetrio pulled it out with his teeth. He drew out the poison with his mouth. So, you see. It wasn't such an ugly wound. Now you know, I think, that I'm not a little girl.

He says, Stupid fucking kid. How're you going to raise a baby? With some spineless coward father. Can't even show his spineless fucking face.

I call him a son of a bitch and he raises his hand. I blink my eyes. He lowers his hand.

I sent him away, you son of a bitch.

I get the slap and crawl to the corner, sitting with my back against the wall. The dog comes to me, and I draw him close to my body.

Don't ever call him a coward. He's not.

Outside, the rain pours and night enters as my father talks about Chicago. He talks about his job at a tire company, and his girl-friend, Bette, whom he loved before he met my mother. He took a job leasing oil land in Wyoming, which is how he came to meet Willy Behr, formerly Willy Chastain.

Sometimes there are new shadows in the cabin, as when my father sets his logging saw on the kitchen counter, or when he hangs our washed clothes on the line to dry. If I wake in the night I'm sometimes shocked by these new shadows. Who's here? What's that? But why do I need to know about everything that's hidden?

Can I find the patience to be still? My blessings can be counted. When it rains, I'm dry. When I cook, I can eat. Wood on wood makes a spitting fire. Why not watch the night come in and fall to sleep, then wake and fall back easily?

He works for the forest service. Planting trees. A good job this time because it's not so far away. One of the other crew men drove to the edge of the path and took him to work in his truck.

He didn't come home last night, but now he staggers in at dawn. His face is as angry as a badger, his jacket torn at the sleeve. He stumbles toward me in my bed, picking me up half by my waist and half by my legs. The dog barks. He thinks we want to play. I scream, and the dog barks harder. My father swipes at the dog with his leg, misses, and falls. He stands round-shouldered like an ape. His arms are hooplike in front of his body, as if he carries an unseeable bundle. Mumbling about dying out there. He drops me half on the bed and half off. When he staggers toward me again, I have the fireplace poker. I back him up to the door, and he falls to his knees. Not out of cowardliness. There isn't an ounce of fear in his eyes. But he's drunk. He crawls to his cot. He mumbles something about no forgiveness, no confession. Then he snores.

She believes in miracles, I say.
    She does, does she?
    Three summers ago she saw the Virgin sitting in a pine tree, wearing a purple robe made of silk, with satin piping. The Virgin's face was long and square, and her hair was on her head, wound around and pinned up. On each wrist she wore a corsage of orchids. Or no. They were dahlias. And silver bangles around her ankles. Small white moths on each toe. Their wings were open, not closed. She sat on the limb with her back against the tree trunk. The foot resting on a branch. The robe was open, and bared her thigh. Mother held her hands up as if the Virgin would lift her there, like a mother taking a child from its crib. Mother thought she should confess her sins. Do you know what sins?

He gets up from his place on the floor and walks to the counter. He pumps water into a bowl, and pours lentils from a jar into the bowl of water.

She has plenty, I imagine, he says.

Do you know what sins?

Sophie, do you remember what happened to the black-headed lambs in our flocks?

They were killed.

You saw them killed?

I've seen it.

The black-headed lambs are defective in a flock of white heads. Your mother's repelled by Antonio's arm. Have you ever seen her really look at it? She can't. Do you catch my point? It's not so much the killing of the lambs. She ordered their killing because she was repelled.

Was she repelled by my webbed foot?

She likes things just so.

My tear ducts that didn't work?

Some of the lentils spill on the floor. The dog sniffs them and crawls back next to the hearth on his braided, mud-soiled rug.

Did you ever know a man by the name of Marty Halahan? No, you were about two when they left town. He owned a motel. It wasn't hard for him and your mother to check in and check out, so to speak. His wife gave him a choice that they sell the motel and move, or get divorced. The little girl, the one your age, saw her father go into a room in the middle of the day. She sat on the black-top around the corner and played jacks, waiting for him to come out. She told her mother.

How do you know?

The wife called me.

Is that why you left?

Partly.

What's the other part?

He stretches his arms over his head and lumbers outside, leaving the door open for flies.

Talk about cowards! I shout.

Hands on his hips. What did you say? He comes at me with long strides. I slam the door and pull the oak stick through the ring. I stand trembling on my side, and listen for a creak in the steps. My ear to the door.

Why did you marry her anyway? I shout through the door.

Because she was fun! he shouts back. She was a boozer! We had fine sex—in the truck, on the floor, like dogs. We laughed at each other's stupid jokes! Do you have any idea what that means?

Have you got an extra blanket? I ask.

He doesn't seem to have enough blankets to satisfy my coldness in the night. I've piled his wool sweaters over me, and the dark green pants that look as if they're left over from some war. He owns a navy blue pea coat with a hole in its rear side, as if he backed into a lit candle. Around the hole there's a burnt crust. But it's not so much the warmth the wool provides. It's the weight over me that I need. It's the weight that's so comforting.

Do you have another blanket? I ask again.

I bend over and cough so hard that I can't get my breath. I think I might die. My father makes tea from pine needles, powdered ginger, and honey. My nose is stopped up. It makes me afraid when my senses don't work.

Here. Take this.

Keep your onion juice, I say harshly. Sometimes I want nothing from him.

What about a doctor? Shouldn't you see a doctor for the child? For that arm? What about that cast?

What do you think cave women did? They had babies without doctors.

That's the most ridiculous thing I've ever heard.

Sometimes I walk and walk. The trees are like a curtain parting as I go through. They whisper behind green leaf hands: Make way for the elephant. Make way. The sky is deep blue and unstained of clouds. The sun slants through trees and makes everything very white and green and black.

Knight runs in circles, sniffing crazily. He's on to something. I see tiny five-fingered prints of a white-footed mouse whose house might be nearby in an abandoned bird's nest in a tree. The dog is after the grouse who has left many tracks in the mud from yesterday's rain. Partridge, drumming grouse, birch partridge, drumming pheasant, mountain pheasant, ruffed grouse. The names stand for changes in the species. But these are the tracks of a spruce grouse. A different bird altogether. We're in evergreens. These are the tracks of a spruce grouse.

My stomach growls. I lumber less, and step ahead with a certain lift of my knees. If I think I'm an elephant now, what will I be in four months?

From here I smell roasting meat. I can't run fast enough. I spring into the house and greet my father by taking the bowl from his hands. It's filled with mashed potatoes. I eat one fingerful after another. My father eyes me suspiciously. He must wonder what kind of creature has returned from the woods. It's only the creature who houses the baby, and the baby needs food.

The baby kicks. Yes, little lamb, I'll feed you more.

A half jar of watermelon pickles. A gingerbread heel from the loaf my father made yesterday. Raw cabbage with salt. A block of chocolate from the second shelf. A handful of walnuts, a dish of black beans, a cup of lemon tea.

I pull on my coat and sit satisfied on a log, smelling the late summer air. Dried leaves, dull grass, a hint of rain. My father comes out and we watch the sky cloud over. I touch the lid of my eye for clearness. I see the breath of my father like small butterflies. But the air is warm. I hear a rabbit nibbling on grass. I reach beneath my rib cage and touch the baby's fist that's found its way there.

Where is my father? Gone to town early with murdered rabbits in a burlap bag. Now it's almost midnight.

I sing in my unelegant voice. Catch a falling star and put it in your pocket, save it for a rainy day. An old Perry Como song. I'd rather hear Muddy Waters, not Perry Como, sing that. I crave music as much as I crave venison, baked yams, olive juice, and cooked oats with cocoa. Bob Dylan, Mick Jagger and Keith Richards, James Brown, Joan Baez. Rock Me, by Muddy Waters, Patsy Cline and Waylon. I want to hear the Stones sing Chuck Berry.

I stoke the fireplace and set a pan of water on the rear eye of the stove to make oatmeal. He has three dozen books. Among them: *Chekhov's Plays, Psyche & Symbol, The Waves,* stories of Roald Dahl, an anthology of poems.

I wish my father had a dictionary so I could look up the word cantilevered. I trim my toenails. I think of why I never painted them red as Edwina painted hers. Why draw attention to such an ugly part of the body? I miss her. When I go to town I'll call her and she'll go on about Max and his Harley. She'll tell me the kind of sex they're having. She blames me for losing her virginity. She can't blame me.

I grow madder at my father's absence. I'm like an old wife waiting for her husband to come home. I understand my father had a life before I came here. I take the poker from the wood box and set it on the floor next to the bed.

In my dream, Pablo has wings. We land on top of a quiet volcano and eat a basket of seaweed. The underside of one of Pablo's wings has a lightninglike cut. The edges are pink with infection. I put seaweed on the cut.

Sometimes I cry at night. I can hear myself in my dream. I touch my cheeks and taste the salt on my finger.

My father pops some of the mushrooms that will cause a person to hallucinate. He chews with a look of bitter-taste. Over the next hour I watch him change.

I eat alone. He springs to his feet and rolls his hands. He gives his piece of trout to the dog. Laughing, laughing, laughing. An infection.

The next time he springs to his feet, he flies outside. His feet kick up under the full moon. He looks like a mirage.

You forgot your coat, I whisper. He's moved to the meadow by now, and stirs roots of fireweeds and black-eyed Susans.

Mushrooms, in general, aren't well digested. You shouldn't serve wild mushrooms to old people or to little children. You need to cut them in half and check for insects and worms before eating. My father calls them shrooms. We all have certain words we make into our own language. Rebby, our dog, came from the name Rebel. I miss him. He was a talkative barker.

I hum It's All Over Now, Baby Blue. On that album Dylan played acoustic guitar on one side. The other side was rock-and-roll. I tuck my feet under my nightgown and hold my one arm down at my side. I have to see a doctor and ask him to take off the cast. I hug the dog and bury my nose and mouth in his fur. I pull his paw to my chin. I feel his heartbeat through the middle pad. I hold his paw to my breast. Can you feel my heart? I ask. Now I'm talking to a dog and asking questions of no importance to him.

The oven is red hot. I boil water and wash my hair. I lather it, rinse, towel it down. I'm pulling a comb through it when my father bursts in. I watch him carefully. His eyebrows hop up and down. I can't make sense of his words. Something about coyotes raising babies. He digs in his pocket and comes up with a fist, throwing some coins against the wall. He's done this before. When they land on the floor, he raises his knees in the air and dances.

He stops suddenly and whirls around. Where's your mother? His face creases. His arms stiffen and he opens and closes his hands, stretching out his fingers.

Bluerock, I say, my heart knocking hard.

When he's touching his forehead many times with the back of his thumb, I touch the fire iron between the mattress and floor, at the edge.

It's not a good sign that the dog doesn't want to play. He's backed into the wall as if trying to make himself smaller. My fingers and toes tingle with the illness in my stomach. On a scale of one to ten, I'm at an eight before I get sick. I think when I'm afraid to this degree, the sickness stops growing.

He leaps onto the bed and straddles me. The whiskey breath. As I reach for the poker, he knocks me off the bed. I scramble up, but he only needs to take one step in any direction to catch me.

I'm not Mother! I scream.

He puts his hands over his ears and shakes his head from side to side as if trying to clear demons. His moan rises from a low part of his throat, and after he takes his breath he moans again. The dog charges out the front door ahead of me. The door slams behind us.

I'm in my flannel nightgown. Cold air sinks in. I might catch cold or pneumonia, and if I do the baby could die along with me. No, my baby won't die. I run into the house, go to the bed, and reach under. When he lands on top of me, I collapse stomach first into the mattress. I think his weight will give a signal to the baby to come out. He kicks me in the back and leg. A heavy kick. Pushing bones. His hands close around my throat. The dog barks. My eyes feel as if they will burst. I reach down, bring the poker up, and let it fall on the back of his head. I move to the side and hit him again. He crashes down on me.

I push him off and roll him over. I check the place in his neck where the blood bumps. With fishing line I bind his hands behind his back. I tie his ankles together. Don't think my hands are steady.

I've been sitting, my back against the logs, for more than three hours, watching him sleep. He isn't some werewolf. He's my father who becomes crazy when he drinks whiskey and eats mushrooms. The truth is that I thought by coming here I'd find my father and life would be safe. I feel a sudden quickness in my stomach that has nothing to do with my baby.

He moves to get up, and feels the knots that bind him. He moans.

What's this all about? Goddamn, I don't remember much. Do you want to enlighten me? He shakes his head to clear the hair from his eyes.

You almost killed me.

He snorts. That's an exaggeration.

You tried to strangle me.

Don't look at me like that. Like you're scared to come near me.

It's not safe with you. Not for me and not for the baby.

You can see I'm fine now.

Why did you leave us?

Why are you starting that up again?

Why did you leave us?

Sophie, this isn't the time.

Good-bye then.

See you. Good riddance! Goddamn!

I pick up my duffel and open the door. A warm wind strikes me.

Sophie!

But I keep going.

I hear him call my name. My father is an animal, and somehow an animal's voice can carry against this wind. Or he is as if part dirt and trees and water. I don't know. One day could I metamorphose into something similar?

Come back, Sophie. I'll tell you anything you want to know. Come back. Sophie!

He's made his way off the bed and lies facedown on the floor. He says with misery in his eyes, You need to untie me.

I can see now that his pants are wet.

If I do, you won't keep your end of the bargain. You'll run into the woods.

I won't.

I don't care care why you sleep in trees. But why did you leave us?

He stares up. He's silent.

Good-bye, then.

Don't go. I should tell you. I should.

I turn to him.

Hell. Where there's no confession there can be no forgiveness. It's too late to make amends, but if I don't confess, I'll be tortured.

I told her redeem and reclaim. Don't destroy. I told your mother that.

Then we don't talk for some time.

Two hours pass. I set a bowl of steaming onion soup on the floor and he, on his knees, arches forward, touches the soup with his mouth, and sucks. He asks if I'll untie him so he can change into some clean pants and go into the woods to relieve himself. I untie him with the promise that he won't run. When he returns, he sits on the cot, his legs crossed at the knees.

In the yellow glare of the kerosene lamp, his eyes and cheeks and mouth are dark. His nose has taken on the sad yellow light.

If she could have loved a thing so ugly. So helpless and weak. She would have been something then. But she didn't want to care for a sick baby. Shut up! I said to your mother. Quit screaming. It was a devil child, she said.

Me?

Born from evil, she said. Not you, Sophie. I'm in pain, she said, you're in pain, the baby's in pain. This baby isn't even an hour old and it's torturing us. Your mother didn't want any torture.

What torture?

That year we lost a truck of sheep on Loveland Pass. The brakes failed on the semi, and it went over the side. Your mother's father died the year before. Her pregnancy was rough. She was in bed the last six months. Awful sick. Couldn't keep her food down. Clements was seven when it happened. You were three. I thought he'd have talked to you about it. When you didn't say anything I thought, well, I guess he hasn't. Thought maybe he'd put it out of his mind.

There was another baby?

A little girl.

Something presses on my heart. A stone. A frozen leaf. A finger.

I said, That's not my baby. I could never be the father of a baby like this. She was born with eyes set wide apart. Her nose was flat. Just didn't look normal. When I put the flashlight on her, saw her like that, and your mother saw her like that, she started hollering. I said, That's not my baby. But maybe it was.

I can see my breath, he says, standing, it's so cold in here. He puts pine cones on the embers and when they flame he angles the logs onto one another.

I stay up most of the night, he says, because night brings out guilt. I suppose I need that. To feel it. Night brings out the memories.

What's your guilt?

Your mother suffered something awful during the pregnancy. She lost weight. She was weak. The snow came. It dropped five feet in two days, and we had to go out into it at two in the morning. I woke you and Clements, and told him to dress you while I helped your mother. The contractions were close. It's so goddamn cold in here, he says, going back to the fireplace. He puts two more logs on the fire, kneeling before it, his back to me.

We got into the truck and started for town. You know, the one thing she didn't do was drink during her pregnancy. It was a relief when she was pregnant, because thankfully she stopped drinking. But now she was at it full bore. Whiskey. Guzzling. She had brought the pint with her and it was almost gone. Jesus, it was snowing. Your mother wanted to push and I told her it wouldn't be much longer before we got to the hospital. She cursed me. I couldn't see five feet ahead. Snow in the headlights. Hypnotic. At DeWolf's pasture we went into the ditch. I got us stuck so that in the end a wrecker had to lift us out. No winch could've pulled us out of that ditch. The back end was higher than the front, all angled down on your mother's side. She already had her bottoms off. The baby was coming.

You and Clements were on the floor on your mother's side, crying your hearts out. I remember Clements kept asking, Is she going to die? I finally had to tell him to shut up. Just shut the hell up. Her head was against the door and her feet were up on my window. I was between her legs with the flashlight, trying to watch for the baby's head.

When it didn't come right away, I thought the worst. I thought the cord was wrapped around, or it was breech or something. I had to shut the motor off so we didn't die from the fumes. I told Clements to come over to my side and shine the flashlight so I could help his mother. It was cold. The windows were fogged up. She was panting and sweating, and pretty soon the baby's head crowned. I told her so, and she gave one last push, and out it came screaming.

I cleaned around its face and took off my shirt. Wrapped it around the baby. Then I set it down on your mother's chest. I took the flashlight from Clements, opened up the shirt and looked at it. Its little hands were shaking, and it was screaming. I saw it was a girl and I told your mother. Then I saw that she wasn't right. She was breathing funny. I thought maybe she was going to die right there before we could get to the hospital. I set her back down on your mother's chest. I thought by holding her I'd only hurt her.

Your mother, I think, saw the look on my face. What's wrong? she wanted to know. I told her. She looked down at the baby. Then the afterbirth came. I kept thinking if there was a God—

Then your mother—she started to cry. She said, That poor little thing. That poor little helpless thing.

Clements wanted to know what was wrong, and I told him the baby wasn't right, and to hush and to go back by you on the floor so the two of you could stay warm. Your mother asked me to take the baby from her. I said, But, Willy, maybe she's hungry. Maybe she needs your milk.

No need for that, she said.

I asked her what she meant by that. She said there was no need to feed the baby because the baby wasn't going to live anyway. You could tell she wasn't going to live, she said, by the way she was breathing. I said to her, Someone will come along and help out, and in the meantime we have to try and help the baby.

You kids go outside, your mother said. She spoke so calm, and it scared me. Go on. Go sit by the tire out of the wind. Clements, take your sister.

Then you started crying again. You used to do that. If Clements cried, you cried. It didn't matter if you knew why he was crying.

You went outside. I told you I would come out and get you in a minute, if you would just stay out there one minute.

Joe, I'm not going to raise this baby, she said.

Maybe they can help it. Maybe there are operations.

This baby is a Mongoloid.

I'm not blind, I told her.

It'll never spell, or write, or have children of its own. It could be deaf and dumb. Blind. An idiot. Something's wrong with its lungs.

We don't know that.

I want you to take the baby into the middle of this pasture and leave it there. Bury it in the snow, bury it all the way down to the grass, and don't come back till it stops screaming.

She talked about the medical bills, the special schools, caretaking a baby until it finally died, as she knew it would in short time. I was convinced she was right. The baby would suffer. And, I justified, this baby wasn't mine. Come on, Joe. Do something courageous for once in your life. Pick up your feet. This baby's ten minutes out of me and already torturing us. I'll tell you what it is. Punishment. Oh, God. Take it away, and I'll never do anything deceitful again in my life. It's nothing but the devil's child. Get it out of my sight, Joe. Do it now, or I'll do it myself.

The baby was bawling like I've never heard a baby bawl. I put her under my jacket and took her out of the truck. The snow had buried the fence. Some winters you could see field stubble through the snow, but nothing there, only white. I told myself, This is mercy killing, just as your mother said.

I'd read that when you freeze to death, it's not such a bad thing. The fingers and toes go numb. The arms and legs. The lips and base of the skull. I don't doubt that when I cleared the snow and laid the little thing into it, and pushed the snow back over her to let her pass quickly and so as to muffle her cries, she would have fought but for a minute. She couldn't know what was happening. She could've had instinct, I suppose. Hell. Do you think your baby—do you think it hasn't sensed a world in the womb? I once read that a feeling of peace comes over you when you freeze to death.

I knelt down and listened, my ear to the snow. I could save her now, I thought. But to bring her back to the truck, what would happen then? Take the child back out there, you coward, she'd say. Within minutes I could only hear the wind, and I perceived she'd slipped away. Gone to a better place. I sat in the snow and cried there, and asked God to forgive, asked that He might one day let me forgive myself. What more could I ask for? Only that.

I walked back from the pasture. My arms seemed frozen that way, as when I carried the baby there. You and Clements were huddled next to the tire. Your arms around each other. I cleared the snow behind the tailpipe and started the truck so we could use the heater. Around dawn a truck came by. Somebody who worked for the county, on his way to plow. He took me into town and I hired a wrecker to come back and lift the truck out of the ditch. Then we went home. I had to clean out the truck. If I'd used the hose, the water would've froze. I had to clean it out a little at a time, washing, wiping it dry.

We told Clements the baby died in the truck, and we buried it then and there. We told him he must never speak about it again for all of his life. We told Dr. Glauser we'd gone to Chicago. That the baby was born there dead. That's what we told everyone but your grandmother and Uncle John. We told them the baby was stillborn here.

In the next year I drank too much and was violent with your mother. I hated her and I hated myself. Finally I left. Your mother was so unpredictable, Sophie. So unsteady. She could've told anyone it was me who put the baby in the snow. It wouldn't have been a lie. I ran and ran, and tried to lose myself, and finally when I ended up in jail over putting that man Waldrop's eye out, I felt I deserved it and more. It was a relief. I almost told the judge what I'd done to the baby. I was this close to telling him.

I tell my father, She used to rock in the chair. Her belly was big. Her belly button stuck up through her shirt.

My father sits back to the fire with his hands against his face. His fingers clawlike.

In the next several hours my father tries many times to speak. He opens his mouth then closes it.

I had a sister. There's mournful awe in that.

Light moves through the windows, slips away, and moves again. Our gloom kills the light.

The trees tell secrets. My baby kicks and kicks. Let me out, it seems to say. Let me out.

In Bluerock I went back and forth on the school bus, seeing that DeWolf's pasture was almost always without animals, and heavy with grasses. Do senile people forget their names? The grasses in his pasture were thick with purple and orange flowers. His black cow came through the bad fence. She stepped into the prairie aster, yucca, buffalo grass, and got a surprise.

Is there, in the whole world, a promise of relief? I'm talking about relief. And what about my father and mother? I'm not so sure they shouldn't both suffer a lot.

My father says he's going to the cellar to get vegetables, and in two minutes I'm running across the avalanche meadow and heading to the road. He was my hope for so long, but think of what he did to a baby fresh from the womb. Sometimes I think his story is just a lie.

I don't know what to do with the information he gave me. I don't know if I should hide it, tell my grandmother, or write to Clements. Clements, I would write, is it true? Should I tell a judge? What's the definition of mercy in a courtroom? What's an infected response, and what's natural, and what's kind when a baby comes out with wide eyes and a broad nose, screaming, and the mother wants the father to put the baby in the snow, and the father does?

part Five

W HERE TO?

Mesa City.

Hop in. Say, are you all right?

I'm all right.

The Jeep's floor on my side has small green- and brown-filled plastic bags. Take care, the man says, please not to step on those. Move them back if you'd like. He adjusts his thick glasses.

He's been up, madam, he says, to Silverwood Pass, checking on flora, fauna, and scat for an environmental study that will in due course enhance Mesa State College's publication record. Where are you coming from?

A cabin back there.

And where are you headed? Your final destination, shall we say?

Chicago.

What happened to your arm?

Broke it.

He hands me a black and red hankie. I wipe the tears from my face and blow my nose. I think he doesn't want the hankie back. But he does. He talks to me about flora and fauna and scat. He says that lockjaw can be deadly. It affects the human nervous system. The symptoms—spasms and convulsions—are caused by a toxin that infects wounds where oxygen isn't available. Its spores are in dirt and animal shit. Six cases of lockjaw in this county in the past ninety days, he says. Stiff arms and legs. Fever. Sore throat. Have you had a tetanus shot, madam?

I don't think so.

You'd remember, don't you think?

You'd think.

I turn my face to the window and tell him I'm looking for Rocky Mountain sheep. He tells me he has scat samples of those animals in a bag at my feet. Then we don't talk.

My father was a mystery. No more. He lives life as he wants. He sleeps where he likes. He doesn't have responsibility to anyone but himself. He's childlike. Uncourageous. I guess we all have truths of un-courage.

I think of the past when things were good. When I was six and eight and ten. A cotton and metal windup snake the dog chewed, then spat out. A box of a hundred Crayola crayons and my unwillingness to use them because I didn't want to wreck the tips. A picture book of fairy tales. Monsters, gnomes, and devils. More scary than anything. I read with a flashlight in the closet.

In half an hour the man brakes his Jeep in front of the Trailways stop.

Thank you.

Take care. He pats my shoulder.

Inside I buy a ticket, then go out and get into the bus. A boy seven or eight climbs in and sets his blue luggage on the seat next to mine. I help him put his luggage up. He slides in and sits in my seat. He presses his nose into the window and his breath forms a halo. He sighs a long sigh. He waves at a woman in a station wagon who waves back with a white hankie.

The bus moves like a bear, and as we swing to the right and out to the highway, the boy sits back in his seat, lifts his chin, and straightens up. He's going to visit his father in Denver, he says. His parents are divorced. Who did you leave?

My father, I say.

His name is Buffalo Billy. He names a river where he trout

fishes, and tells me the weight of the elk his father bagged last year. For half an hour we talk about his school, his friends, and a water balloon fight. The bus groans and climbs as the driver shifts gears, and we make our way up the pass.

Do you know you can see the Continental Divide from the top? he asks. My dad and I stopped once in that hotel and had lunch. There's a ski area up there. Did you know that?

I didn't.

I'm an excellent skier. Where are you from?

Wyoming.

What happened to your arm?

Broke it.

How?

Fell off my horse.

Are you going home?

No, I'm not.

At the top of Monarch Pass the bus stops struggling. We start down the other side. I feel as if I'm rolling downhill without the bus. My baby rolling inside my belly that rolls as my body rolls.

I ask the boy, Do you mind if we trade places? I didn't think I was tired. I'd like to rest my head against the window and fall asleep.

But if you go to sleep, you're going to miss the place.

What place?

The place where the bus went over the edge. A school bus went over and killed everybody. You can see where it happened. The trees are still broken. Do you think that could happen to us?

I don't think so.

He stares at my stomach. I lean my head against the window.

Billy—

Buffalo Billy.

—Buffalo Billy. I'm going to close my eyes now.

My grandmother's directions to me: I should walk straight out the terminal. I should keep my eyes to the ground and hold my duffel with both hands. I shouldn't tell the cabdriver I've never been to Chicago.

A line of yellow cabs waits in the pouring rain. I run into an open door. The big-haired Negro has a match-thin mustache.

Where're you from?

Wyoming. Colorado.

You've been to Chicago before?

No. But my grandmother said I shouldn't tell you that. Take me the right way, will you, not the long way? Will you do that?

He turns around and smiles. Don't worry. Do you like Greek food?

I know what spanakopitta is.

You ought to go to Greektown while you're here.

All right, I say, looking up at the skyscrapers. I can't see the tops for the fog and for the rain that shoots down at an angle. There are thousands of people on the sidewalks and street. Cars honking. Buses. Miles of umbrella people.

Your grandmama's neighborhood—that's going to be a good neighborhood. You've got your Polish people there. Is she Polish?

Yes.

What happened to your arm?

Broke it.

Gosh. Sorry. You've got your Ukraines the next neighborhood over. Hospital nearby. You've got some fantastic restaurants on that side of town. Polish, Russian, Ukrainian. They're all about the same as far as food goes. Borscht. You like borscht?

I don't know.

Me, I don't like soup too much. Now I like blood sausage. You've got some excellent meat markets in that part of town. It's not too much longer. Turn left up here and go about a mile. You like strudel? Take this restaurant, Krazinski's over there on Norman, a few miles up. Best apple strudel in town.

I won't have a car.

Buses run most anywhere. You've got trains, too. Here. Let me write this number down for you at the next light.

At the red light he hands me a slip of paper. Weather number, he says. So you know what to wear before you go out in the morning. Very handy number.

Thank you.

You like fresh fish? You've got Nick's down at Monroe and Dearborn. Do you want to write it down?

I can remember, thanks.

Okay, we're almost there. You want to get the money out of your pocketbook, looks like it's going to be six bucks, just under.

My grandmother's going to pay when we get there.

All right. Fair enough.

The house is small and boxlike. Ugly turquoise. The house next door is hot pink and the one next to that is yellow. Down the street they're red and orange. In case I lose my way, I can ask a person, Excuse me, but where are the ugly-painted houses on Bellevue Street?

When she answers the door she almost smothers me with hugs and dry pink-lipsticked kisses that must polka-dot my face. The cabdriver steps back and puts his hands behind him. My grandmother pays him.

Good luck to you, young lady, he says.

You too.

She takes my duffel and leads me down the green-carpeted hall.

This is the room your father had when he was growing up. He and Johnny shared it.

She says she doesn't recognize me, then angles herself in front of the mirror. You can't recognize me either. Menopause lent me forty pounds and—was I gray when you last saw me?

Your hair was black.

Now it's thin. Well.

Her cheeks come down from the sides like small weighted pouches. My eyes are drawn to them by her dangling earrings. Her face is in makeup too orange. Eyebrows have been painted on in brown crescent moons. Her eyes are black and the glasses over them are square like ice cubes.

The bedroom is a space the size of a barn stall. Two twin beds are pushed together. The bureau is dark and old, the floor made of wooden slats painted the color of egg yolks. She stands near the doorway in a closet of sun.

You said you wanted to go to a doctor.

Did you find someone? I ask.

We'll look tomorrow. But we'll need two, won't we? A baby doctor and a bone doctor?

One for now, I think.

What about your arm?

Will the baby doctor put a speculum in me?

Oh. I imagine. But, dear, think of what must come out eventually.

In three months, I say.

Are you afraid?

Not yet. Can we find a woman doctor?

We can try.

Have you ever had a speculum inside you?

Not for many years. Yes, we can look for a woman doctor. I don't blame you. I no longer want a man doctor pushing his nose in that direction.

One of them almost got me in Bluerock.

Lord have mercy. The way you say it. Yes. It's more a woman's business, it is, looking up your tunnel than a man's.

What did you say? You call it a tunnel?

I used to call it a cave, but your grandfather told me I was crass.

I want to talk to you about my mother. Did she drink? Was she a drunk?

She used to get drunk.

What did she drink?

Her eyebrow comes up. Anything. She drank anything, dear.

Her face holds a look of astonishment. I think she's astonished at everything. I don't know why I think that.

• • •

Dear Clements,
I'm at our grandmother's in Chicago, and this is where I'll
have the baby. Our father told me about the baby girl, our
sister. About the night in the truck during the snowstorm when
I was three and you were seven. You must remember. I don't
remember but you must. I wanted to run from the cabin when
he told me, but I had to make a plan. He was drunk and on
mushrooms again. He threw me on the bed and tried to kill
me. I almost killed him with the fireplace poker. Clements.
Why didn't you tell me?

The beds have soft mattresses and my back hates the mornings. I sleep late, then meet my grandmother in the living room. Sunlight melts through the picture window.

She reads the *Chicago Tribune* and shakes her head at war stories. She shakes her head at racial conflict and calls them niggers. I hate that word. If I tell her not to use it, if I make her mad, if she tells me to leave, where will I go?

She tells me the numbers of the Dow Jones industrial average. She works the crossword puzzle. Clips coupons for the grocery store and files them in a recipe box. She doesn't believe in horoscopes. She wishes she could write a column of advice. The movie reviewers have terrible values, she says. She reads *Time* magazine and wants to know how these beautiful models in magazines can wear such ugly things as granny boots. My grandmother wants to know why the younger generation acts so urgently. She's anxious for football season to start. The cat's name is Mac. He's orange and fat from eating too many birds, and his ears are notched from cat fights. He sleeps in a scrap of sun by the living room window on the yellowed lace doily of her couch arm. The living room furniture doesn't match, but it looks nice like a pasture of flowers.

In four days I haven't been able to tell her why I left my father. She knows about his whiskey. If I don't want to tell her about the dead baby, I can let her think his whiskey was the sole thing to come between us. The soul thing.

• • •

Billy went home injured, Clements wrote me. A bullet hit his foot. But there wasn't much in the letter. I want to know more. If I call Aunt Alice's, someone will answer the phone standing on the floor of their house that sits on the red dirt that's the same red dirt as on our ranch. Those memories. That's why I don't call.

My grandmother tells me my father's called twice. He wants to know if I'm all right. She says, I asked your father what went on, why you left, but he won't talk. Was he drinking, Sophie? Yes. Did he hit you? Yes. Then she cries.

Today, September 12, I'm sixteen. My grandmother's making a day and night of it. We'll go shopping at Marshall Fields'. I can have anything I want. Anything? I don't think *anything*.

I can picture it. The salesclerk will say the dark green jumper I'm trying on is big enough for the baby's growth, and after the baby's born I can belt it. I'll pick out a white blouse. In the shoe department I'll look to see what the other women are buying. High heels. No. I can't. A pair of loafers. The salesclerk will call the color cordovan. She'll say the trend is to put a penny in the notch of each shoe. I'll tell her I'm not too big on trends.

Tonight we go to the Barnum and Bailey Circus. The minute we walk into the lobby, I smell animals like mud and lemon urine, and their straw and old shit.

The first act is four elephants in the ring. They hold on to each other's tails and trot in circles. A stupid trick. A feather-capped woman rides the head, then the trunk of an elephant. She does a backbend on the elephant's back, twists around, and stands on her hands.

Dr. Marilyn Carr is my baby doctor. She told me to stretch my arms and legs twice a day. Don't bounce with your head at the knee. Go down gently. When you hurt, stop. Stretch every day, Sophie, until the baby comes.

I feel like the elephant. Not the woman acrobat. My due date is December 10, according to Dr. Marilyn Carr. In my own calculation I was only twelve days off.

• • •

Some of the children walking by my grandmother's wear uniforms. They go to the Catholic school, my grandmother says. Would I like to attend the Catholic school? I would not like to attend school at all. Very well, she says. Maybe next year. I'll take care of the baby while you finish high school.

At my school I didn't sing in the choir. I didn't write for the newspaper. I didn't even give a vote for homecoming king and queen. Cliques. Groups. Circles. Life isn't singing and voting on things like whether the school should buy an apple machine.

There are thousands of protesters on Michigan Avenue, blocking traffic. Hell no, we won't go. Cops on horses are prowling. What a place for horses. I'm afraid to join the protesters and I'm ashamed to stay out. Why am I afraid to join? The protesters have their own club. The cops have their own. The signs say BABY KILLERS. What if Clements is one of the baby killers? What if he gets shot in the head? If he dies over there, all the hope I had for being friends with him will be gone. Just when we started. I can't go with the protesters. Call me a coward.

My grandmother and I baked breads. We played Monopoly. We went to the museum with two white lion statues on the steps, I waddled up the stairs, we paid the entrance fee, took the elevator upstairs to see Monet's haystacks. We put on coats and scarves and mittens and sat on a bench at Lake Michigan. We browsed through a used book store near the University of Chicago. My grandmother searched for cookbooks and I looked for picture books of fairy tales, as if they'd take me back to when Pablo was a forever horse. We didn't go to church. Sunday nights we watched *The Wonderful World of Disney*. We visited Dr. Marilyn Carr, and Grandmother paid her bills. We washed and ironed and dusted. I wrote letters to Demetrio, Clements, Billy, and Edwina.

I worried about Billy. My grandmother pickled corn. The wind was heavier than Wyoming's. In the autumn months we took turns mowing the lawn, and in November we shoveled the sidewalk.

Sometimes I thought of catching my mother asleep, tying her hands and feet with wire, and putting her head in a vise. She screamed help murderer, and to shut her up I stuffed her mouth with poisonous mushrooms. *Amanita phalloides.* If I didn't suffocate her while I was stuffing them down her throat, her liver would go bad from the *Amanita phalloides.* Yellow liver. I learned that at the library.

What in the sun and stars was I thinking?

Six days before my due date, the pains come under my belly button. My belly's going to split like a watermelon and the baby will swim out with seeds for eyes.

My grandmother calls a cab.

At the hospital a nurse hands me a gown and I change into it. In a minute another nurse comes with things on a tray. The whir of floor fans are like trains. Why are there fans in the middle of winter?

The nurse: Will you lift your gown, please?

Why?

I'm going to shave you.

Over my dead body.

She grabs my gown and pulls it up so that my naked lower part shows.

I punch her in the chin.

My grandmother exclaims, Oh! and the nurse puts a hand over the place I've hit. She takes her razor and other things and leaves.

Another nurse comes in and says I must be shaved for hygienic reasons.

My grandmother didn't shave when she had babies.

The nurse looks to my grandmother who stares with an astonished face toward the hallway.

Very well. I'm going to have to give you an enema, though. This I'm going to have to do.

Over my dead body.

Sophie, dear, feces are full of bacteria.

Don't explain. No shave. No enema.

Would you mind telling me why not?

They aren't natural.

Well, but neither are pain relievers, and, dear, we do offer those sometimes for mothers in pain. You, in fact, may need them.

It's hot in the room as if the windows are open and it's a hundred degrees, as if the heat comes in, summer evil heat. But on the ground there's snow.

Go away, I tell the nurse. She does.

They take me away on the cart and my grandmother is a blurred body in a rabbit-collared green wool coat and rubber boots. I have to be sitting up when the pain comes. Sitting up will help the baby come out.

What kind of pain is this? I'd like to claw out someone's eyes. The fat nurse with a bubble nose who won't bring me water. Would she like to lose her eyes? Is my baby stuck? Can someone say the truth? Is its head big as a skillet?

I need some water, I moan to the fat one. She walks away.

My feet are lifted into stirrups. All right, I'm here and close to having the baby. I'm at their mercy. I ease out a crude low cry and one of the nurses steps back. I'm part water buffalo and part gorilla. Get away. Don't hurt me.

The fat one bends to my ear and I smell her eggish breath. Listen, honey, the more you fight, the worse it's going to be. Buck up. Enjoy the ride.

Witch, where's your broom? I draw back to punch her between the eyes, but she's quick, and catches my fist.

You try that on me, she says at my ear, and I'll knock your block off.

I understand. I'm a problem. Sophie says no to what they say, but she's dangerous too. Isn't there a nurse who can help me? Hello. Please. My baby's coming. That nurse's eyes are kind, aren't they?

Can you help me? Oh, sweet blue eyes. Pearl skin.

What do you need?

Water. Some medicine for the pain. Where's my doctor?

I can't give you water, she says. I can bring you ice chips.

That's good. Yes. Thank you.

Then a pain with such force that I'm swept away in its river and think I'll drown. Stay away from me, hog bitch! I stupidly made nurse-enemies. I'm defending myself! Then the ice comes in a plastic cup. Thank you. The chips melt on my tongue. They coat my mouth with thrill. Shocking and cold, I want a cold river to shock the baby out of me. But thank you for the ice. Thank you.

What a fool to think I was in the last lap of this run. Can anyone tell me? How much longer?

Dr. Carr just came in. She stands at my stirruped feet. I tell her maybe my baby's head is stuck. I tell her to go in and get him and I tell her this unkindly. One of the nurses smiles. I'll get up and box the gray from her brain. But no. I'm tied into these stirrups.

My doctor explains forceps. Her mouth and nose are covered by a white cloth mask. Her eyebrows are plucked to nothing.

I say, Put in the whole kitchen. I don't give a fuck.

Sophie, my doctor says, you need your strength to push.

The fat one again. I hope a crow plucks out your eyes and spits them out in horseshit.

Then a push. It's all I have left. Maybe not. Maybe there are dozens more pushes needed. Where will I find the muscle? The breath? Another. And another. Then a rush of weight that leaves nothing. As if a big bird flies from my womb. Heart, don't go away. The baby cries.

Is he all right? I try to sit up. I can't.

This isn't a boy, my doctor says. This is a girl.

Oh, a girl. Bring her to me, please.

She's being weighed, my doctor says.

Bring her to me, please.

Sophie. Settle in for a moment. Here. Your hair's all matted and wet. Nurse, come here with a towel, will you?

The baby is laid on my chest. Pink and prune-faced. Pigletlooking. She must look at me and see her mother sweaty and weak, and a bubble-nosed nurse, and a doctor without eyebrows. But can my girl see yet? No. Nature's way that she doesn't see so much so as not to shock her back into my tunnel. Frances. This isn't the boy who would grow into the deep voice. This is a tiny baby whose vagina is red and sore-looking. My doctor tells me it's normal. Her head is bald as the moon.

Look at her nails no bigger than an O on a book page. Look at her ears, tender as two lima beans. Dr. Carr.

Yes.

Can you call somebody to come and take this cast off? My arm's healed.

Well, I don't—

It needs to come off. Is there a bone doctor somewhere in this hospital? I'm so tired of this cast. My skin needs to be scratched. I need both arms to lift the baby. Would you, please?

The boss's wife went on her horse to the field where Demetrio was taking up beets, and she told him I had a girl. He rode back with her to the boss's house and called me.

Her name is Frances, I say.

Es el mismo que St. Francis, he says.

No es el mismo. She's Frances. Our baby girl.

You would like St. Francis, he says. He loved all of nature. He preached to birds.

I wish you were here.

I wish I were there.

I hate it when you wake me in the night to suck just after I've gone to sleep. My nipple's cracked and sore enough to send me to the ground. You suck and soil your diapers and cry and smile your gas pains. I change your diaper. You soil again. The washing machine's broken. Grandmother has to go out into the snow and wash your diapers at the laundry two blocks away. She has to carry the dirty laundry over ice and snow.

My bones are weak. They feel swollen as my breasts are, and

ache like blisters. Look at her on the pink blanket next to me. My angel. I'm sore between the legs where my doctor stitched the tear. My grandmother calls these grapish things piles. My anus throbs from them. Hour by hour my belly loses its roundness.

This is your aunt Alice. How are you? How's the baby?

She's beautiful, I tell her.

Your mother told me. Your grandmother left word for your father. He called—

Queasiness circles my stomach when she mentions my mother. Her name is Frances, I say.

How was your labor?

I had a few pains.

Do you have stitches?

No.

Hemorrhoids?

None.

That's fortunate.

From what I hear.

She wants to know details: Frances' weight, and if she has hair. Then she comes to the point.

Sophie, your mother's not managing too well.

I grow stiff in the back.

It's strange. She only eats bread and drinks wine. It has to be red wine, Sophie. She spends a good deal of time in the barn on her back, in the straw, staring up. What do you suppose she's staring at? Bats? Cobwebs? She quit smoking. One day, cold turkey. You know Clements is due home on leave the last of February. She keeps wanting to call him over there. Call him on a telephone.

She laughs. A nervous laugh.

As if America runs telephone lines for those boys so their families can dial straight in.

How's Billy? I ask.

Well, he's all right.

Can he walk?

He's having a hard time, Sophie. I have to tell you, the men—Julian, Piraté, Antonio—well, bless their hearts, they're doing it all for your mother. I have to run to the bank once a week to transfer money so I can pay bills. I don't know what made her get so deep into debt. But everyone's in the red, anyone who owns a ranch.

Aunt Alice talks on and I think to hell with my mother's craziness. That she should grow crazier and crazier is no surprise to me.

Aunt Alice sniffles. It's one thing after another. You can't imagine. I spent Thanksgiving rescuing her from a tubful of eggs.

Hmm, I say.

She cracked a dozen eggs in the tub. You should have seen that mess. All over her. Is that your baby? Is your baby crying?

Yes.

Why don't you tend to her. Sleep on this. I'll call you tomorrow.

Sleep on what?

All I've told you.

Aunt Alice, I don't know what to do with her.

I mean, she's just letting it go. What do you suppose the men think? Nobody's telling them what to do, and they're used to being told what to do. All right, I'll call you tomorrow if that's all right. Go now and take care of your baby. Everything will turn out. It always does.

Say hi to Billy for me.

After we hang up I feel awful for lying to her about not having stitches and hemorrhoids. I don't want her saying anything to my mother. I don't want my mother knowing anything about me.

My milk comes all the way down and Frances quits to take to her dreams. I worry for my impatience. My grandmother lifts Frances from my arms and lays her sleeping on the blanket on my bed.

My grandmother says next week she'll draw a hot bath and lace it with salts. She wants me to soak three times a day in order to heal.

She comes into my bedroom. Your father's on the phone.

Tell him I'm busy eating a box of chocolates.

• • •

On New Year's Eve day I have a letter from my father. He writes, I was thinking that when Clements comes home, the three of us can get a room in town. What do you think?

I blaze words onto a postcard: No. No. No. When I put the stamp on and slip it into the mailbox, I touch my throat where a lump has formed like a spool of thread.

My grandmother comes to the door and lets the cat in. The cat weaves between her legs. She stands against the doorjamb. Your father used to collect salamanders from window wells. He used to sleep with them. His friends were putting firecrackers in their little salamander mouths, but Joey would have no part of it. Maybe someday you can tell me what happened there.

Maybe.

I think the worst when you don't tell me. I think he did something to you. Something unspeakable.

He didn't do anything like that.

I mean sex.

Nothing like that.

Thank God.

Maybe I hope the truth about my baby sister is like the hair on my head that comes out on my brush in clumps. Dr. Carr says my hair falls out because of hormones. The truth about my baby sister, the truth of my father, might go into my hair roots, and when my hair comes out little by little, the truth about my baby sister might go away.

My grandmother watches westerns on TV. I don't. They remind me of home.

The moon through the picture window is half full. It hangs over the elm in my grandmother's front yard. The city is bright. Where is the moon? Hidden by electric lights. I knot three dish towels and make a papoose for Frances. She fits tightly inside the papoose. Her head is against my heart.

I lay her in the drawer. The phone ringing is a harsh sound in the darkness of the house, and it makes my heart quicken.

Hello, Sophie.

Clements. Where are you?

At the ranch.

You're home early. Is everything all right?

Listen, Mom's in a bad way.

When did you get home?

Day before yesterday. But how're you? How's the baby?

Fine. How are you?

Making it.

What about Mom?

She's in the hospital. I had to take her. She hadn't come out of her room for six days. She's not talking. This morning I found her next to the bed, on the floor. Her eyes are open but she don't blink. You know anything about that?

I haven't talked to her.

She was pissing in her bed. Wrecked the mattress. Piraté went into town and bought a new one. We put a plastic sheet on it. Then she asked Antonio to bring her a lamb. She wanted a lamb to suck from her own teat. She must've forgot, we don't have no small lambs now. I don't think she'd bathed for more than a week. I called Aunt Al and she come over and saw how bad it had got. Then I called Dr. Glauser. Tonight I drove her to town and checked her into the hospital. She ain't speaking. I don't think she can.

Nothing?

Nothin'. And I should tell you. I signed up for another tour. That's why I come home early.

You did what?

Signed up for another tour.

Why?

What I'm concerned about is the situation here. You know Aunt Al's been taking care of some of the bills. They was three months past overdue, some. The thing is, you got to think about coming back.

Are you coming here?

I might can make it for a few days on my way out. Truth be known, I'd rather be in Saigon than here. I know the ins and outs of Saigon so good, I'd rather spend my time there trying to forget all this bullshit. The thing is, I mean, Julian and the boys are running it by theirselves with no one to boss them around like Mom could. Aunt Al's all wore out from it. You know? I should ask— how's Grandma?

I don't know how I could have done without her.

Well, you're fairly iron-willed.

Are you coming to Chicago?

If you want.

I want.

What's the saying? Don't wish too hard or you might get what you want. She doesn't have an L-shaped house with a green lawn on a corner lot. But she's in town. Corners. There are four on her hospital bed, the sheet tucked away. Applesauce and beef broth and canned corn–air when the nurses bring food. Huey's Shoe Repair at the corner on the other side of the hospital. Maybe she can see it from her window.

In two days Clements is at the door lifting his feet in the cold. He looks like he's lost weight. Maybe all that walking has turned him into muscle and he only looks thinner. He holds my face in his hands. And this is Frances, he whispers looking into my papoose as she sleeps. She's beautiful, Soph. His red-brown hair is a match-tip long.

Grandma Irene calls out, Is he here? She runs thundering to the door and throws her arms around Clements. She cries softly and kisses every part of his face. Then she steps away from him.

My. You look so much like your father.

I knew she'd say that.

Clements tells the story of our mother. Our grandmother listens with her astonished face glowing in the dark that's come into the picture window so that my grandmother turns on a light. I think Clements is going to cry. His nose turns red and his voice shakes.

My grandmother stands and leaves the room. She comes back with a pint of Jim Beam. He holds out his empty teacup and she pours.

Thanks, he says.

According to Clements, our mother went into what the doctor calls a catatonic state.

There wasn't nothing more I could do, Clements says.

Of course not, Grandmother says.

After supper the four of us sit in the living room. Frances is attached to my breast. The television is on but the volume is off. Some kind of game show. I ask him to tell me about the war. He does. I say, Do you really believe you're doing the right thing?

What do you mean do I really believe I'm doing the right thing? Me, individually? You mean do I think our country's doing the right thing?

Yes.

We're fighting to eliminate communism. Don't you know that?

He tells me about the things he likes in Vietnam. The women in Saigon are beautiful, the food in Saigon is good, and he has his boots shined there. There are movies to see, and there's gambling to be done.

Our grandmother says it sounds like Babylon.

Yeah, he laughs. Clements looks over at Frances. Jesus Christ, she sure does sleep a lot. Can I hold her?

I hand her to him. He looks upon her tenderly. I wonder if the war could have made him more tender.

Our grandmother has gone to bed. Clements' leg pulses all the time. I ask him to tell me about Billy's injury.

Hell, he got shot in the foot, he says.

The way he says it makes me think I shouldn't ask again.

He carries Frances into the bedroom and we lay her in the open bureau drawer. She moves, but doesn't wake.

We put on our coats and boots and go out for a walk.

Boy, this air feels good. Hell, it feels good. Hey, how about the color of her house?

I smile.

Like to blind me, he says.

He tells me more about the war and wants to know why there are so many protesters here. He wants to know why the country doesn't band together and support them over there. I think he wants me to say something he'll like to hear. I can't give him an answer like that.

He tells me how sorry he is about Pablo.

Let's not talk about it, I say. Why'd you sign up for a second tour?

Sophie, you're very anti-American. Do you know that?

I'm not anti-American.

We walk silently down the street. It's dark and quiet, save for corner streetlights that make the snow bright and sparkly as if it could talk.

Why'd you say that? Because I'm against the war?

There's a big world out there. You've never seen none of it, Soph.

I'm here, aren't I?

Chicago ain't the world. Hell, if you saw some of the—let's not talk about it. I'm so tired of the goddamn war. Can we talk about Dad?

I tell him we should turn around and go back. The wind will be at our faces going home. I tell him about our father trying to strangle Edwina. Our sleeping in the truck. The time when I saw my father naked, standing at the kitchen sink.

He says, That must've been freaky.

I say, You don't see your father for eleven years and he tries to strangle your friend, and when you wake up you're in a truck. You walk back and see him naked at the sink, and his nakedness makes you think he's gentle, and that last night was a crazy dream.

We talk about him until we're only a block from home.

• • •

The grandfather clock in the living room chimes eleven times. Clements and I sit across from each other. He's in the chair and I'm on the couch. My arm rests on the doily.

Look, I know you got no reason to help her out, but I'm gone, Dad's gone, you're here. I can't be here 'cause I'm over there for another year.

You should've thought about that before you signed up again.

Yeah, Sophie, well the bottom line is, I want to go *home* after the war. Okay, he throws up his hands, we might as well put it up for sale. Piraté mentioned him and the men were thinking of forming their own company. They could buy the ranch. You know, those guys never spend their money on nothing but whores and cheap wine. It's all saved up at the bank. They could buy the ranch, you know.

The image of Piraté sleeping in my bed. The image of him getting up and walking to our toilet that he would own makes the blood rise hot to my temples. To think of Piraté owning our land.

Well, I don't want that, I say.

Do you need some coffee? I ask him.

What time is it? Christ almighty. Almost two. No thanks.

Then he yawns and stretches his arms over his head.

We haven't talked about the baby sister.

His leg stops its rhythm as if all night it's been keeping pace with a fast song. He sits with his mouth a little open. His hands are on the outer part of his thighs.

You don't remember any of that? he asks quietly. We weren't supposed to talk about it. Mom said, Never talk about it.

You didn't tell Billy?

He shakes his head.

Didn't talk about it with Mom?

She came into my bedroom the next day. She got into bed with me. Under the covers. She called me her strong little man.

Oh God.

She says, You're perspiring, Clements, I remember she used that word perspiring, and she blows on my face. Her breath stinking of wine. She says, The baby died of its own accord and we buried it. It rose to heaven, and you're not to tell anyone. It's a private matter. A family matter. We're never to talk about it again. If you do, I'll get mad. I'll hit you till you're bloody and can't see.

He stops talking and sits forward in his chair. He puts a hand over his ear. Then he says, Her fruitiness got worse a little at a time, and we got so used to the way she was, we never noticed when it got really out of hand.

She favored you, I say bitterly.

I don't know why.

Because you were perfect.

Yeah, he half laughs, in her fruity eyes. That's a compliment.

I was ugly and not perfect.

She's psycho, Soph.

You're not a person to keep a promise, Clements, so tell me why you kept your promise to Mother and never told me about it.

What do you mean I'm not one to keep a promise?

You've lied to me.

Everybody lies sometimes.

Sshh. Don't raise your voice.

He paces to the hallway and back again.

What do you mean I don't keep a promise? he whispers. All right, they haunted me, the baby's cries. At night when I was in bed I thought I heard that little baby crying. I didn't want to talk about it. Never again. I was scared shitless of the whole thing.

Do we tell someone?

What do you mean?

I mean someone. You know.

Look, Mom and Dad, they ain't mass murderers. They didn't fly into a rage and go on a killing spree. Christ, Sophie, if you can't remember.

I said I can't.

He cries into his shirtsleeve and reaches up to turn out the light.

He says, When he comes back, his coat's a whole lot less bulky and I'm thinking, Oh shoot, he didn't, he didn't.

I say, But it was always you and Mother, Mother and Clem. You had a secret. It made a bond between you.

No, no, no. His head moves back and forth. His shoulders heave as he weeps. I bring him the Jim Beam and he unscrews the cap. He draws on the bottle and wipes a sleeve over his face.

Clem, have you killed anybody over there?

He takes his time to answer. I'm not going to start now and tell you what goes on over there. You just couldn't understand. You couldn't.

How many men have you shot?

I don't know. Christ, I don't want to talk about it. Why are you hitting me up with all this?

Do you think you've killed fifty men?

Hell no.

Twenty?

No.

Under ten?

Probably under ten.

I wonder if he's killed more than ten, and if maybe they're not all men, but women and children too. If he tells me he's killed women and children, I'll jump on him and beat him with my fists. I'll never speak to him again. Then I think, But enough. Think of this. We only have each other in our growing-up memories. There's no one else.

He yawns again.

I'll get some sheets and blankets, I tell him.

He stands and comes to me, and holds me. He's never held me like this. It's nice.

I'm sorry, he says. God, I am. It was wrong for me not to talk to you about it. He looks down. He sighs. He moves his hand, palm up, palm down on his thigh. I was scared.

All right, I think. Enough. That's enough.

You know, I used to have that job at Bilky's. No-brainer, right, throwing food into a sack. I told Mom I quit, but, you know, I was late one day and Bilky put me on probation. That pissed me off, and I ended up yelling at Mrs. Jamison for asking me to put her ice cream in a separate bag. I'll tell you what. I don't know if I can fit into civilian life, hold down a real job. Even on the ranch. Me and Billy'd go shoot rabbits when I was supposed to mend fence. So far, Vietnam is the only thing I can do.

It's okay, I say.

It's okay?

I don't agree with it. Over there. Can we stop now? I pull at the waistband of his jeans: I've been wearing your jeans. These are yours.

You got that big?

I told you. Forty-two pounds. I couldn't wear them at all toward the end.

I'm glad you got use out of them.

Aunt Alice says that two weeks ago my mother came home from the hospital where she was fed by a tube and wore diapers. In the four weeks she was at the hospital, she lost thirty-one pounds. As the pregnancy weight leaves me, my mother is taking it off, too. We've always had different ways of doing most everything.

But I can't keep on, Aunt Alice says. Look, she fell out of bed, and there's something funny with her ankle, so now I have to take her in for x-rays. To tell you the truth, I don't think it's broken. She doesn't move ninety-nine percent of the time, then she falls out of bed. I don't understand.

I say nothing.

Sophie, I know you and your mother—well, I don't blame you for feeling as you do, but I can't keep on. I've got to tend to my own family.

What about a nursing home? I say. She could go to a nursing home and I could come home and take care of the ranch.

Send her to a nursing home? I will not. Not my sister. And who has money for that?

How much is it to keep her in a nursing home?

You don't seem to understand the financial nature of a working ranch. You think I'd send my own flesh and blood to a state nursing home? Not on your life. We could maybe sell to Julian and the men and I could take Willy in with us, or you could come home and take care of the situation yourself. This is your land more than it's mine.

The week before Easter my grandmother and I take Frances to Marshall Fields' eleventh-floor auditorium. Frances is too young to know why Easter means lambs, ducks, yellow goslings, chicks, donkeys, and bunnies. There are lilies by the thousands. Ferns. Colored eggs. Marshmallow rabbits.

The ewes and their lambs are black-faced, and look to be Suffolks. A Suffolk's face and ears and legs are free from wool. Suffolk ewes are good milkers, and they almost never have trouble lambing. Their wool has a fine texture.

Frances coos and wobbles her head. She squirms and cries. I sit on a yellow-ribboned bench with green balloons tied to each bencharm, and gently put her on my teat. My grandmother buys Frances a stuffed duck animal. Look here, she says to Frances. But Frances sucks on.

I watch the children and their mothers. Balloons are tied to the children's wrists, their small hands petting animals, and small legs carrying them from animal to animal. I like to watch the children's faces. Some of them scream with happiness and some of them scream with fear. Do you know that an open-faced mother ewe, that is one with no wool on her face, will raise more lambs and heavier lambs than a woolly-faced ewe? Do you know that an open-faced ewe won't suffer wool blindness or collect burrs on her face? Soon it will be lambing season at our ranch.

part Six

THREE NIGHTS AGO, two nights before leaving my grandmother's house, I dreamed about a bear. Its breath was hot on my neck, and he made a growl. I was behind the loafing shed at the ranch. There was a shot. The bear fell dead on the ground. Blood made a circle at my heart. I looked up and saw my mother floating naked toward me. There was a gun in a holster on her waist. Her lips were red, and her crow's nest hair was drawn up as if magneted in fistfuls toward heaven. I woke up sweating and ran to the drawer to look at my baby. She was asleep.

You can learn anything at the Chicago Public Library.

When in your dream you know you're dreaming, it's called lucid dreaming.

The caduceus was the wand of Hermes, a Greek god of chance. The wand was made of braided olive wood and gold, and there were wings above. The wand had magical powers over waking, and sleep, and dreams. Hermes put the wand over the eyes of those being called to the hereafter.

Do you know what Freud said? If someone constantly frowns or grinds her teeth, or dreams that someone is being killed, then that person is angry. Some discovery.

People born blind dream in all the senses but seeing. For example, they hear their dreams.

Humans will have one hundred thirty-six thousand dreams in a lifetime.

I have a dream that someday I'll visit the ocean, and from there I'll visit the Amazon River. The Amazon's flow is so big that it dilutes the Atlantic Ocean a hundred miles beyond shore. The Amazon Basin has two million kinds of insects, a hundred thousand plants, two thousand kinds of fish, six hundred kinds of mammals. I'll start my trip at the Pacific Ocean. I'll love the ocean. I'll hate to leave it. The hypothalamus controls love and hate.

In my stomach I have a thousand rusty nails. My grandmother said, I know you have to go. Patting my hand. Don't be scared. Thousands of people fly in airplanes every day. You have a better chance of getting hit by a car than you do crashing in a plane.

I wasn't scared of flying. I was scared of leaving.

She stood at the terminal window. I was in my seat. A beehive-hairdoed stewardess asked me to fasten my seat belt. Two days before, when I told my grandmother I had to go, she said, I know. Her face wasn't astonished.

If there's a God, let Him or Her make a miracle. Show me in a dream the night of the snowstorm when the baby was born. Lost memories should be made whole. Like broken pottery glued to make a cup whole. Miracles? Show me one. The little baby of the snowstorm might have been no better than a cabbage, but she could have lived. Maybe it's better that she died.

The Wyoming snow is deep, unlike last year when it snowed the last of February and never came again that spring. The snow comes to the top of the fence. Aunt Alice drives our truck because the tires on her station wagon are bad. She's thinner than I've seen. Her hair's twisted into a French roll. Dark berry lipstick calls attention to her drawn mouth. She tells me we had three feet of snow last week and a foot the week before. The headstones at the cemetery are snow-covered. When I look over there I think of little Jo-Jo Oucker's parents who died in a fire. After that she had to live with her aunt in Trenton, New Jersey. I wonder if old DeWolf has gone to his grave.

A flatbed comes from the other way and the man behind the

wheel lifts his hand. Bedeker. I turn around and see he's got a hog in the back, lying down, its fat jiggling. A line of red around its neck.

With the fence lines invisible, I think for a minute what a place all this never-ending land makes. Seamless. That the expanse is so beautiful. Or maybe not. Maybe it's only a snow mirage.

Smoky lives in the house next to Mona's parents' two-acre place. She graduated last year from high school and works sometimes at Calley's Doughnuts. She likes Smoky. I know she does. He's older. Smoky rides his palomino bareback. Now his horse stands alone in the corral where he's hoofed away a clearing so he can hunt for food. I heard that Mona watches Smoky through her binoculars.

Guy Larksman's alfalfa field is high with snow. In three or four months he'll have violet-blue flowers.

Has Pastor Fabila been out to see Mother? I ask, slipping off my coat, unbuttoning my blouse, lifting the flap of my bra for Frances.

He came to the hospital, Aunt Alice says. He prayed for her.

We drive by DeWolf's land. Frances firmly takes to my teat.

Is DeWolf still alive?

Things around here don't change that much. Not in eight months. But I don't know. I don't hear much about him.

Here's where a dead tendon-glistening cow lay in the ditch. I want to remember my father going into the field and coming back empty-armed when I was three.

How's Billy? I ask.

Adjusting. We were told it would take some time.

What happened exactly?

Well, his foot got shot. He's got a limp. You come over when you get settled and have supper with us.

There's something in the air of our house. Maybe dust from curtains and furniture. A muddy floor. When I open the refrigerator to take some juice, a bitter smell flies out. In the cupboards, mouse dirt.

Antonio and Aunt Alice and I, holding Frances, walk into my

mother's room. If I try to describe the smell. Sour. Old. Human shit and urine. My mother lies face up on her bed. Her face is snow-white and her cheekbones poke into thin skin. Her hair is combed flat against her head and held back with bow barrettes at the sides. Unblinking eyes. The scent of Chanel No. 5 is gone.

Antonio goes to her bed and lifts her shoulder to square her up against the pillow. Her face skews for a second. A flicker. Then a look of nothing. I have a flood of pity. I take her hand. It's cold. Oh. Cold as her heart. Best not to feel too sorry. One day she'll rise up fit as a young ram and start passing judgment. There's a reek of soiled diaper.

Hello, Mother. I'm here. Sophie. This is Frances, your grand-daughter.

Nothing. Not a flutter of a lash.

Hungry, Willy? Aunt Alice asks.

Not a twitch.

We have some soup, Antonio says.

Nothing.

I stare at her for a few minutes and leave.

Here's my old room. Everything in place. When I run my finger across the record player, I leave a mark in its dust.

As I change Frances' diaper, she kicks and bucks. I speak to her in meaningless gibberish words. She could learn this only-mine-and-hers language in time. A SoFran language. Or FranSoph. Is it possible that my mother talks when no one's around? Does she drool and whisper words in the night when no one's watching? Do hissing snakes crawl from her mouth?

In my mother's bedroom, Aunt Alice changes my mother's dia-per. Her pubic hair is flat. Thighs scrawny. Her legs white and muscleless. Jungled with black hair. She hasn't been shaved.

Aunt Alice washes between Mother's legs, wedges the wash-cloth beneath her, and runs it along her behind. My mother's face wears no look of shame.

Where do you buy the diapers? I ask.

The hospital, Aunt Alice says.

My mother all this while is blank. Blank as the land outside her window. I wonder how often her bowels move. Pretty soon it will be Sophie changing diapers. Sophie asking, Are you hungry? Feeding time.

The sound of bleating ewes is both nice and bad. I like to hear them, but I don't like to think they're in trouble. Maybe when they're in labor, their pain is easier than a human's. The snow is an added danger for our lambs. Newborns come out of their mothers' tunnels wet. If a lamb is stiff and unable to rise, and its mouth and tongue are cold, the lamb needs to be warmed. It needs to be dipped to its neck in a warm-water tub. It needs to go into the barn, out of the wind, or into the men's trailer where it can bottle-feed.

A newborn lamb has almost no body fat under its skin. In five days its wrinkled skin will fill out. Sometimes you don't need to cut the skin of a dead lamb and cape a live one for orphaning. Sometimes you can rub the orphaned lamb with the dead lamb's birth fluid, and the dead lamb's ewe will take the orphan. Maybe this year we won't lose a single ewe to her lambs. Not a single lamb, either.

At supper I ask Julian, What is the state of things? I need to know about feed and repairs and shipping costs.

Feed has gone up. You can be sure of that. We need another truck. We need a man to take Demetrio's place.

Demetrio's coming, I say.

They don't look surprised.

En dos meses. O tres. Más o menos.

Bueno. And what do we do about Climax?

We hire someone there, or rent some land here.

Oh no, Julian says, land is too expensive here and we can get no more from the BLM. I can ask around. Maybe in Nebraska. Maybe on some piece of land with a hired man there. We should buy ewes in the fall, he says.

Can we afford to? I say.

On credit.

Piraté sits across from me with an orange-section grin on his face. I shoot him a look and he clamps his mouth. His face sickens up as if the food suddenly doesn't agree with him. Maybe he didn't understand that I'd come back and sit here at the supper table eating lamb chops and Brussels sprouts and *pan con mantequilla,* and ask these questions.

After supper Aunt Alice comes over. We look at the ledger to see what checks have been written. I learn we're about seventy thousand dollars in debt.

Everyone owes, Sophie, she says. Now your mother's medical bills have been floating in. Insurance pays most of it.

My mind adds and divides numbers. I get a pencil and notepad from the desk drawer. The men stand and put on their coats and gloves, and go out to the sheep.

I haven't told you about the night. What your mama needs. You have to spoon-feed her. Applesauce, hot oats, scrambled eggs. She'll take milk shakes, and I've bought some baby food for her in the past, strained liver and peas and such. She'll eat anything, she's not fussy, but it's getting it down her throat. I'll tell you what. I'll stay the night.

What do they call her condition?

Catatonic.

When did you know the truth about the baby?

I guess about two years after your father left. I told her she should talk to you about it. I believe she thought that poor baby was a punishment from God. I believe over the years the circumstances of that baby made her this way, the way she is now, in there right now. That's what I believe.

Does Uncle Edward know?

She shakes her head.

How could you not tell him?

I made a promise to your mother that I wouldn't.

Protecting her.

You might say that.

What kind of parents did you have? What did they do to her to make her this way? Was she born regular and got crazy?

Our parents weren't bad people. I think we were brought up right.

I tell her about my father. I tell her about when I hit him over the head and tied him up, and that's when he told me about the baby sister.

My mother can still cause harm. Maybe harmfulness will have built up over these days that she couldn't use it, and she'll roar out of bed and explode with it.

Aunt Alice coaxes her with a spoon, Come now, open up, here's food to make you strong. Open up. That's it. A little more so I can get the spoon *in*.

There's a rumble in my mother's stomach. A burp.

Good girl, Aunt Alice says.

There's no smile of pride and no embarrassment-smile from my mother. Nothing but the taking in of food and holding it on her tongue until Aunt Alice can coax her, Swallow now, come on.

She groans as Aunt Alice pushes her from one side to the other. She needs to be moved every two hours to keep her body from bed sores. Her eyes stay open. Even in her thinness she's awkward to move. She's maybe fifty pounds thinner than when I left the ranch. Now and then she twitches or wriggles her toes. She's loose-skinned. I think she is as innocent and intelligent as a cabbage.

Her hand falls into my chest and milk comes out of my breast. It makes a circle on my shirt.

It was in the middle of lambing that the sun came out and took away the snow.

My cousin Billy captures a horse for my ride, and ties him to the post ring by the barn. Billy's face is rockish and windburned. His lips are full and damp. His shark-fin nose is at an angle when he slants his head and shapes his eyes pie-wedged at me. He limps. His knee stays bent. His hair is three inches long.

The horse inside the barn is a big chestnut stallion three years old. Billy keeps him in a stall so he can go straight to him every day and not have to catch him in the pasture or in a corral. The horse whickers low as we come into the barn.

He's not muscled up yet, Billy says.

Who's he for? I ask.

Ricky.

Ricky is their hired hand.

Did you get enough to eat? he asks.

Meat loaf isn't my favorite. But don't tell your mother.

You're awful thin. Your baby's nice and plump.

She eats a lot. Am I too thin?

No. No.

He brings the horse into the barn, hooks him to two rings, one on each side, and brushes him down.

I been trying to get him ready for Ricky, but he's a ornery boy most of the time and my patience wears thin. You'll see, unless he's on good behavior.

With roughness, he slips off the halter and eases a bridle over the horse's head. He shoves the bit into the horse's mouth.

Ricky pushes open the low half-door and walks across the barn. His boot heels are determined on cement. His knees are like big hammers punching when his toes come down. He pulls off his shredded straw cowboy hat and says hello, nodding hard once.

How are you? I ask when I see black circles under his eyes.

We put our daddy in the grave last week, he says.

I'm sorry.

Yep. It was his heart. Our oldest brother Chet took it hard. Him and Daddy run the truck stop all by theirselves and Chet's wife don't want nothin' to do with it, and none of our other brothers don't neither. Our granddaddy owned it before our daddy. But there you go.

All my life I've said words of sympathy to near strangers like Ricky, but I haven't shown sympathy. Why can't I? I should have shown sympathy to Jack the bus driver when his mother was in the hospital dying of cancer. How do I show it? We were a family of nods and murmurs. When someone died, it was my mother's nature to say, I'm sorry. Then you could see her back thicken up. I've seen people at funerals touch hands or grip shoulders. They weep into each other's arms. I think of going to Ricky and holding him. I don't know him too well, though. I can count the times on the legs of a horse that my mother has held me.

Were you thinking about going up there and helping out? I ask.

Not me, he says, spitting tobacco on the cement. His hours there's god-awful. Chet's kids don't want nothin' to do with it, neither. They's going to have to sell out, plain and simple.

I'm sorry.

I feel stupid that I've said it again. I think of putting my arms over his shoulders and across his back. He's short and thick in the neck. It seems more that his back and neck fuse together. It seems less that they're separate body parts.

Thank you, he says. A smile of sadness. He lifts his chin toward Billy. When do you think he'll be ready? He runs his hand down the horse's face front and the horse's eyes round up. His head lifts high and back.

Another two weeks, Billy says. He needs more muscling.

You got a name for him? Ricky asks.

Naa, Billy says. Couple more weeks to get him muscled up.

I thank you, Ricky says. He turns around and tramps out, heel toe hard, heel toe.

When Billy has him saddled, he walks him outside where the horse I'll ride, a white-yellow, stands doing nothing. Billy walks back into the barn. His walking power comes from his hips thrust forward. But his spine seems curved, not holding him straight. His chest is narrow and sucked in. Beanpole they called him in high school. He saddles her while I hold the stallion by the reins. Then we get on our horses. We cluck to them and lift the reins and ride east where the hills are steep. There's a stream deeper and wider than the one on our property. The beautiful saddle creaks.

Billy likes to run the stallion up hills, but I don't want to run mine. Billy gets to the top and sits waiting. The day is about sixty degrees and humid, with gray-white clouds overhead and black clouds west that seem unsure whether they'll move east. Sometimes low-hanging clouds make me nauseous. The color over the plain is still brown. It's as if twilight has come already because of the cloud-shadows.

Billy's horse seems dared by hills, and wants to win the dare. Billy seems neither angry nor grief-full. He didn't talk much at supper. I don't know why he limps. The full story. He looks blank as if he's been left behind, not knowing where everyone else has gone.

The plain is lush with brownness and the blue-green of sage. We stop for a minute and silently look west at rain fingers, and at all the land around us. Our horses' rears hump as we ride down and canter to the stream. Billy dismounts and lets his horse drink. I dismount. The horses suckle water and Billy pinches his lips together and sighs. He's maybe six feet five inches tall and thin as a grass blade.

He tells me thank you for all the letters. I tell him I don't know how they helped, except that he was in touch with his girl cousin back home, and home is a safe place. He touches my hand. Thank you. He says he would like to tell me something. A secret, Sophie. I don't want you to tell anyone.

Are you sure you want to tell me?

You don't want to be burdened by a secret? he says.

If you want to tell me. I won't tell anyone.

Then a smile as sorrowful as Ricky's smile in the wake of telling us about his dead father and the family's troubles at home.

There's no courage in signing up and going there. That was easy. I stepped into the arena. Me and Clem. The first secret is that I never knew for sure if I could go all the way. I thought it was fifty-fifty whether I could stick it out.

He laughs nervously.

My sixth night there they brought this guy in by chopper. He'd been shot in the face six times. See, they didn't want to kill him. They wanted to shoot his nose off. His jaw and his mouth. It came clear to me then, I'd have to get out of the arena. Do you know who shot me in the foot? A buddy did, Sophie. He did. Do you think I'm ashamed because of it?

I don't know.

His voice has a forced deepening.

They all asked me. My platoon captain asked me if I saw who shot me. Hell, no, I said. I wasn't ashamed. I was proud.

He swallows twice.

You think people judge people by their faces?

Then he says something I can't hear. His voice is soft.

Sorry. I didn't hear.

Do you think people judge people by their faces? The way they dress? Their voice? How they comb their hair?

Yes, I say.

No, he shouts. No, he says quietly. People judge people by the way they walk. He lifts his face, his eyes green and bright and damp. How you walk into and away from a place. This is how I'll be judged, and don't you forget it. People's going to stare and whisper. Was he born that way? Was he in the war? Is he a hero? And I'll stand tall, a war hero fake.

He doesn't stand tall. His chest is sucked in. Lips nearly unmoving: Do you know what they did for me?

I think: I don't know who they are.

They gave me a medal to hang on my chest. So I can have pride. Well, I have pride without hanging no medal on my chest. Do you see a medal here? No. Because I have pride. I went there and stayed forty weeks longer than I thought I could without going nuts. End of story. End.

Did Clem shoot you?

I'm done talking about it, Soph.

I drop to my knees. His body is humid and hot. Our lips brush and his tears wet my face. Our lips meet again and part, and his breath touches my lungs, and my breath touches his. My back is on the dried mud of the bank, and he's hard on top of me. When I set my eyes back, I see the horses, their heads bowed along the shore, mouths searching. Billy lifts my shirt and cups my breast, and milk comes out. He says, Oh. That's all right, I whisper. He lowers his head to my cheek. He moans my name. I love you, I whisper. Only one tear comes from my eye.

He lays his head on my stomach and rests a hand on my thigh, and strokes my face. I kiss his mouth and hair and cheeks and eyelids.

I tell him, When I say I love you, I'm saying I'm sorry for what you've been through. It's the way I know how to say I'm sorry to you, that all this has happened.

The horses stay near. They graze and lift their heads, and bow them.

Billy. Billy. Look at me. Don't misunderstand.

His body moves slowly, with urgency.

Billy.

I don't misunderstand, he says.

Is it all right?

Yes.

He lays his mouth around my nipple, but doesn't drink.

My mother's eyes go back into her head and her body writhes. She flails herself to the floor.

Dr. Glauser comes to the house with a black bag. He takes her blood pressure and asks me questions. Now her eyes are closed. She seems to be sleeping. A line of drool hangs from the corner of her mouth. She needs to have tests, he says, and we'll need to take her to Denver, to a specialist.

I can't take her now. Are there drugs you can give her?

Phenobarbital. She needs to see a specialist. She needs to go now.

When I look up, the men are standing in the doorway.

She is going to die? Antonio asks.

Dr. Glauser explains this illness. The men leave. Dr. Glauser looks at the inside of her diaper. The urine's dark, he says. Concentrated. You'll have to get more liquids down her. How much are you giving?

A glass of water is never a glass. Half of it spills down her chin.

How often are you changing her?

Every four hours, I tell him.

But you need to do it every two hours. You see, she's urine-burned.

Do you think she feels pain? I ask.

She responds to pain tests, he says.

I think: Good.

It's not easy for Antonio to carry a lamb tucked under one arm to a pen.

Coffee's made, I say to Antonio and Julian in the corrals.

Julian walks to the trailer. I think he's going to tell Piraté the coffee's made.

We four drink silently from our cups. We eat from a package of sugar cookies. Is Piraté so stupid that he thinks I've forgotten he shot my horse? He obeyed orders so he's innocent? Maybe if I told him to jump off a cliff, he would. If he obeys orders so well.

I tell them, Tomorrow Antonio and I will milk the sheep twice a day. Every day for the next five months, until September. We'll make cheese.

The men are quiet. Even their chewing has stopped.

You know how to make the cheese? Julian asks.

I don't. Antonio does.

Antonio stares at the floor, as if he's betrayed his comrades. As if there isn't already enough to do.

The only way to work this is to stand behind the ewe and pull between her legs on her teat. The milk streams into a pail. Antonio and I each take two pails into the kitchen and pour the milk through a cloth. Flecks of dirt and wool stay behind. Antonio brings down the stainless steel kettle and heats the milk. He adds enzyme from the lamb's stomach. Rennet. To test the temperature, he spills drops on his wrist, as a mother does with a baby bottle. The milk turns solid. He cuts it. I cut it. We stir and cut again. He says something in Spanish. I tell him, *¿Qué? No entiendo.* But I see now, he means curds and whey, and he scoops them out and presses them into the mold. He presses and presses, and the whey runs out and down onto the counter, and he pushes the whey with a spatula into another pan. More pressing. Turning the cheese over. The curd goes firm and dry.

He laughs.

What's funny? I ask.

Queso. Tenemos queso.

The darkest and coolest place of the house is the pantry. It's where we line up our cheese, and it's where it will get ripe.

When we finish, Antonio goes to the couch. He lies down and pulls a newspaper over his head. The paper lifts and falls with his snores.

I have little time to watch the clouds, or the sage blown by the wind, or the moon growing and shrinking. I have little time to sit on the cement steps and listen to the crickets, or thunder as it tumbles across the plain. I have little time to sit at my open window after a rain, and smell the *borregas'* wet wool, and I don't bury my face in the mane of a horse, or follow a vole as it tunnels its way along. When I was five, I told my mother I could smell a vole coming or going, and she told me I was foolish. When I told my mother I wouldn't take my vitamins because the rocks gave me vitamins, she said I couldn't ride Pablo until I decided otherwise. So I took her vitamins with my milk, and licked the faces of rocks when she wasn't around. I don't need the rock vitamins so much now. But sometimes I do. I know I do. I have little time to hunt for the beautiful ones.

In my sixteen years, I've seen a lot of *oveja* bonfires. The heap of sheep is gasoline-soaked and a match is struck. I watch from my bedroom window, changing Frances, watching, pinning her diapers, watching with a lonely-heart feeling. Flames whip and rise.

I had to come back to this ranch. Plants are attached to the earth by their roots, and I'm attached to this land by my feet.

I throw all the ashtrays away.

I reach back and touch my mother's neck. I push. It's full of ropes. Massage is what you do for someone you love. You massage as if your love will pass from your hands into that person's body. Maybe my hate goes as easily as love from me to her. I watch her dull unblinking eyes. Does she blink when I'm away?

Demetrio used to pinch the ache from my toes and run his thumb along my heel. Side to side, top and bottom, as if drawing a cross. When he pushed the foot-edge and brought his finger down to the heel, that's when I got up from the bed and moved to him, and ate his swollen lips, and looked into the mirror-blade of his knife to see my lips red as blood.

Piraté, with his filthy beret in both hands clasped to his chest, speaks Spanish with my mother. I think he thinks she might come out of this sickness speaking only Spanish, having lost her English for good. He doesn't want to learn more English to speak with me, the person who's over him now, and he wants her to come alive so she can give him his orders. Don't think he can't read the layers of a tree's girth. He knows truth from invention, unless he doesn't want to know the truth. I let him into my mother's room whenever he likes. I have the pleasure of watching the red-brown beret fold and circle in his hands. I enjoy hearing his Spanish comfort words as he tries to will her well.

In the next three weeks she doesn't have another fit. Maybe one will come again. I don't sit around waiting for it. I know my mother. If she were talking, she might say the devil came into her body and threw it around.

I have to rub petroleum jelly into her lips and feet because they crack from dryness. Dr. Glauser took blood from her to test her thyroid, liver, and sugar levels.

•　　•　　•

Demetrio is the kind of man who feels he has to finish his farming contract. Skipping out would be the same, to him, as cheating. I tell him, Cheating is better than not seeing your daughter. And I miss you.

He promises to come by July. With the money he's earned, he put a new floor in his mother's house. He bought his grandmother a hearing aid so she can understand the needs of her rich customers when they ask her to make velvet capes. He paid for the wedding of his seventeen-year-old sister. In his time there, he saw to it that his little brother quit his friendship with a pack of boy-thieves. He became godparent to the eldest sister's, Juanita's, son.

I'm trying to learn more about what makes a sheep ranch earn money.

Uncle Edward tells me the key to profit is to make good use of all possible sources of income. I have to know that all my ewes will lamb, that a high percentage will twin, and a low percentage will die. If we can do all our shearing and not have to hire the shearing company to come in, this will keep expenses down. Uncle Edward says I should publicize our sheep. Their pure-breddedness. I have to control parasites.

My uncle says I should advertise lambs for Easter, especially to Greek Orthodox people. I should advertise in Greek newspapers.

An old ram tastes even stronger than an old ewe, and the best thing to do is sell the old rams for dog food. We can feed ground old ram to our dogs.

Maybe Julian can tan sheep hides. A reason to keep sheep free of ticks is that tick bites cause cockle, and cockle makes an ugly, unsmooth pelt. I wonder if I can find a seamstress in town who would like to come to our ranch and make goods. I can put a seamstress and her sewing machine in Clements' room, and she can make slippers and coats.

A hundred pounds of sheep milk will bring twenty pounds of cheese, twice what cow's milk will make. Suppose you have one hundred ewes for a total of twenty thousand pounds of milk worth thirty to forty cents per pound. Total it up for yourself.

We use sheep manure in our garden, but what about selling it? It's more powerful than horse or cow manure. For example, sheep manure contains twenty pounds of nitrogen per ton, horse manure contains eleven pounds of nitrogen per ton, and cow manure contains nine pounds of nitrogen per ton. Sheep shit does not have the bad-smelling sulfides that cow shit does.

What about sheep soap? Measure six pounds of clean tallow, heat it slowly, add water and lye, and heat it up again. Be careful that the stirring is slow and gentle or the mixture will curdle. I can make perfume soap by adding oil of lemon or lavender. Oil of sage? If I add vitamin E I can make deodorant soap. If I add honey I can make face soap. I can grate the soap into flakes and use it for the laundry.

Candles. And waste wool for insulation. Wool in comforters. Maybe Demetrio's grandmother will want to insulate her quilts with wool. What about handspun yarn? A sweater company.

But I can't think of doing these things now. Not today. Thinking about them makes me tired. Tomorrow or next week. I'll think about them then.

Frances lies back in her bouncy chair, and I tell her the things she needs to know about planting hotbed tomatoes. Here's the dirt. The tomato will grow from it, with sun and water. I can put dirt on your knee, but I shouldn't put it in your hands or you'll eat it.

The morning air is crisp and smells cornlike. But there is no corn on our land. I hold my baby on my hip and we walk to the horse pasture. I have an idea that I'll fence off some of this land and plant oats. I know that when you plant oats, you can also plant clover, and it comes up in a thick undergrowth. The oats in September will be shoulder-high, and the clover will be ready to harvest. The horses will have plenty of feed. I know this because Tin and Rudy plant oats and clover in their pasture every spring. Tin and I walked through the oats. She was wearing shorts. Never mind, she said, that my legs will rash up, but the itch will go away after a bath. I took off my boots and walked barefoot. The undergrowth of clover was cool and soft and beautiful. When we got to the horses, we tore up handfuls of dark green waist-high oats, their fruit hanging like beads. The horses' heads were high over the fence, their ears forward, noses drawing full and narrow, full and tight. Some of the oats came up from the roots with clumps of dirt, and we had to beat off the dirt. The backs of my fingers were cut.

First there is the barbwire fence that has to be put up to keep the horses out. We have no planting machines and I'll have to do it by hand unless I hire someone and his machine. I need to call Tin's hired man, Leeland. If she could let him go for a few days. What would he charge? How much will harvesting cost? Maybe it makes bad financial sense. I should go back to the house and get on the phone.

Uncle Edward and Billy lift Mother, and by her arms and legs carry her to the blanket on the grass in the sun. It's my mother's forty-fourth birthday. The wind carries napkins to a tree trunk and holds them there.

Also, we're celebrating my second cousin's, Jeffy's, fourth birthday. Every now and then my cousin Glenna gives him a couple of whacks on the back, and he coughs a little. There isn't anything good about having cystic fibrosis, except that if his father left him forever, or his mother, and if he never remembered anything about them, even the color of their eyes, he'd know that he has the illness because his parents both had the genes that gave it to him. They hope he lives to be twenty-four. He'll die of lung disease. Look at his freckles, like sugar ants on his face.

The sun is so healing. Aunt Alice says this three times while we eat. One of Sabrina's boys, Michael, watches me breast-feed Frances. He sits with his shoulder into my arm. Can I try? he asks. No, precious, I say. You got two of them, he says. This is all Frances' milk, I say. He wanders off to look for the horses.

Billy's eyes are light green like Indian jewelry rocks in a ring, and they watch me breast-feed Frances. His hair has grown over his ears, and is on its way to his shoulders. He wears a leather strap across his forehead to keep the hair out of his face.

He helps bring leftover food into the house. Limping.

I throw paper plates into the garbage, and knives and forks into soapy water. Potato salad into the refrigerator and hot dogs into the freezer. The men have taken the day away from the ranch. They've gone into town to see a movie.

In the kitchen he rests his back against the wall and asks if I want to talk about his letters to me from Vietnam. What did you think of the dead girl with the flies on her face?

He always wants to talk about those letters.

It was bad, I say. I wrote you not to be ashamed to cry. Men can cry just as well as women, and there isn't anything wrong with it. I wrote for you to take care. To watch your back. To think the good thoughts, and when you came home you'd start ranching again. Remember? I wrote that you should think about the weather. If it's raining, think about the day when it will stop. If the sun's out, get it on your face and close your eyes. Pretend you're home in your backyard. Try to smell your mother's cooking. Listen to the grazing cows.

You're beautiful.

I'm not.

I love you.

Don't, Billy.

He turns and walks outside and into the backyard, and I'm ashamed.

Julian and I drive to a horse auction in Laramie where I buy a two-year-old Arabian stallion. When I take him by the halter he pulls his head back, then throws it in my face. I knock him on the head. He nuzzles my arm and I pull away. I like you. I don't love you. Let's get that straight.

To Piraté, as he crosses the yard toward the trailer, I shout, Piraté, *ven aquí* and show me your knife please.

He pulls his beret down over one eye.

Eh?

Por favor, come here and show me your knife.

He walks with his shoulders back and his head cocked to the side. I stab a straw bale with a pitchfork and carry it into the shed, then scatter the straw and face him. Your knife. *Cuchillo.* I don't know if there's a word for pocketknife. *Cuchillo,* I say offering my palm to collect it.

He pulls the blade from the body and lays the knife on my hand. *Bueno.* The blade is sharp. *Cuando* you slit the *garganta,* you must do so quickly so the *oveja* does not suffer. Do you understand?

Sí.

Bueno. Me alegro mucho. I hear you're thinking of going to Spain for two weeks. When were you going to tell me?

Tomorrow, when I make the airline reservation. If you say yes, I will go. Only if you say yes.

All right. So you'll be gone for two weeks. Two weeks only? You can go longer if you like.

Solamente dos semanas, he says, then turns and walks toward the trailer.

During the night my mother doesn't wet her diaper. It's only the second time I've found it unsoiled by morning. Maybe I'm not giving her enough liquids. I've been rubbing petroleum jelly around her eyes and over her cheeks. The skin is dry, and flakes there.

This morning there's thunder in the distance. I try to fall asleep while Frances sleeps. Just two hours more, from six-ten to eight-ten. Please. Sometimes I can't fall asleep because I'm too full of thoughts from the night, and am past the point of tiredness. I hear Frances' little breaths. My cousin Glenna gave us this crib and there are small tooth marks in the wood.

I step outside for air, and my face is cooled by a thin drizzle. I walk into the pasture. The Arabian at the cottonwoods stands upright with his forelegs on the tree. I've seen stallions stroke their hindquarters on a fence post until they self-satisfy.

Some ranchers say to fit a stallion ring on the cock, an inch behind the glans because, they say, a horse's self-satisfaction lowers his fertility rate. The metal cage fits around the glans. I know that stallions self-satisfy when they're alone, and they do it at night. But I couldn't clamp metal around a horse's *huevos,* even if I were breeding him.

When Piraté comes home from Spain, he speaks in half English and half Spanish. I went to my bed, he says cocking his head. But there is no bed.

No, there isn't, I say.

He looks right and left. And again. I don't need to stand and face him. I see him from my hands and knees, where I scrub the floor. I see the broken zipper of his pants, the bode bag full of wine across his chest, his teeth brown and gapped.

How is Willy? he asks.

See for yourself. Please.

Hoy más tarde, he says.

All right. You may go now.

Excuse me, miss, *¿pero dónde está mi cama?*

Your bed? We'll have to make a bed for you on the floor of your trailer. There are some blankets in the hall. You know where they are.

When I come into her room, I find her lying on the floor. She's in the same position that she takes in bed. Her head is propped against the wall.

How did you get here? I say, but there's never an answer. Her mouth moves. Open and closed. Open and closed.

Are you going to talk?

Open and closed.

Are you going to talk?

She makes grunting sounds as if she's a rooting pig.

Are you going to talk to Sophie? I bend over and put my face into hers. Are you going to say some words?

The mouth opens and closes.

I sit next to her, my head against the wall. Our temples touch.

Sophie even put Coppertone on Mother's face and arms on Mother's birthday, so Mother wouldn't burn in the sun. Wasn't that good of Sophie?

I move like a cat to the front of her. Her eye whites are red-lined and the color is unflashing green.

When the men come in for morning coffee I turn up the accordion and trumpet music and sit down. I tell Piraté that after coffee he must go into my mother's bedroom and change her diaper. He looks at the others. Julian's ears redden. I turn down the music.

Did you not hear?

Julian looks down at his plate of eggs.

Later in the day she'll need a sponge bath. Why do you look at me that way, Piraté? I'll show you how to do it. *No es muy difícil.* It takes time, is all. *Tiempo.* It's her favorite moment of the day. You'll see the smallest flicker of light in her eyes when you sponge water over her arms and between her legs. The smallest flicker.

By morning Piraté is gone. Julian tells me he's gone north to find work.

To Alaska? I say.

North Wyoming. That is all.

He doesn't smile. When it comes down to it, men stand up for men. I understand. Standing up for someone doesn't have to equal respect. In my heart of hearts, I don't think Julian had much respect for Piraté. But maybe he did. If I'm going to have half an ounce of respect for Piraté, it'll be because he left quickly and quietly, and because he didn't ask for an extra week's wages.

It's the second time in a month she's fallen out of bed.

Her reddish eyes narrow and her mouth moves, but words don't come out. Her clawlike fingers on the right hand move. She makes the words ka ka ka ka.

Clements? Is that what you're trying to say? Do you want to know about Clements? That evil war is far from over. I had a letter from him only last week. He didn't ask about you. He never does. Ka ka ka ka. You sound like a baby.

Ka ka ka ka.

Frances cries in her crib. I get her and bring her into Mother's bedroom. She sits up and talks baby language. I lift her into my arms. Frances seems to be taken with my mother, and touches her face.

What's that? I say. That's a nose. Give Grandma's nose a little poke. Like this.

My mother doesn't blink.

Frances giggles wildly and looks to me for approval. But I'm suddenly pulled down with shame. It fills my stomach and lungs and womb. My mouth overflows with it. Look at me. I'm as hateful as my mother was. If I keep on, will my face sag at the jowls, and will I use blue eye shadow and black liner? Will I trade in my boots for ballet slippers? Will I draw red lipstick over the lines of my wrinkling mouth, and shower on hairspray?

I have the power to gag her with cotton and stop her up for good. I can fill her with a poison mushroom malt and ruin her liver. There must be other ways that don't leave wounds or bruises, ways that would go unnoticed except for the fact that she was ill, she's dead, and must be set into the ground. Dirty, earth-eating worms, Mother. I could kill her not all for hate, but for mercy, too. Look at her. But if I kill her, how and when would I ask, Sophie, did you do it out of hate or pity? Would I know the truth?

In these thoughts and deeds, I'm lower than my mother. She's pitiful on these sheets. The rotten smell from her diaper. The room stinks of stale lungs and old food and sour poisons sweated out from her feet. Look at her. Look. Her hair is brittle and gray. Her eye whites are red or yellow, depending on the day. There's a stain of food on her nightgown. Blue flies light on it and rub together their forelegs. Sometimes her mouth is open and I've seen flies land on her tongue.

When I feed my mother three times a day, I notice no change. I depend on Dr. Glauser to tell me otherwise. The day before yesterday, he said her ability to swallow has gotten worse. If it gets much worse, we should start her on another medicine. You can crush up the pill and put it in her food, and it will help her swallow.

Why don't you invite your family here? I ask Antonio. Ask them to come and visit.

Oh no! he says.

¿Por qué no?

Because they like it in España.

Don't they miss you?

How do I know? He shrugs and pounds the bread with his fist.

There's a knock at the door. I stop breathing. It's Demetrio standing on the other side of the screen with a suitcase. His hair combed back. The smile showing a silver tooth.

Ah, Demetrio, Antonio calls.

He opens the door and comes in. His eyes shift to Antonio and he raises an eyebrow. His eyes come back to my face. He puts his arms around me. His kiss is long and moving. His breath is the scent of coffee and sweet bread, as if he's just come from his silver camper. He pulls the braid over my spine and kisses me again. From his shirt pocket he pulls a strip of pictures from a Bluerock picture booth. Pictures of giggling Frances and me.

Hello, Sophie.

The long kiss makes me what I think is the definition of drunk.

Where is my daughter? he says softly.

Sleeping, I say.

Let me see.

But I want to hold him longer.

While we walk to my bedroom, he tells me of a strange ride he had from Nogales to Phoenix in a yellow Cadillac. The driver was a young woman who asked him to talk dirty to her in Spanish, although she said she knew no Spanish. When she dropped him off, she gave him her business card and asked him to call on his way back through.

It seems odd for him to have told me that story. I don't know what to say.

He peers over the crib at Frances asleep on her stomach.

I want to see her face.

Sshh. We'll wake her.

After a few minutes I ask, So did you talk dirty to her in Spanish, and do you think she was lying, that she knows Spanish and could understand everything?

He stares at me for a moment. I'm angry. He has ruined the moment of my happiness by telling me that story.

Of course not, he says.

I turn Frances gently over. Her fists go to her eyes and she rubs them.

My God, Sophie. How beautiful she is.

I want him here and I don't want him here. I'm scared I'll stay confused.

The pasture is patched with daisies and blue columbine. The Arabian's tail stands like a lightning bolt as he gallops away.

I have the papers for his bloodlines, I tell Demetrio. Look at his strength. The hindquarters. I'll buy a good mare for breeding.

Will she not be stung by a bee? he says as Frances crawls forward through the pasture. He runs and lifts her, and she wails.

But she doesn't know you yet, I say.

Papa, he says to her. She wails. Papa, he says. Papa. Papa.

He puts her down.

She is so fast, he says, although she isn't. I missed you. I want to start working. Not tomorrow, but the day after. I want to be with you all day tomorrow. What work will I do the day after tomorrow?

There's a fence that needs to be fixed.

Yes. Do you love me?

Oh, Demetrio, I say. I'm tired at the thought of starting this now. Frances. Frances! Come back. But she keeps crawling. I catch her. The horses' ears are pricked forward. They wander away. We spend a minute close to the Arabian, who won't give us the time of day, and walks off.

When we get back to the fence I look into the sky.

Do you see the clouds up there? Do you see the dirt here under our feet? The sheep to the west? There are crows in that tree, and there's a dog by the garden who barks when antelope come. I don't know how all of the things of the earth came about, but I don't believe there's a God who made them.

Estúpido.

Don't call me stupid.

Do you see the dirt under my boots? he yells. The trees and horse shit? How do you think all the beautiful and ugly things of the earth were made?

I don't know, and I don't care. Demetrio, Demetrio. This year I turned sixteen. I drive the truck now, to town.

Bueno.

But sixteen is a young age to try and understand everything.

Who asks you to?

Some people.

It is not important for you to understand everything. What do you feel in your heart? He pushes the tip of his boot into the ground. He grinds the red dirt around.

What I feel is that I want to lie in the pasture and watch the clouds change.

We walk to the far side and lie down in oat stubble and clover and purple flowers, and watch the clouds shift. Frances curls into my side and sleeps.

Look at the moon, I say.

A scrap, he says.

It's so pale in the day.

It is just the moon, Sophie. I wish you were not so passionate over a scrap of moon.

I don't know how to make a grain feeder. I watch quietly with my back against the barn door while Demetrio builds. The plywood for the bottom boards is one inch by ten inches. The dividers are one inch by six inches. There are five sides. A star.

I make one. We make six, and line them up in a corral, and fill them with hay. Some of the hay is bad. I ask Demetrio to order fresh hay, and ask why did someone not cover it against the snow and rain. He says this is Julian's job. I tell him, This is your job now.

Sí, señorita, he says standing straight, clicking his boot heels, saluting, not smiling.

We feed our *ovejas* in the corrals once in the morning. I take the night shift and feed an hour before dark. Sheep aren't like cows and horses. They don't like to eat when it's night, and they need time to eat before the sky drops with black. If you don't feed your sheep at the same time, they can bolt their food and choke. During a ewe's pregnancy, strange feeding hours can bring toxemia. I ask Demetrio to bring whole grains from town, but not barley. Not rolled oats. They're full of powder and can cause sneezing. A little corn and wheat too, I say. Then I tilt my head toward the earth. Listen. I put my ear to the ground.

You look like a bird hunting for food, he says.

The strangest thing. I thought I heard a train. Thought I felt it in my feet. But that's impossible.

You are crazy. All right. I will go to town now.

Don't call me crazy, I say with a prick in my voice. When you come back, will you change the oil in the truck?

I know almost nothing about trucks, he says.

Piraté did it all those years. All right, I'll do it. I wish you wouldn't look at me that way.

I will change the oil, he says. That is easy.

Demetrio, please go to town.

The deepest problem lies not in who will do what jobs here. The concern is what I must do to keep things going, and what I must sacrifice in order to do that.

My single bed is so small for the comfort of two, no matter how woven together and in love we seem or are. The night is hot and sticky, and the window is open. Lace curtain edges crease in the breeze.

Maybe lovemaking is the strongest force in bringing honesty. Sometimes the smallest flinch or moan of desire can lead to the crudest note-making. It's strange and beautiful, the ways one can bring another to pleasure. The pinch of a toe and a blow on the ear. A candle's flame makes beautiful gold light on the face.

When we're lying in each other's arms and our breaths finally slow, I'm tempted to say things on my mind. But he hushes me with a finger to my lips before I can even speak. He must know that the most honest time of life is after lovemaking, and he must not want the truth. Maybe he's like the earth, and I'm like the moon. Maybe he believes at this minute, because he doesn't see or feel my back, there isn't anything to me other than my breasts and hips. But there's more. The moon has another side. I've been thinking about the ocean. Maybe I don't want to go. The ocean is like the fluid in my belly where Frances swam for nine months. It reacts like my menstruation to the tug of the moon. It's the ocean that can swallow people whole and put ships into rocks. I can't be sure, but maybe the ocean is too scary.

Maybe the moon touches crazy people and makes them crazier.

¿Qué piensas? he says softly.

I'm thinking about the ocean and the moon.

It was not difficult to change the oil in the truck?

It was easy.

It is only that I have always been around sheep, cattle, horses, and dogs. Vegetables and fruits. I am going to take the truck apart and put it together. I am going to learn.

I have no doubt that you can.

Then, we don't talk.

I think sometimes that he believes the moon is half alive or even dead. If he thinks the moon is dead, he's only afraid of the deadness in himself. When he looks up and thinks nothing of the moon, he's sensing his own emptiness.

He nuzzles me. Does he want me to say I love you? If I keep saying it, then I'll be in love only with the language. That's a form of unlove. What I don't want to do is send him away so that my daughter never knows her father.

Demetrio. Are you awake? Demetrio.

I am awake.

But I don't talk. I hear the crickets and the distant weeping coyotes.

I would lie awake two nights in a row, then sleep all day. Then lie staring into black for two more nights. I would snap at my workers and forget to change my daughter's diaper, and put off washing clothes, and bring milk shakes to my mother at strange hours. I would forget to take joy in watching my Arabian graze and run, and there would be no pleasure in hearing my daughter coo.

We planted two blanket lengths and widths of clover, not for my horses' pleasure. Demetrio and I lie down and look into each other's eyes. For a moment I only see his shoulder and the small rip at the seam. Maybe I'm afraid that if I say the words, he will get angrier and angrier, and I'll cave in and tell him he should stay. His eyes are full of mercy. With the edge of his hand, he wipes away a side of my tears.

In the middle of the night I reach out to him, but only touch a pillow. On the kitchen table there's a note: I want to come back, and you must say when. Do not make me wait too long. I will miss you and Frances. You might think I am weak for writing only a letter. It is the easy way out, no? But I am not weak. You will see.

The tiny struggling moans of my daughter draw me to her crib. She's asleep and dreaming. Where is the moon? The window is so stained with dirt and straw and dried raindrops that I can barely see it. Do thin clouds stain the sky? I'll call Jack and tell him, Please come and wash our windows, all of them, every one. My mother used to do it, but she can't now, and I don't have time. Could you come right away? Where is Aunt Alice to tell me everything will be all right? She sleeps in her bed next to her husband, Edward. I can't call her each time I need to hear, But, Sophie, it's going to work out. Everything will be all right.

• • •

The rolling plain at this time of day seems quiet and harmless and at ease. The forms of the antelope fit like puzzle pieces into place. The large jagged sections of gray-green stream and pale brown rocks and thick grasses slide together and connect.

I've walked an hour and let my thoughts drift. I can walk down to the stream and sit there and think about nothing, but let the pleasant sights push my dullness away. I can put my thoughts not on me, but on this place.

For a minute I fall short and think of all the times I used to be on the plain, on Pablo's back, wondering why my father left. He was pushed by a wind down the road to the blacktop. All the wondering I did.

The plain rolls and dips and stretches in the same manner year after year. The seasons are irregular, but you can know when the grasses will come in and the colors of the earth will change. The insects and snakes and animals act accordingly but for some strange habits you might see from time to time. Demetrio and I once saw two hawks mating in the sky, clinging and at first looking like some prehistoric bird with two heads and four legs, curling about, and that strange dance was beautiful.

The screen on the door bows out and I make a note to tell Julian. There he is, at the barn with the farrier who is shoeing my Arabian horse's small black hooves. It will take forty minutes, more or less, to shoe him. I think of going there and watching.

It's beautiful here at twilight. The clouds' undersides are pink. I think whoever the creator is might own heaven, but that creator must crave the earth. I don't know on whose or what toe the ring of Saturn lies, or whose or what fingers hung the Milky Way, and scattered the dust of heaven, feldspar dust, breathed fire into the sun, and blew winter cold winds across Wyoming to freeze words.

I should think of a name for the horse.

I believe happiness can only come because of unhappiness. As soon as happiness is over, or the force of it becomes edgeless, I need to look for it in something new. Newness isn't so hard to find. If you look.

Julian comes to me bow-armed, a piece of straw hanging from the nook of his mouth.

You are going to ride him tonight?

Not in the rain, I say.

I think I broke him pretty good.

I saw. Thank you.

In the middle of August, two teenage boys show up at my door. Their cowboy hats are bent and sweat-formed. There are faded leather pieces around the hats. Their boots are square-tipped and black, with raised etching on the toes. Their truck is old and red with pits and dents, and half a bumper gone.

You speak Spanish? one asks.

Poco, I say.

They want a job. I ask, What do you know about sheep?

They understand a lot about sheep, one of them says.

Who told you to come here?

Our uncle.

And who is your uncle?

A worker of Larksman's.

I nod. Do you want to come in? *¿Quieren café?*

They wipe their boots on the door mat, take off their hats, and set them on the floor next to the chairs. Their names are Juan and Antonio Hernández, and they're from near Casa Grande, Arizona. Before that, Tepehuanes, Mexico. Juan is seventeen. Antonio eighteen. Their black hair is gelled back. They have long arms and wide shoulders. Antonio is taller. I'm ashamed to be looking at them as if they're bulls at an auction, but then I'll be paying their wages.

I tell them I'll bring groceries once a week, and they'll have to share the tin sheep camper. Juan says he prefers to sleep outside. But in the winter you'll come here and stay in the trailer over there, I tell them. Do you know anything about trucks? Engines? Broken fences? Can you catch fish in a pond and bring them to Antonio to cook? Have you fished through the ice?

They look at one another and Juan says, I am sure we can.

Very well.

268 \ Karla Kuban

But, miss, what will our wages be?

Two hundred each, including food and a roof over your head.

You would not settle for two-fifty?

I would not settle for two-fifty.

Two twenty-five?

All right. Two twenty-five.

Very well, Antonio says. Our uncle says your mother is sick.

Yes. Her name is Willy. Are your things in the truck? You can put them in the trailer for a few nights until I get the camper ready.

Miss, can we see the camper?

It's out back. And my name is Sophie. You can call me that.

We walk through the hallway and pass my mother's bedroom. I look in and see Frances in her playpen, and my mother sitting up and staring blankly ahead. The boys with their hats in their hands glance into the room, then put their eyes ahead and wait for me to walk on. We step outside. Rebby barks. I say, *¡Siéntate!*

I think we'll call this one Antonito.

When we get to the camper door, I tell them to go inside, but I have to get back to my baby daughter in the house.

The truth is that I can't go into the camper now. I'll have to change Demetrio's sheets from when he was in Climax, and scrub the floor, and maybe I'll replace the pillows. Maybe the coffeepot is full of his grounds, and maybe a bird has flown down the stove's flue. Maybe a bird came in to find food, and became trapped, then starved.

There is only a half moon. My Arabian and I step more slowly when the light isn't bright. The smell of rain veils dusk's air. If I believed in heaven, I'd say that the moon is hanging between heaven and earth. The astronauts have not been to heaven. John Glenn orbited the earth in *Friendship 7,* but I know he didn't make it to heaven. If there is one. It's the moon that transforms day into night.

Darkness is so visible. A nighthawk screeches. Antonito is away with the flock. He likes to sleep outside with them. As the Arabian and I come near the camper, the moon is covered by clouds, and a pale rain begins to fall. In the distance there is thunder. I'm not sure which way the wind blows.

Hello, I say, knocking on the door.

Juan opens it and stands in holed jeans, and without his shirt. In the back, by his bed on the small ledge, a candle burns. There is a book open and facedown on the bed.

Will you come in? he asks. Do you want coffee?

No, thank you. I'm just riding. Thank you anyway. Is everything all right?

Very good. Very good.

Do you need anything?

Thank you, no.

Your brother?

With the flock. North, I think.

He doesn't mind the rain?

He likes it. And you?

My hair is soaked, and my face, and clothes. I like him more than his brother. There's something about him. I think the something about him is really the something about me. That I'm sad and want the rock on my heart to go away. I need to get back now, and let Aunt Alice go home to her family. I don't want to say much here and now to Juan. Maybe my reason for coming is that I wanted to see life inside the camper here on the plain.

Rain. Sometimes it falls like worms, sometimes like needles, and sometimes like iron swords. Tonight has been a rain of tears. It came warm at first, and slowly cooled, and now it's wiped away.

My horse is fifteen hands high, tall for an Arabian. His chest and hindquarters are thick, his back is short, his legs are thin and small-boned. His face is sweet as a child's. His color is red-brown or bay, and that color in Arabians isn't so prized as a gray or white. He and I can probably go at a full gallop from this camper all the way home, and he wouldn't get winded. I wonder if his ancestors a hundred years ago were from a Bedouin desert.

We could gallop home, but the moon isn't too full, and I need it full to lead the way. It's come out from the clouds. The rain is gone. There are mole and prairie dog holes. Do you know that the moon is four point six billion years old? When it's full it has a stony face, and keeps scarring up with cosmic weather. In the future, the moon's face will be more and more bashful in its sleepy sneer.

Half a dozen times I have seen antelope at night. I wonder where they hide. They're like deer, but they're closer to cows. Antelope chew cud. They don't have biting teeth in the upper front jaw, and they have to tear off grass by using force with their lower teeth. I don't know how fast a deer can run, but the antelope can go sixty miles an hour. I haven't seen the mountain lion.

Tomorrow I'll go to the pens and ask Julian if I can bring him something to drink. He might ask, The baby is asleep? I might say, She's been sleeping all afternoon. I suppose it's the heat. Look. It could rain. The rain will make it cool.

It rains so many afternoons this time of year.

I'll walk to the small fenced-in pasture of my oats. They will be knee-deep, and the clover will be soft as stockings. I'll lie back and watch the clouds shift like flocks of sheep. I'll close my eyes, and when I open them the clouds will still be there, shifting. I'll close my eyes. When I open them, they'll still be there. I'll close my eyes.